TWISTED LIES

Twisted Lies

Georgia Blake

Dedication:

To my amazing editor.
Kelly, you took me on a wild ride when you asked me
to revise the entire plot, but girl...it worked! We did it!
You never steer me wrong.
Thank you for making me a better writer and laughing
at my quirky characters.

Contents

Dedication   iv

Content Note   vii

1   7

2   15

3   22

4   31

5   43

6   51

7   71

8   90

9   100

10   115

11   130

12   138

13   144

14   159

15	167
16	176
17	180
18	194
19	206
20	213
21	218
22	230
23	239
24	245

Epilogue	250
Kartoshka Recipe	252
Bird's Milk Cake Recipe	255
Sneak Peek Of Twisted Vows	259

| *Acknowledgements* | 265 |
| *About the Author* | 267 |

Content Note

Twisted Lies is a work of fiction solely from the twisted mind of the author. Any characters, names, places (real or imagined) are written from the author's imagination.

Warning: this novel deals with dark themes including human/sex trafficking, prostitution, human auctioning, learned helplessness, and illegal activities by the Russian Bratva. It contains explicit language and sex scenes. If you are sensitive to these subjects, please use this information to make the best judgment for yourself before you proceed with this story. Your mental health is most important.

Prologue

Kate

8 years ago

Bam! I went flying face-first into the locker, then fell onto my bottom on the vinyl tiled floor. Laughter, shrill and rude, faded down the hallway as the group of eighth graders headed out to go home, not caring that they'd knocked me down.

"Kate! You okay?"

Warm hands grasped me under the armpits and hauled me up. I turned to see the concerned green eyes of my best friend and forced a smile even though I wanted to bury my face in my hands and cry in frustration. "Of course. Eighth Grade-itis is hitting hard this year. Literally." My reply was flippant as if I had no care in the world when really the weight of life was starting to crush me at the tender age of thirteen. Seventh grade hadn't been the best year. We were like the middle child of the middle school years: forgotten, pushed to the side. Not brand new babies like the sixth graders and not the top dogs like the eighth graders. We had been coddled last year in sixth grade. The teachers were sweet and everything was shiny and new to us. The seventh grade teachers weren't exactly mean, but they were definitely more strict. I was a pretty good student, though, so they kept off my back. The worst part was the other kids. I was so glad I had Lex in a few of my classes.

I could tell by Lex's frown that she didn't believe me, but she wasn't going to argue. We'd been inseparable BFFs since meeting at a playground at six years old, so she knew me well enough to just leave this alone. I'd talk about it if and when I felt like it, and I'd shut up tighter than a clam with lockjaw if someone tried to pry it out of me. It's just how I was, and it was one reason in a thousand why Lex Wilder was my best friend.

"How about we skip the bus today and walk to the park? Dad gave me some money for doing chores yesterday, so we can get ice cream," she offered, linking her arm with mine.

Ice cream was my kryptonite.

"Deal," I replied with a grin and hefted my heavy backpack onto my slight shoulders. My parents always joked that my backpack weighed more than I did. I was beanpole skinny, all gangly arms and legs like a puppy who hadn't quite grown into its big paws.

We walked in silence, side-by-side, out the front doors of Theodore Sneed Middle School and down the wide brick steps. The park wasn't far, and we often ditched the bus on Fridays to hang out on the monkey bars and share the latest gossip and secrets only teen best friends could dream up.

It was an unusually warm day in April. The bright sun criss-crossed the sidewalk with afternoon shadows, and a light breeze caused our uniform skirts to whip against our knees. I loved early spring and despite the incessant sounds of city traffic, I started to feel better—less burdened—outside in the sun and fresh air. Especially with ice cream on the horizon.

I sensed, rather than saw, Lex casting glances in my direction. She was a quiet soul, just another reason we were kindred spirits. I knew she wanted to ask me what was wrong, but she wouldn't. With an over-exaggerated sigh, I decided to put her out of her misery and let her into my thoughts.

"I think my parents are getting a divorce." It felt nice to get it out into the open. I had an older brother, but he was away at college, and I didn't want to bother him with this. He often gave me the feeling that my problems were beneath him. I knew what he'd say if I called. *Parents fight, Kate. Stop being a baby about it.*

Her soft gasp was a balm to my senses. "Why do you think that?" she asked.

"Well, I overheard them arguing, and mom said the word."

"Divorce?"

"No, the *wooord...*" I said slowly, drawing out 'word' as if that alone could lead her to my meaning. I didn't want to say it out loud.

"What word, Kate?" Her voice showed her usual good-natured exasperation with me. There were things I just wouldn't and couldn't say.

"You know...the word."

"I have no idea what you're talking about. The only word that means divorce is 'divorce.'"

"Ugh! Why haven't they developed mind reading tech-nology yet! I don't want to say it, but I will for you...it's...." My hand wrapped around Lex's arm to bring her to a stop. I leaned up to her ear, lowered my voice to a barely audible whisper and said the *word*.

She blinked in the silence afterward, then slowly turned her face toward mine. "Fuck you?"

"Shhh!" I frantically looked around, but we were alone on the sidewalk. "Don't say it so loudly."

After rolling her eyes, Lex leveled me with a stare, "I don't believe 'fuck you' means divorce. If it did, the statistics of divorce would be even higher than they already are."

"Yeah, but—"

"No. Your mom was probably just pissed at your dad about something, and the only way to get her point across was to curse at him."

She resumed walking, and I hurried after her. "Yes, but—"

"No buts. Don't borrow trouble. I've told you this before, right? Don't make a big deal out of something small."

I didn't consider my mom dropping the F-bomb to be something small. She grew up in a very strict, no-cussing household. For her to use that kind of language at my dad meant big trouble.

Though I didn't agree with Lex one hundred percent, I did feel a little better. I also hoped she was right. Several of my friend's parents were divorced, and though they now had two Christmases, they were sometimes used against each of their parents in one way or another. I didn't want to be put in the middle like that.

We soon reached the park and dropped our bags by the sidewalk just as the blaring melody of the ice cream truck grew louder. It rounded the corner and stopped in front of us. We each bought our favorites: a Firecracker popsicle for Lex and a Chipwich for me, and then walked to the old jungle gym and climbed one-handed to the top where we dangled our legs and savored our frozen treats.

Our friendship didn't require us to fill the silence with incessant chatter, and we were happy to snack quietly as the late afternoon sun warmed our hair and faces. By the time we were ready to go, I was feeling way more positive than when we'd left school. I wasn't sure if that was a result of being outside or eating the ice cream. Probably both coupled with being around my BFF.

As we began climbing down from the jungle gym, I saw a large white van slowly rolling down the road. It came to a stop near our backpacks. I tossed the ice cream wrapper into a trash bin and headed for my backpack, but Lex's hand snagged my shoulder. She was staring at the white van.

"I think we should leave our stuff here and have one of our parents drive us back to get it," she said.

"Why?" I asked. "It's probably just someone doing work on the playground. Someone has to keep it up, right?"

"Does it look 'kept up' to you?" she asked, and I glanced around, noticing the shabby state of the playground equipment. Rusting chains on the swings. Peeling paint on the tall red slide. Several missing monkey bars. I shrugged uncomfortably.

"I have a ton of homework, and I need my bag. I don't want to waste time waiting for someone to bring me back. And I don't want anyone to steal it. I'll be right back. I'll grab yours, too."

Her unease was contagious and skittered through my veins as I approached our backpacks next to the van. There was no window on the side of the van, and the passenger window was tinted dark, so I couldn't see if whoever was sitting there was watching me.

What happened next was like watching a movie in slow motion.

As I bent and curled my fingers around the strap of my backpack, the van's side door slid open and two men climbed out, reaching for me. I dropped the bag and turned to run but arms encircled my waist and pulled me back against a hard chest.

"Kate!" Lex's scream cut through the air making every-thing speed up.

I saw her running toward me, and I shook my head. "No! Go, Lex! Run!" A hand clasped over my mouth and nose, stifling my words and my breath, causing panic to rise in my chest. I screamed and screamed behind the hand, kicking to try and trip the man behind me. Anything to get away.

Lex managed to grab her bag and used it like a weapon, swinging it wildly at the man who was now trying to grab her, too. No! I wouldn't allow both of us to be taken! Blood smeared my mouth when I sank my teeth into my captor's salty palm. He released my mouth and let out a curse that burned my ears.

"Run, Lex! Go get help! Ru—" The air around me shifted, and all sound ceased except for a ringing in my ears. My body went completely limp in the wiry arms that held me. It took a dizzying moment to realize I'd been punched in the face. Not slapped, punched! I was so stunned by the act of violence that I had been knocked dumb by it.

Pain, sharp and nauseating, radiated from my jaw, but it was the least of my worries. Lex running away down the sidewalk was the last thing I saw as the van door closed with a click.

Chapter 1

Kate

Present

"Are you sure this is the right place?"

"Yep. This is the address you gave me." The Uber driver said. It was my brother's address according to Misha, but it had to be wrong. That high rise was extremely...high. And fancy. I always knew Derek would make something of himself, but this was outrageous.

"Okay. Well, thanks." I tipped him on the app and hopped out of the car. The door to the high rise swung open, held by a doorman in a gray uniform who smiled at me as I passed. There was another man waiting behind a desk in the entryway. I felt a little lost, unsure of how to approach this situation.

"May I help you, Miss?" the man behind the counter asked with a professional smile. He was an older man with kind eyes that immediately set me at ease.

"Um, yes." I stepped up to the counter, returning his smile. "I'm here to see my brother, but I don't know his apartment number. We haven't spoken in a long time. His name is Derek Lancaster."

The man's smile remained in place until I uttered my brother's name. His eyes sharpened, and he squinted at me before saying with a hint of suspicion, "Derek Lancaster is your brother?"

"Yes."

"And what's your name, Miss?"

"Kate Lancaster."

"I will see if he is at home."

I knew that was code for *I'll see if he wants to see you.* I watched him dial from a landline phone and listened to the exchange. It was swift and over before I could blink.

The man hung up and offered me a keycard. "Use this for the private elevator to the left."

"But what apartment is he in?" I asked, taking the key from him.

"The Penthouse, Miss. The elevator takes you straight there."

The *Penthouse?* I had to scrape my jaw off the marble tiles before turning to find the elevator which blended in with the fancy wood paneling of the walls. I pushed the button and waited. It seemed ridiculous that after everything I had been through in the last eight years, reuniting with my older brother was what caused the butterflies to twist and swirl in my stomach. Would he look the same? Would he recognize me? What if he thought I was a crazy person after his money?

Ding! The elevator door opened, and I stepped inside. I slid the keycard into the slot, and the elevator smoothly rose up to the nose-bleed section of the high rise. When the door opened again, I stepped out into a bright foyer, and there was my brother, looking so much like the college kid I remembered, but older. A man now. People always said we could be twins if our ages weren't so far apart. We were both tall and slender. His blond hair was darker, more golden blond while mine was a white blonde. But it was our eyes that matched the most. A blue so dark they could be navy.

"Kate?" His voice was hushed as if he said it louder he might frighten me away.

I felt my lips curve into a wide smile, and tears prickled at the corners of my eyes. "Hey, big brother."

In a whoosh of air, I was swept off my feet in a massive hug. All I could do was wrap my arms around his neck and hold on tight.

"Put her down, it's my turn!" Another voice interjected. I hadn't known someone else was in the room.

Derek set me back on my feet, and I brushed my shaggy bangs back from my eyes to peer at the woman standing next to Derek. It was on the tip of my tongue to ask who she was, but I would recognize those green eyes anywhere.

"Lex!"

We collided in a hug, laughing, and jumping in excitement as if we were thirteen again instead of twenty-one. It struck me as odd that she would be there with my brother. They hadn't really known each other when we were kids since he was so much older. How had they even gotten to know each other and for how long? Did my disappearance bring them together? I put the thought out of my head for the moment. I would delve into it later when the time was right. The hugging went on between the three of us until Derek finally pulled away and grabbed my hand, tugging me toward the open door.

"Come inside. Lex and I were just about to have breakfast."

My brow wrinkled. "Why are you two having breakfast together?"

My brother and my childhood best friend looked at each other from either side of me. Both were smiling, and pink began creeping up Lex's neck to her cheeks. I narrowed my eyes, scanning her. She wore a robe that looked way too big for her and had a bad case of bed head.

"Oh. My. God." My whisper cut through the sudden tension. "You two are banging!"

Derek laughed and pulled me into the kitchen. "We are a lot more than just '*banging.*' Alexandra is my girlfriend."

Girlfriend.

The word shocked me into complete silence, and I allowed Derek to draw out a chair and seat me at the large table in the open kitchen. "Since when?"

Lex escaped the conversation by burying her head in one of the largest refrigerators I had ever seen. She began collecting items in her arms: eggs, cheese, milk. I blinked and turned my attention to Derek. He was sitting in the chair next to mine, his eyes focused completely on me.

"We've known each other for seven months. It's complicated, though."

"Complicated how?" I asked.

"I think it's a story for another time. What I want to discuss is where you've been and how you're magically here after eight years. Where the fuck have—"

"Derek." Lex's voice was soft, yet effective at cutting through my brother's tirade.

And though his words sounded angry, there was pain behind them. "Sorry," he muttered, his large hand wrapping around mine on the table. "I missed you so much. I've been searching for you for years. I never gave up on finding you."

I had never seen my brother cry, and seeing his Adam's apple work up and down as he tried to get his emotions under control was disconcerting.

I squeezed his hand tight. "Thank you, Budder." It was my childhood nickname for him since I hadn't been able to say 'brother' correctly when I was two. His eyes grew misty, so I gave his hand another tight squeeze. "You have no idea how much it means to me that you didn't give up on me."

The crackle of bacon sizzling on the stove caught our attention and Derek released my hand to stand up. "I better help her before she burns down my kitchen. Again."

"I heard that!" Lex sent him a glare over her shoulder, but I caught the hint of a smile curving her lips.

"Seems like there's a story there," I said, watching the two of them move around each other in a comfortable dance. They were a good looking couple: both tall with dark blond hair. A real life Ken and Barbie.

A sudden weariness came over me, and I closed my eyes to steady myself.

"You okay?"

Lex's face swam into focus when I opened my eyes. I smiled at her with a nod. "Yeah, just overwhelmed."

She reached out and wiped her thumb against my cheek then showed me the tear she'd collected. "It makes sense to be overwhelmed. I bet you have a lot of different feelings hiding in there." Her finger tapped my breastbone.

She had no idea.

"I haven't had time to process them all," I confided with a shrug.

"We won't rush you," she said with a meaningful look at Derek who plonked a plate full of eggs, bacon, toast, and cut fruit in front of me. "Right, Derek?"

His mouth tightened, but he nodded and set down a second plate before heading back for more. His nod was good enough for me, and I began to relax a little. I hadn't realized how tense I had become until that moment. I took a deep breath and released the tension in my back and shoulders.

Lex poured three cups of coffee and placed them on the table with forks, then took the chair across from me with a smile. When Derek returned with his own plate, he sat next to me again at the head of the table.

"So where have you been all this time?"

"Derek! You said you wouldn't rush her!" Lex admonished. Her fork was halfway to her mouth, a piece of scrambled egg jiggling on the end.

"Are we supposed to pretend she didn't just show up here after eight years? I'm allowed a couple of questions, Alexandra."

Alexandra. It was weird to hear her full name on his lips. Not even her parents called her that.

"It's okay," I interjected before Lex could respond. "I was in Russia 'til a few weeks ago."

"You've been back a few weeks and didn't think to look me up?"

"It wouldn't have mattered, Budder, since you were in prison." I smiled sweetly at his shocked expression. "Yeah, I know you went to prison for human trafficking. I watched the news for a solid week straight to find out what the heck's been going on in the world. I was certainly surprised to hear news that my big brother's prison release date was coming up. Want to talk about that?"

"No."

I knew he wouldn't. He could be as close-mouthed as I was when it came to spilling his secrets.

"That's fine. I'm not ready either." As a victim of sex trafficking, knowing my big brother had been convicted of it made me positively sick to my stomach. "But I will satisfy a little bit of your curiosity. I was voluntarily released and sent home with some money and your address."

"Have you contacted the authorities? I wouldn't allow Mom and Dad to list you as deceased because I knew you were out there somewhere. But you are still declared a missing person," Derek stated.

"No, I haven't done that yet. I don't want them to question me, and you know they will."

"Why wouldn't you want to answer their questions? What about talking to a therapist?" This came from Lex. There was something behind her green eyes that I couldn't interpret.

"Because I don't want to." My voice was firm. The thought of reliving everything from the past eight years was emotionally exhausting. I wasn't going to do it, and I wasn't going to be pressured into it. I'd had enough pressure for a lifetime. "I really should be going," I said.

"Going? Going *where*? You just got here, and you haven't touched your food." Derek's hand wrapped around my wrist to hold me in place. I jerked my arm away, but Derek held on.

"I'm staying at the Hilton downtown."

"I'll send someone to get your stuff. You are moving in here."

"I am not! Let go!"

Lex's voice of calm reason cut through our argument. "Derek, let go of her arm. You're hurting her."

He instantly released me, and I quickly stood and backed away from the table. "I'll call you soon. I just... I need some space." It felt like a vise was tightening around my throat and I recognized it as the beginnings of a panic attack. I needed to get out of here this second. I ran to the elevator and when I reached it, I mashed my finger into the call button. Gratitude swept over me when the doors immediately opened for my escape. After quickly stepping inside, my fingers fumbled with the key card before I managed to push it into the slot.

The last thing I saw as the doors closed was my brother standing in the foyer, fists clenched at his sides with Lex's arms wrapped around him in what must have been comfort. It was a bittersweet relief to be alone in the elevator as it descended to the ground floor.

I closed my eyes and willed the rising panic to cease before the elevator reached its destination and spit me back out into the world. I thought I had been ready to face my past, but I hadn't been prepared for how different everything would be. I needed to get a grip on reality before coming back here. I just didn't know how.

Chapter 2

Kate

Present

Breakfast with Derek had gone well. Better than I'd expected. I'd reached out to him as a peace offering since I'd left so abruptly, and he'd accepted.That had been two days ago, and I hadn't heard anything since. I didn't know if he was giving me time to process everything, or if he was the one who needed the time to deal. I had, after all, surprised the heck out of him.

I picked up my phone and scrolled through my contacts. Derek. Lex. Mom. Dad. That was it.

Four people. And only two of them knew I existed in Chicago right this minute. Unless Derek had outed me to my parents. The Derek I knew from my childhood wouldn't have, but adult Derek was a stranger to me.

I dropped the phone to the mattress and took a deep breath. I laid in bed staring up at the ceiling since I got back to my room. Being with family again was supposed to make me happy. Supposed to heal me...right? But I didn't feel healed. I just felt the same. Always the same. I hadn't really let myself cry since I'd been put on that plane headed for Chicago. I needed to cry. Scream. Rail. Grieve. But I couldn't. I felt numb. Maybe Lex was right that I needed to talk to somebody. Tell them my story. Get it out of my mind. My soul. The very fibers of who I'd become.

But I didn't want to.

I didn't want to tap into that well of emotion. It felt good to be numb to it all because that meant I was surviving it, right? Did I want to heal? It was a sorry state of mind I was in that I wasn't even sure if I wanted to feel better.

I scrubbed my hands over my face in exasperation before sitting up and grabbing my phone again. I hit the call button and pressed the smooth glass to my ear.

"Kate! I was hoping you'd call." My best friend's voice was light and welcoming. Relieved. It made me feel bad that I hadn't called sooner.

"Sorry, Lex. I just have a lot on my mind."

"I know, friend. That's why I didn't reach out. I thought you could use some time where Derek and I weren't all in your face. Ya know?"

"Yeah. Thanks for that. So, um, would you like to...uh...go somewhere?" Why was it so difficult to ask my best friend to hang out?

"Yes, Kate, I'd love to hang out. I'll swing by soon. And Kate?"

"Yeah?"

"Take a shower."

I scowled at the phone. How'd she know? I ended the call to the sound of her laughter, tossed the phone to the bed, and headed to the shower.

***

"Lex, you are a goddess," I said around my mouthful of pizza a few hours later. This was the real deal: Chicago style deep dish. It was built the right way with thick crust, cheese, and a mountain of sauce, peppers, and sausage.

"Only with your BFF can you pig out on Giordano's pizza and drink cold-ass beer in comfy pajamas," Lex said.

"While watching Deadpool."

We clinked the necks of our chilled bottles and chugged the rest of the beer. "It's the truth though. I've missed this so much. Missed *you* so much," Lex said, balancing her plate on her pizza-engorged belly.

"I've missed you, too." I let the silence stretch between us as we watched Ryan Reynolds prance across the screen in his superhero getup. Finally I set my pizza aside and snagged another bottle. I popped it open with the funny palm tree shaped bottle opener on Lex's keychain and took a fortifying sip.

"Why didn't you contact the police when you got home? I know you said you didn't want to talk about it, but that's not really an answer, is it?"

My face flamed in awkwardness. Busted. I should've known my best friend would call me out on a lie. "No, you're right. It isn't. I just don't see the point in it. I don't know who exactly kidnapped me. I never saw their faces. Without any evidence, how would going to the police help? I'd rather just not deal with that mess." And a mess it would be. I was afraid that if I went to the police, I'd eventually be hounded by reporters, and my parents would find out I was here. I wasn't ready for any of that.

None of that would bring Misha back to me. I'd been trying so hard not to think about him since that horrific day. Misha. Now that his name was a whisper on my lips, I could feel them wobbling at the corners.

"Oh, Kate...Kate, tell me."

"I don't know if I can," I whispered.

"Don't take this the wrong way, friend, but I think you have to. Think about the leeches that doctors used to suck out sickness in the Dark Ages."

I wrinkled my nose and a rusty chuckle escaped despite the sorrow twisting my insides into rope. "If I remember seventh grade History correctly, the leeches actually made it worse."

"I guess that's why I failed History. Anyway, you know what I mean. Let me be your leech, Kate."

"Gross!" I laughed again and threw a pillow at her which bounced off her face and then the floor. I collapsed backward on the hotel bed, my hair fanned the flat mattress where the pillow had lain. "I don't really know where to start."

"Start with whatever is on your mind. That makes the most sense. This doesn't need to be a night of spilling your soul. I think we would need something stronger than beer to get through that."

"Okay..." Start with what was on my mind, or in this case, my heart. Misha. "I fell in love while I was in Russia." I paused to suck in a deep breath. "And now he's gone forever. He's dead."

***

My hand smoothed the steam from the mirror, and I stared at my foggy reflection. My eyes were red-rimmed and shadowed with purplish circles, but the tears were gone. At least for now.

I could see Lex's sleeping form in the dimly lit bedroom behind me. We'd stayed up long into the night talking. Drinking. Crying.

Lex had cried with me. For me. Before last night I don't think I'd ever seen her shed a single tear, but she had shed them for my heartache. Heart break.

We had both fallen asleep around one in the morning, too emotionally exhausted to go on.

"Kate?" I turned and saw Lex stirring in the bed. She sat up and looked around. Her golden hair was a messy halo that made me smile.

"I'm here. Just took a shower to help wake me up a bit." I walked from the bathroom and paused to flip the switch on the coffee maker. "Don't worry, some unexceptional hotel coffee to the rescue." I grinned at her as I hopped onto the bed. "It was nice to have a sleepover with you again. Felt like old times."

"Yeah, but I don't remember having a hangover like this after our sleepovers," she mumbled as she lay back down and burrowed into the blankets.

"Of course not. We didn't drink at thirteen."

I received a grunt from her in response which made me giggle. "Come on. Go take a super hot shower. The coffee will be ready when you get out. And I'll even scavenge for Danishes or whatever they have in the continental breakfast."

That got her moving. She threw back the covers and headed to the shower. "Okay, but I get first dibs."

By the time I arrived back in the room, my arms loaded with plates, Lex was standing at the sink using my brush to comb out the kinks in her hair. A steaming cup of coffee was on the counter in front of her.

"Okay, they had a surprising assortment this morning. We have a cinnamon roll, a Belgian waffle, and some fake eggs and floppy bacon. They really outdid themselves today," I said with cheerful sarcasm.

"Waffle will be good, thanks." I set her plate down on the counter before sitting on the bed with my cinnamon roll, sub-par eggs, and bacon. I didn't mind. "I think talking with you helped me a lot," I said around a mouthful of bacon.

"Yeah? I'm glad. You know I'm not the most chatty, forthcoming person, myself, but even I found it helps."

We ate in silence, both of us lost in our own thoughts. Mine centered around my friend and my brother. I still couldn't get the fact they were together to make sense in my head. It was weird and slightly uncomfortable. I decided it was best to get it all out in the open. "Can I ask you a question about you and Derek?"

"Sure."

"How did you recover so easily from him kidnapping you? You seem like you've got it all together, but it wasn't that long ago."

"That's...a complicated question. I guess my recovery went hand-in-hand with forgiving him. And I'll tell you that didn't come easily. I was so fucking mad at him!" She glanced at me with a self-deprecating smile. "Sorry for my language."

I found my smile again as my BFF lightened the mood. "S'fine. Keep going." I had to know. I needed to know this was possible. That everything would eventually be okay.

"I guess I realized that Derek wasn't out for blood with everyone, just me. And he went through Hell during court and in prison. I figured he'd suffered enough. And he practically groveled which helped a lot." She sent me a grin.

"How did you deal with the kidnapping itself?"

"The judge in Derek's court case forced me to see a psychologist, but I continued seeing him long after. Dr. Reynolds specializes in kidnapping and trafficking victims, and he's amazing. I can set up an appointment for you if you'd like." She turned to face me, coffee cup in hand.

I still wasn't sure about seeing a psychologist, but I supposed if Lex could do it, I could, too. "Yeah, that'd be great."

"I'm glad you're ready. I really think it will be good for you. And if you want, me, Derek, or both of us can be there with you for support. You just let us know."

I nodded, a lump in my throat. I was truly lucky to have a best friend as amazing as Lex. I knew that with her help, I would start to heal.

Chapter 3

Kate

Past

I wasn't just sick, I was seriously ill. Like, maybe dying, and I wished I could get the dying part over with and have some peace! My stomach was so cramped it felt like it had twisted itself into a knot that throbbed angrily with each breath. Every muscle ached like I had run a marathon. And if that wasn't bad enough, my skin felt like the boiling surface of the sun. I was wracked with chills so intense I felt like my bones would shake right out of my body.

I wanted to die. I *yearned* for death.

A horrible sound invaded my misery, and I realized it was coming from me. I groaned, turned on my side, and threw up until my stomach was empty. Cool, gentle hands helped me settle onto my back once more, and a damp cloth wiped my mouth and chin. I tried to open my eyes, but I felt too weak to lift my eyelids. The hand returned to smooth across my cheeks and forehead, cooling my blistering skin. I drifted off to a fitful sleep.

Time was an unknown entity as I drifted in and out of sleep. I would wake up to my entire body shaking. The only solace I found was in the cool hands which dampened my lips with cold water and stroked my hair. She—the voice which accompanied the hands definitely belonged to a *she*—spoke to me in soft whispers and even sang me to sleep like my mom used to do when I was little, but I couldn't understand the words.

Eventually, my eyes opened. My body hurt like I had been in a car accident, but thankfully the throbbing muscle aches of before were now only a memory. Everything before now was hazy and muddled in my mind, so I turned my head to glance around and gauge where I was.

The room was tiny with sunlight filtering through white lace curtains. The only other furniture in the room besides the bed was a trunk and a small chair by the bedside. Where the heck was I?

The sound of footsteps outside the room drew my attention, and I slowly gathered myself to a sitting position. It was just in time because the door was pushed open and two women entered. One carried a wooden tray which she set on the foot of the bed. There was something about the older of the two that drew my attention. My eyes skated over her elegant black updo, noting no hint of gray despite faint lines at the corners of her eyes which crinkled in a smile.

"Hello." Her voice was rich with warmth which immediately soothed my raw senses. I tried to place her accent. German? Russian?

"Hey. Where am I?"

"You're in Russia, child."

Holy guacamole! What the heck happened to me? Flashes of memory lit up my mind, but none of them stayed long enough for me to grasp. Tears pricked at the corners of my eyes, and I blinked rapidly to keep them from spilling over.

"Who are you?" I sniffled softly.

The woman rounded the bed and perched in the nearby chair. Her hand was soft and gentle as it gripped mine. "I am Irina Bombadine of Madame Bombadine's Exotic Treasures. I procured you from a salesman to be one of my rare and beautiful treasures."

I wasn't sure if it was her accent or her wording, but I was seriously confused. "I don't understand."

She gave my hand a reassuring squeeze and said cryptically, "It will come in due time, child. You have much growing up to do first." She motioned for the younger woman to come forward. "This is Emmeline. She speaks some English and can interpret for you until you learn Russian."

"Why would I need to learn Russian?"

"This is your home now, child."

"No! My home is in America! I want my mom and dad!" I vaulted out of the bed and stumbled as dizziness overtook me. But I wouldn't be defeated. Once I was steady, I ran for the door, threw it open, and launched down a narrow hallway. My ears strained for pounding feet behind me, but it was silent. In fact, the...house?...was quiet as could be. My footsteps slowed to a tiptoes as I approached a staircase and slowly walked down.

That's when I realized why no one was coming after me. A huge man sat on a stool by the elegant, wooden door. His arms were crossed as he warily watched me. Why did a house have a bouncer?

We stared at each other, me on the stairs, him on his stool as I slowly dropped down each step until I stood on the last one. Energy gathered in my muscles, and I sprang for the door, my feet barely touching the runner on the tiled entryway floor. My fingers grasped the doorknob, twisted, and...nothing. I tugged as hard as I could! But still nothing. The door was locked. I turned and glared at the bouncer. He was still sitting there, arms crossed, eyes on me.

"Let me out." My voice grated out between clenched teeth.

No response.

I refused to give up. I turned from the door and raced from room to room. The adrenaline pounding through my veins made my legs strong and fast. The rooms I peeked into were ornate—almost gaudy, a term my mother had used numerous times when speaking with decorators. She had a habit of redecorating every three years or whenever she and my dad were arguing, something they'd been doing a lot lately.

I knew in my heart that my disappearance would either bring them together again or break them apart for good.

I raced straight into the kitchen where several women sat at a table, hands white with flour and dough. Since I hadn't been able to find a back door, my heart leapt when I found the room. Most kitchens I'd seen had a door leading outside, and I hoped this one would be the same. And it was! A white-painted door was perfectly framed against the far wall.

One of the women stood from the table and planted herself in front of me so quickly I had to dig my heels into the linoleum to not run into her. I narrowed my eyes and studied her sturdy frame for any weakness.

"*Ostanovka!*"

"Please, let me out!" I whimpered. "I want to go home!"

The hard look from the woman's face softened, and I dared to hope she would move out of the way. But then she slashed her hand downward with a soft, "*Niet.*"

I knew enough that she was denying my escape. My freedom! She made a shooing motion back toward the hallway I had come from only seconds before.

Something happened then. I grew a backbone I didn't know existed. I mirrored her position with legs splayed and balled fists on my hips. "Niet." The foreign word felt odd on my lips as I attempted the exact inflection.

Don't hit me, don't hit me, don't hit me! The prayer rushed through my head. I didn't know what the consequence was going to be for my bravado, but I wasn't backing down.

The woman and I stared at each other for a long minute before the corners of her lips pulled up into a smile. Her booming laugh startled me out of my stand-off stance. "*Ty rebenok,*" she said.

I had no idea what she'd called me. I uncurled one finger from a balled fist and pointed at the door behind her.

She shook her head.

Okay. I was close enough to the flour and dough covered table to touch. And touch I did. I reared my hand out to the side, fingers scrabbling on the wooden table, and then I shot forward with one large ball of dough. I watched in complete satisfaction as the dough whirled through the air and splatted right against the woman's chin and neck.

Her smile was gone now, replaced with an angry, mottled red. I had seen that look on my teachers' faces when a student talked back, and I shivered in unease. That didn't stop me from reaching for another dough ball which I lobbed directly at the woman again.

Then I made a mad dash for the door.

Elation surged through me as my fingers curled around the doorknob, but my heart began to beat in desperation when a strong arm wrapped around my waist. I screamed in frustration and failure as I was yanked away from my prize and my freedom.

The next moment I was flat on my stomach on the floor, barely able to breathe with the woman's weight on my back. I shoved against the floor, kicked my legs. Anything to get some leverage, but I couldn't move.

A sharp pain on my bottom ripped through my desperation. I paused in my screaming and struggling wondering what had just happened. And then there came another slap to my bottom! And another! This time I howled for a different reason entirely. I hadn't been spanked since I was a small child and stole a cookie from the jar before supper. Now I was brought back to that moment of pain with the cracking whacks against my bottom and thighs.

When the spanking stopped, I was hauled to my feet and marched from the kitchen with a death grip on my arm.

The woman who had brought food to my room was standing on the bottom step of the staircase. Her calmness told me that this situation wasn't new to her or this place. Nor was it new to anyone else, if my guess was right. The bodyguard hadn't even moved from his post by the door. What kind of low life treated people this way?

I was marched right up to Madame Bombadine, and I listened to the rapid-fire Russian spoken between her and the cook who still had her meaty hand around my bicep.

When the conversation was over, the cook walked away without a backward glance, but my attention was fully focused on the woman in charge.

"Did you get it all out?" she asked gently.

"What?" I added an extra edge of sass to my tone.

"Your need to prove yourself an unwilling victim. If you manage to leave the property, not so many out there speak English. And less will care. Russians care about two things: Russia and their own survival. You, little American girl, are nothing."

You are nothing. I was alone in a strange country where I didn't speak the language or know the customs. And my survival skills were negligible at best. I had never felt more like a kid than I did now. If I was going to get out of this, I was going to have to grow up.

Lesson one: Survive.

It didn't take me long to learn lesson two: eat the food immediately. When Madame Bombadine was finished speaking, I crawled onto the bed next to the tray of food which looked even less appetizing than when it had first arrived. There were potato dumplings swimming in some type of cream-based broth that was beginning to congeal and a beet salad with a vinegary dressing so strong, the smell was burning my nose.

"Eat up. You won't get more until supper, and we eat late around here," the matron said, sitting down in the chair beside the bed.

I dipped my spoon into the broth and lifted it to my mouth. It didn't smell as bad as it looked, thank God, but my stomach still flip-flopped in distaste. I slid the spoon into my mouth and drew it out clean. The texture and consistency weren't great, but the taste wasn't bad. I could eat it.

Survive.

Survive.

Survive.

I ate the entire bowl of soup, the crusty bread, and the salad because I knew I had to keep my strength up.

"Now that your belly's full, let me tell you my expectations."

Expectations. The word rang like a bell in my mind foretelling an awful future.

"What is your age?"

"Thirteen."

"And what is your name?"

"Kate."

"No. It is Sveta."

My brows drew together in confusion. What the heck? "You can't just change my name. It's my *legal* name. It's on my birth certificate."

"Darling, you're not home anymore. Who you were is not who you are now, nor who you will become. You are Sveta. That is all."

I pursed my lips and decided to hold in my arguments. It wasn't like she was going to listen anyway.

After eyeing me sternly for a moment, she continued, "This place is a high end brothel." At my confused expression, she explained, "A place where women sell sex for money."

Oh, my goodness! I felt like my lunch was about to show itself again.

"Don't worry, Sveta," she patted my knee warmly, "you are only thirteen. A child. I don't sell children here."

"But you do *buy* them," I shot back at her.

"Yes, but that is because you are safer here than in other places. Some wouldn't care that you are a child. They would sell you to the highest bidder regardless of your age. Anyway, I can still make use of you. You will earn your keep by doing chores: laundry, dishes, prepping food in the kitchen for meals. Then when you are eighteen, you will earn your keep like the rest of the girls here: on your back."

S.E.X?! How was I supposed to be a S.E.X. worker if I couldn't even say the word?! My mom's version of teaching me the birds and the bees was by making me read *Are You There God? It's Me, Margaret.* by Judy Blume every time I asked a question. "For how long?" I asked, dubiously. I was already looking at being here for five years which sent my heart racing in panic mode again. My hands trembled as I plucked at the quilt.

"Until your beauty runs out or you earn a sum of five million rubles. Whichever comes first."

Holy cow! I was never going home. I had no idea how much five million rubles was in American dollars, but a million of *anything* sounded like an astronomical amount. The only thing I could count on was my beauty—or lack thereof—getting me out of this ordeal earlier than five million rubles would. My best friend had the beauty, and I had the brains.

Madame Bombadine patted my knee and stood from the bed. "Get some rest. Tomorrow will be the first of many long days."

Chapter 4

Misha

Past

"Happy birthday, Misha, darling!" My mother said as she dropped a kiss on my cheek and passed a serving plate of my favorite orange rolls to me. As a growing boy does, I plopped three huge orange rolls onto my plate and bypassed the healthy stuff. The only time fruit should touch my plate is if it is rolled in sugar and dough.

"Thank you, Mother," I said with as much maturity as I could put into my manly tone. It was a big birthday for me. In the Family, fifteen meant you were entering manhood and could start learning the business. I wasn't an idiot. I knew my father was head of a Russian Bratva. I had grown up with frightened teachers and whispering school children. The only friends I had were the children of other Family members. Kids I called "cousins" who weren't actually blood-related.

"There you are, Misha." My father set down his newspaper and studied me with a gleam in his dark eyes. "I thought you were going to sleep through all the festivities."

"Papa, you know Misha takes a shower for a full *hour* every morning and then takes another hour just to do his hair."

I glared at my twin and kicked her under the table.

"You all do realize that it's *my* fifteenth birthday, too, right?" she whined. If she wasn't such a brat sometimes, I would have felt bad for her seeing as this day wasn't as special for a Bratva princess as it was for a prince. Especially the heir.

"Of course, Valentina, darling. You and I will go on a shopping spree later while the men do their thing," our mother replied, patting Valentina's hand.

"Can I get a tattoo like Misha?" She asked hopefully.

"Absolutely not, my dear," Mother responded, lifting her teacup for a sip. "Ladies don't get tattoos."

Valentina snorted. "I've seen plenty of ladies with tattoos. Cousin Pelka got one when she turned eighteen."

"First of all, there is a world of life experience between fifteen and eighteen. And second, Pelka is not a role model you should aspire to be like." She took another sip of tea and then muttered under her breath, "She will be pregnant before she's wed, most likely."

Obviously Mother's voice wasn't as soft as she thought because Valentina snorted her juice in response and sat back with a coughing fit. In brotherly fashion, I couldn't pass up the opportunity to annoy my sister, so I rounded the table and began helpfully whacking her on the back.

"Misha, stop hitting your sister. She stopped coughing a full minute ago," Mother stated. I gave Valentina one more "pat" on the back before returning to my breakfast. I turned to Papa who was studying me with a small smile. "What's on the agenda today, Papa?"

"A number of surprises. Eat up."

***

"That tattoo isn't going anywhere, Nephew."

I glanced up into the mirror to see my uncle's smirking face behind me in the bathroom doorway. Reluctantly, I replaced the tape over the gauze patch on the tender skin below my right ear, and I turned to face him.

"What's up, Uncle Yuri?" He was my favorite of my three uncles because he always gave me a birthday gift. I hoped this birthday would be no exception.

"I have a special surprise for you since you are becoming a man today. Meet me in the garage in ten minutes."

It had been a day full of surprises between getting my first Bratva tattoo, a driving lesson in Papa's Lamborghini, and dinner at Valentina's favorite restaurant. I was tired but also excited about what this next surprise could be.

My uncle's eldest son, Pavel, and my youngest uncle, Grigori were waiting with Uncle Yuri next to a sleek, black SUV.

"Where are we going?" I asked when we piled into the car.

"You'll see!" My cousin grinned at me in a way that made me nervous and excited at the same time. Where the hell were they taking me? "It's a Belov family tradition! A right of passage."

Clearly no one was going to give me a straight answer. That was fine. I liked to delay gratification because it made the reward that much sweeter.

I watched Moscow race by as we drove toward the edge of the city. I knew the riskier businesses like gun smuggling, prostitution, underground fight clubs, and gambling happened there. So I wasn't surprised when we eventually slowed and parked on a side street next to a tall row-house.

"Come on, Misha," Pavel, only two years older than me, said. "It's time to get your dick wet."

They had brought me to a whorehouse! I wasn't disgusted by the idea, but I also wasn't excited. Honestly, I didn't want my first time to be with a whore! It sounds lame, but I'd always hoped sex would happen with someone I actually liked. Or loved. I'd had girlfriends through the years and a computer with fast internet. So I wasn't completely ignorant about sex, but going to a brothel was a huge jump from a clumsy make-out fondle in the back of a car with my girlfriend.

The sound of a concerto drifted from the multi-story row-house. I would not have considered classical to be the music of choice at a brothel. Then again, I'd never visited one before now. Knowing how much my uncles loved the finer things in life, maybe this brothel wasn't the seedy kind. Was there such a thing as an upscale brothel? I didn't know.

The doorman—bouncer?—nodded to Uncle Yuri and opened the door for us. The air was spiced with heavy perfume and the lamps cast a dim, warm glow. The place felt comfortable. Cozy, even. My nerves began to drain away.

We followed the sound of male and female laughter to a large room with an abundance of furniture situated in quiet, cozy gatherings. Men and women were sprawled in all manner of undress. There was no actual sex happening that I could tell, but I imagined it was only a matter of time. Several men were talking together at a side table over drinks. The women were never together unless they were with customers. Yuri led us to an unoccupied section of sofas, and we all sat. It wasn't long before an older woman with black hair walked to us with a large smile.

"Mr. Belov! So lovely to see you as always." She took his hands as he stood and kissed both of his cheeks in greeting before turning to smile at the rest of us.

"Madame Bombadine, I'd like you to meet my nephew, Misha. Today is his fifteenth birthday." His hand gripped my arm and hauled me to my feet.

"Ah, a special day indeed! I remember it was Pavel's fifteenth birthday not so long ago." She winked at my cousin who was too busy making eyes at a dark-skinned woman who had just walked into the room.

"Misha, do you see anyone who strikes your fancy?" Madame Bombadine asked.

I took in the room. One dark haired woman massaged the shoulders of the older man seated in front of her while another fed him small hors devours from a platter. Another woman giggled as her customer whispered in her ear. His sneaky hand caressed her inner thigh. Everywhere I looked, people were involved with each other. I looked back at Madame and shrugged like the teenager I was.

"Still a bit shy, I see. Well, make yourself at home."

I nodded and watched the room with fascination. The women here weren't what I expected. They looked healthy and clean, not like the ones I'd seen on street corners who looked like they would kill you rather than screw you. Or maybe they would kill you after screwing you. I didn't know and didn't care. I guessed these women were fancy prostitutes. Their clothes were made of fine silks and satins, and they looked like they had just rolled out of bed but in the best way imaginable. And they smelled good, too.

Hearing a noise to my right, I glanced over to see my uncle's face mashed up against the madame's as he kissed her. With tongue!

Gross!

I stood and moved away, confident that my family were all too preoccupied to notice or care. A flash of movement caught my eye, and I turned to see a girl sitting on the staircase with her face pressed between the slats in the railing. Her fingers, which caught most of the dim light in the hallway, twitched in time to the music. What was she doing there? Was she a maid? A younger sister of one of the girls? I felt a little sick thinking that a young girl like that lived in a whorehouse. I mean, I wouldn't want Valentina to even know this place existed.

When she caught me staring, she frowned and skittered up the stairs until she was out of sight. I slipped out of the room and found her sitting at the top of the stairs.

I waved.

She hesitated a moment then wriggled her fingers in what I assumed was a little wave.

"What are you doing?" I asked.

She looked down at me, her brow wrinkled in confusion. "I don't speak Russian."

"You're American?" I asked in complete surprise. My English wasn't perfect, but it was passable.

"Oh, thank goodness! Someone who speaks English! I've been—"

"Slow down," I said, alarmed at how quickly she was speaking. "English is not my first language."

"Sorry, I just got excited to be able to communicate with someone other than Madame and Emmeline."

"Why are you here? Is your father in there?" I pointed to the large room I came from, a little horrified at the thought of a father bringing his daughter to a place like this. To wait for him while he...I shuddered at the thought.

She shook her head and tears turned her eyes into lakes of dark blue. "No. I was kidnapped and brought here." Her voice broke, and her lips trembled as she said, "I want to go home. Can you get me back to America?"

My eyes widened, and my jaw dropped. *Kidnapped*! I moved around to the front of the staircase and jogged up to sit on the stair beneath hers. Though I'd never met a person who was kidnapped, smuggling children wasn't unheard of. In Russia, you could buy or sell *anything*, which was a benefit or a curse depending on which side of it you were on. Clearly, this girl was in distress. Her tears sent a pang of sympathy into my heart. I really wanted to find a way to help her, even if she was American. "I can ask my uncle when we leave. I'm sure I will be back, so I will let you know what he says then. What's your name?"

"Kate, but Madame calls me Sveta."

I wrinkled my nose. "Sveta doesn't suit you. I will call you Katya. It's Kate in Russian." That got a smile out of her at last. I couldn't imagine what she had been through, and taking away her identity seemed like an unnecessary cruelty. "My name is Misha. Would you like to learn?"

"Learn what?"

"Russian." I couldn't imagine being in a country where I didn't speak the language, and this seemed a good enough way to pass the time until I could go home. Plus, I was willing to do anything to make the girl stop crying.

She wasn't a pretty crier. Before the tears started she looked like a fairy waif with her pale skin and long, white blonde hair. Now there were misshapen pink splotches on her cheeks, her eyes were rimmed in red, and her nose was running. I dug into my pocket and handed her a blue handkerchief. She patted her cheeks and nose, then offered it back to me, but I held up both hands with a look of disgust. "Keep it."

She twisted the fine fabric between her fingers and took a deep breath which she let out slowly. "Okay. I want to learn. I need to be able to communicate."

Smart girl.

By the time my uncles and cousin were finished with their "business", Kate—Katya—had memorized several common words and phrases. Enough that she could at least ask where the bathroom was.

"Misha!" My uncle's voice echoed in the high-ceilinged hallway. I jumped up and trotted down the steps, pausing halfway to turn and wave, but Katya had already disappeared.

"I noticed you disappeared pretty quickly," my uncle stated as I walked down the stairs. He had my father's penetrating stare that always made me squirm and tattle as a small child. "Did you have a good time?"

My cousin let out a lecherous laugh at his side and I rolled my eyes. "Yes, Uncle."

"Good, good. Happy birthday." He absently turned his attention back to his phone as we walked to the door.

Feeling my cousin's eyes focused on me, I flicked my gaze to him. "What?" I asked through my teeth. The prick was always watching me.

"Which girl did you sneak off with?"

"Some blonde. I didn't bother to get her name." The lie rolled easily off my tongue. I didn't want to draw attention to my new friend. I'd heard a rumor that my cousin liked younger girls.

"Veronika," Uncle replied as he tapped on his phone.

Neither my cousin nor I answered, but I took note of his unsettling smile before I got into the car.

**

Today, the day after my birthday, I was to be initiated. The club I would join was not a country club or a sports club. It was the Bratva. I'd grown up knowing and anticipating this day. Every birthday, my father would comment that I was one year closer to initiation. One year closer to being a true part of the Family. Every year when he said that, a thrill of anticipation and excitement would run up and down my spine, but today...today I felt the heaviness of responsibility like a weighted blanket—but less comforting —wrapped around my shoulders.

I wasn't good with change. Never had been. When I left my black tricycle in the driveway when I was five, it was run over. The ally of my father who had hit it bought me a shiny red tricycle, and I threw such a tantrum that my father whipped me right there in the front yard for the world to see. He whipped the tantrum out of me, but I still hated change.

It was uncomfortable.

What was worse than change was not knowing what to expect. And that's where I found myself as I stared at my reflection in my mirror. I had dressed to impress in a navy suit. My hair was brushed. I had removed the bandage from my tattoo, and the black ink was crisp against the skin behind my ear.

A text buzzed on my phone, and I picked it up from the counter. A one-liner from Father. *Come to my office.* No please. No thank you. That's how the Pakhan of our Family operated. He ordered; you obeyed. It's how I grew up. Mother was much the same, though she had a softer touch and a softer temper.

I walked out of my room and took the stairs at a trot down to the main level. Soon, I was at my father's office door and knocking. Uncle Yuri opened it and stood back for me to enter. I stepped inside and scanned the room of men. All the uncles on both sides of the Family were present as well as the male cousins who were already initiated. No one smiled at me, shook my hand, congratulated me on turning fifteen and being able to join the Family. It was silent and grim. My stomach somersaulted, and I suddenly felt like I was going to puke.

My father stood in front of his desk. His piercing black eyes, so like my own, stared at me. In the back of my mind, I had a vague sense of hoping I could look at someone the same way when I took over the Family. The thought of eventually taking over the Family and business made me straighten my spine in pride. Today was important, and I needed to be brave. I was a fifteen year old man, now, not a little boy. Though it hurt like a bitch, I didn't cry yesterday when I got my tattoo. Surely this would be no worse than that.

"Misha Belov," my father intoned into the silence, "do you come here of your own free will?"

My swallow was audible in the stillness before I answered, "Yes."

"Come forward and place your right hand on the Belov family Bible."

As I walked forward, my uncle picked up the massive book from its honored resting place on the carved wooden lectern and held it out flat. When I was six, I snuck into my father's office. He came in right when I was reaching for the Bible, then he whipped me within an inch of my life after explaining why I should never touch it. After fearing the ramifications of touching this book for years, my hands turned sweaty at the thought of touching it now. I wiped my right hand on my pants before placing it on top of the family Bible. I know I imagined the power I felt thrumming through it. It was just a Bible, after all. A really, really old Bible that had been in the Belov family since before we thought about creating an organized crime syndicate.

"Misha, repeat the rules of the Family after me. I will never betray a member of the Belov Family."

I lifted my eyes from the rough leather of the Bible to my father's eyes which now seemed to burn into me. "I will never betray a member of the Belov Family."

"I will never violate the wife or children of another member. I will not engage in battle if I cannot win. I will be a man of honor. I will respect women and my elders. I will keep my eyes and ears open and my mouth shut."

I repeated all of these verbatim. With each vow, I felt the tie to my father and the other men in the room grow stronger as if an invisible force were tying knots in our unseen connection. This responsibility was heavy and tight, and I felt the urge to roll my shoulders to relieve the discomfort.

"Blood of my blood, we seal your membership." My father grasped my wrist and flipped my hand palm upward. Then he slid the ring off his index finger and did something completely unexpected. With a sharp twist of his fingers, he snapped off the brilliant ruby on top to reveal what looked like a small spike. He brought the spike down onto my index finger. I was proud of myself for not flinching! I watched as a bead of dark red welled out of the puncture. My uncle opened the Bible to the inside cover where an enormous and elaborate family tree was intricately drawn. Fingerprints of dark brown, aged blood dotted the tree like morbid Christmas ornaments. My father took my bloodied finger and pressed it down below where my name was scrawled in his bold handwriting.

I had just signed my fate, literally, in blood.

Chapter 5

Kate

Past

My days were filled with chores designed to keep me so busy I didn't have time to think or do anything else. I didn't stay up late every night like I had the first night when I'd watched my future from between the slats of the staircase bannister with wide, shocked eyes. Instead, I fell asleep as soon as my head hit the pillow when my last chore was complete, and I woke at daybreak to do it all again.

I didn't see Misha until the next weekend. I guessed that made sense. He was a teenager, like me. I'm sure he went to school and had friends. Maybe a girlfriend. He was leading a normal life while I was trapped in a prison of old Russian charm with a sketchy future I wasn't ready to think about.

I had just finished washing the dinner dishes, my fingers like raisins from being submerged in hot water for so long. I felt gross, tired, and starved after scrubbing pots and pans while everyone else in the house ate. That was how it had been all week, so it wasn't anything new. I took my plate out of the refrigerator, zapped it in the microwave, then headed toward the back staircase. Apparently I wasn't supposed to be seen by the clientele.

"Psst!"

The sound had me stuttering to a stop, and I turned to see where it had come from.

"Katya, this way!"

The first smile of the week pulled at my lips as I recognized Misha's dark-haired head peering out at me from beneath the stairwell. A boyish smile tugged at his lips, and a dimple winked from his cheeks. He beckoned me to him, and I glanced around before sitting on the bench next to him in the darkness.

He leaned in and stared at my plate. "What is that?"

"My dinner."

"Mmm... looks like pelmeni."

"I have no idea what that means."

His lips twitched into a grin, and he reached to snag one of the little dumpling ravioli things.

"Dude, that's my dinner! I haven't eaten since this morning." That wasn't entirely true, but I wouldn't call a piece of flatbread around eleven o'clock 'eating'. "Didn't you eat before coming here?"

"Yes, but pelmeni is my favorite!" Misha's melting dark eyes and pouting mouth had me offering my plate before I knew what I was doing. "*Spasibo*, Katya!" He leaned in and brushed my cheek with a dry graze of his lips before snagging two pieces of pel-whatever with his fingers.

I watched him shove both bites into his mouth at the same time and giggled as he waggled his eyebrows at me. Then I snagged one dumpling with my fork and tentatively placed it in my mouth. It was delicious! Suddenly, I was ravenous, and I began to eat quickly.

"It's good but not as good as my grandmother's recipe. My mother makes it a lot. I will have her make some special for you next time I come."

I swallowed the lump in my throat at his kindness. "That's really sweet, Misha. So... your mom knows you come here?"

He shrugged. "We don't talk about it, but I'm pretty sure she knows."

The thought of my mom knowing her son—my brother —would go to a sex house horrified me as much as it would my mom AND my brother.

A change of topic was in order, so I said, "Can you teach me some more words and phrases?"

"Only if you can remember the ones I taught you last weekend."

"Alright. Um, *spasibo* means 'thank you'. *Privet* is 'hello'. *Do svidanya* is 'goodbye'. *Da* is 'yes', *niet* is 'no'. And *gde toualet* is 'where is the toilet'." That last one had taken me a good ten minutes to learn to pronounce correctly, much to Misha's amusement.

"*Otlichnaya rabota*, Katya! That means 'good job'!"

I beamed at the praise. I was the kind of student who sat in the front row, took notes until my fingers felt like they were going to fall off, and worked for every scrap of praise uttered from my teachers' lips.

Even though Misha wasn't an adult, I considered him to be not only my friend, but also my Russian tutor. If I had to live in this godforsaken country with no ruby slippers to click together to send me home, I had better learn to survive.

Step One of Survival: learn the language. Knowledge is power.

"I also brought you an English to Russian dictionary," Misha beamed at me as he presented a small book from the pocket of his jacket.

I shoved the last dumpling into my mouth and set the plate next to me. Then I took the thick book into my hands.

"*Spasibo*, Misha!" I smiled as I flipped through the pages.

He ducked his head with a grin. "It's not much, but I thought it would be useful. Anyway, I want to know some more about my new friend. How are you doing?"

My smile slid from my face as his expression turned serious. I lifted one shoulder in a shrug and pulled my knees to my chest, wrapping my arms around them. "I don't know. I mean, I guess it's okay for what it is. For now." But I wouldn't be a maid in this house forever. Madame was very clear about my future role. As if on cue, moans escaped from one of the nearby rooms, and I shuddered with revulsion. "Misha, I don't want to be a prostitute! That's not me! It's not who I am! It's not who I'm meant to be." My lungs constricted until I felt like I couldn't breathe. Like I was drowning within myself. Heaves of strangled breath puffed against my knees. "I miss my mom and dad," I whispered between gasps, "and even my brother." Black dots danced in my vision.

Misha turned me to him, grasped my wrists, and shoved them up above my head, opening my airway. "Katya, breathe. Panicking isn't going to help."

He was right. I dropped my head back, and tried to suck in lungfuls of sweet air until the muscle-clenching panic began to subside. Once I was back to myself, I gazed ahead at the far wall. "I want to go home more than anything in the world." Risking a sideways glance at Misha, I tentatively asked, "Did you ask your uncle about helping me get home?"

A brush against my cheek had my eyes flicking over to Misha, and I realized he'd stroked a tear from my face. I hadn't known I was crying. I didn't know I could still cry after all the tears I shed at night—every night—when I thought about the pain my family and best friend must be feeling. I could only hope Lex escaped and wasn't in the same boat as me.

Or worse.

I didn't want to think about that, though. Freaking out about my friend wasn't going to do me any favors here. I couldn't do anything about her.

Misha's warm hand took mine, and he squeezed so hard it was like he was giving me some of his strength. "Not yet, but Katya, I promise that one day I will set you free and get you home. I don't know when or how, but I will do it. This I swear." He placed my hand on his heart, his dark eyes boring into mine. The beat of his heart thumped beneath his warm skin against my hand. Strong and true.

The breath shuddered out of my body at his vow, and I slowly nodded my understanding. Each word rang with truth, and I believed him. Patience was going to have to be my best friend until then.

"Okay, well, until then, we can get to know each other. When is your birthday and what's your favorite food?"

Now that the heavy mood had lightened, I could breathe a little easier.

A hesitant smile kicked up the corners of my mouth, and I replied, "December 1st, which I always hated, by the way, because everyone was gearing up for the holidays. My birthday presents usually got lumped in with my Christmas presents." I poked my lower lip out in a pout as I thought back to the not-so-many birthdays I'd had.

Only thirteen. Maybe thirteen really was an unlucky number.

"And your favorite food?" Misha prompted.

"Chipwich!" I exclaimed with a smile.

"I have never heard of this 'Chipwich'. What is it?"

"It's two chocolate chip cookies stuck together with vanilla ice cream in the middle, and rolled with chocolate chips. It's to *die* for. I usually ask for that instead of a cake for my birthday. I know it's not traditional, but go with what you like, right?"

"Right!" Misha responded wholeheartedly. "Where do you get this ice cream cookie sandwich? Do you make it or buy it?"

"I mean, you can do both. I've made my own before, but nothing compares to a REAL one from the grocery store. I guess it would be like making your own Nutty Buddy."

Misha stared at me with his mouth open. His brows pinched together.

"Let me guess...you've never heard of a Nutty Buddy, either." I didn't know much about Russia, but didn't these huge companies like Mayfield and Nestle distribute around the world? "Don't you ever go to the grocery store with your mom? I used to hide out in the frozen foods section just to look at all the glorious ice cream options."

"No, I don't think I've ever been to a grocery store...." His eyes turned distant as he turned to thought, and then he shook his head adamantly. "No. Never."

"What? How? How have you never been to a grocery store?"

He shrugged. "We have a chef who does all the shopping and cooking. When Mother wants to cook something, Chef goes out to buy the supplies."

A personal chef. Dude really *was* rich. "That sounds cool, too. Much better than going to the grocery store. But you also missed out on all the different kinds of popsicles, ice creams, and frozen waffles."

"Frozen waffles? Why would anyone want to eat those?"

"Oh, my gosh! Leggo my Eggo, dude!"

Apparently that was too much for him. He began laughing hysterically, and I had to shush him to keep from catching anyone's notice. But I was grinning, too.

"Okay, your homework for next time I visit is to make me a list of all the foods I need to try." He pulled out his cell phone and began typing. My eyes stared hungrily as his thumbs flew across the smooth glass. A cell phone. For the first time since meeting Misha, I took a moment to gauge if it would be possible to overtake him. Not hurt him, of course, just take the phone and make a call. His eyes flicked up and caught mine in their darkness. "Can you read Cyrillic?"

"No...."

"Then you can't use my phone."

"Aren't numbers the same in every language except for written out or Asian characters?"

"No."

"Why won't you just call and schedule a flight home for me?"

"It's not that simple, Katya." There was an edge of irritation in his voice. "If I could, I would. But you don't have a passport. You don't have a reason for being here. In all records you really *aren't* here in Russia. You don't have money—"

"But you do!" The whine in my voice annoyed even myself.

"My money is closely monitored by my father. I can't help you. We need an adult." And then he changed the subject so fast I nearly got whiplash. "So far I have Chipwich, Nutty Buddy, and frozen waffles."

I was frozen there with my mouth open. How could he just change the subject like that? How could he treat my problem—a very serious problem, I might add—so casually? So carelessly. My dry-throat swallow was audible. The hardness in his eyes said there was no point in continuing to argue with him. My shoulders slumped. "Not just *any* frozen waffles. You need Eggo Buttermilk Waffles. Those are my fave."

"How do I spell that?"

"E.G.G.O. Like an egg with an O."

"Okay. I will give you my personal review next weekend."

"Yeah? You already know you are coming back then?"

"Yes. My uncle made sure I knew this was a regular thing unless I have something else planned. I wouldn't be too excited about it except that you're here."

Heat creeped up my cheeks at his compliment. "You make my time here better, too, Misha."

Chapter 6

Kate

Past

The next morning, I'd been woken at the crack of dawn, tossed a clean dress, and told—in broken English—to come down to the kitchen. When I entered, I took note of the bodyguards, a maid in uniform, and the kitchen staff all eating their fill. Life as usual now.

I found myself scarfing down a slice of fresh-baked bread and a bowl of hot oatmeal with golden raisins and butter as I listened to the foreign conversations around me, trying to pick up on any of the words Misha had taught me last night. Foreign languages came easily to me (Spanish was one of my favorite classes in school), but Russian was something else. The sounds didn't come naturally. It was melodic, in a way, but at the same time there was a rolling of the throat that had Misha's lips twitching as he tried not to laugh when I messed it up.

Once I shoveled the last bite of oatmeal into my mouth, I took my bowl to the sink for a quick wash. Then I stood awkwardly by the sink, unsure what to do. Normally, I'd already have a list of duties for the day

Should I go find Madame Bombadine for directions? I hated bothering her after a long night of work, though. She was definitely still in bed.

Should I try to find some other way to escape? Though the staff hadn't spoken to me while I ate breakfast, once in a while I caught the head baker eyeing me as if she was ready for me to make a move toward the door again. So, that was a hard no.

The maid, a plain-looking woman with graying hair in a bun so tight it gave her a mini-face lift, finally took pity on me. She approached with her bowl and rinsed it as I had, then turned to me, drying her hands on her apron. "I speak little bit English," she said by way of greeting. "You come." She offered a smile and a wave to the others before stepping into the foyer.

She was a fast walker, and being short, I had to nearly run to keep up with her. Luckily, we weren't going far. A few doors down from the kitchen was apparently the laundry room. Ugh, I absolutely hated doing laundry! It was my least favorite of all chores. Give me dishes, vacuuming, and even raking the leaves, but please don't give me laundry!

"Every Sunday, girls put clothings outside of rooms. You go get for me." She eyed me a moment before making a shooing motion. "Right now. Go get."

I blinked and then hurried from the room, toward the large staircase where Misha had found me. I raced up the stairs and meandered down a quiet hallway. The girls were up all night doing "business", as Madame had called it, and were now sleeping. Each door had a mesh bag with a name. Who knew a brothel could be so organized? I guess that's one reason this one was considered 'high end'? Ugh, whatever. According to Madame, I had years to worry about that. Enough time to find a way out of here and back home.

I started at the very end of the hallway and grabbed as many laundry bags as I could hold, then I tossed them down the stairs before returning for more. When I returned to the laundry room, bags in hand, the woman gave me a nod of thanks and showed me how to use the washer and dryer. I wasn't a stranger to laundry, but the dials were labeled in Russian lettering. Cyrillic, I think Misha had called it. Whatever the writing was called, it wasn't in any letters I recognized, so I was grateful for the maid's help.

"Clothings get washed, dried, folded. Put back in bags, then put outside rooms. Yes?"

"Yes, I understand. What's your name?"

The maid looked taken aback for a moment, and then gave me the first smile I'd seen on her face. It made the stern lines around her eyes soften and made her seem younger. Prettier. "Magdalena."

"I'm Ka—" I paused in confusion when she started shaking her head at me.

"Sveta."

Ugh. I hated that name!

"How about Katya?" I tried. Surely Misha's name for me would work.

"Niet. Sveta."

Sigh. It was very difficult to argue with someone who barely spoke your language. "Sveta," I conceded, but I gave her my patented sad puppy dog look that always worked on my dad and brother.

It did not work on Magdalena the Maid (or Magdalena the Miserable, if I was being honest in how she looked).

I turned away from her to start my chore. I was hoping that if I got it all done early, I would have some free time later to explore the house more. The laundry didn't take too long, and in between loads, I swept the stairs and ironed fresh sheets. Magdalena even taught me the correct way to fold a fitted sheet which my mother had despaired I'd ever learn. I used to bundle them up into a lump and toss them into the linen closet.

With every load cleaned, I separated the folded clothes into stacks from the names on the labels. Returning them all was my favorite chore because the girls were sweet and welcoming. Despite their status in life, most of them had ready smiles. Once in a while, they would even give me a coin or trinket as thanks. If being a maid was my final lot in life, I could do it. Unfortunately, that wasn't the case, as I was reminded by the late night music, moans, and pounding bed springs. It was a constant reminder of what was to come when I turned 18.

***

Misha found me again the next Saturday and presented me with a Tupperware container of dumplings which he assured me were way better than our cook had made. I had to agree. They were still hot and melted in my mouth. As my grandmother liked to say, this was the kind of food that soothed the soul. And it did. It warmed me from my mouth to my toes and every nook and cranny in between.

Misha watched me with a soft smile as I devoured the contents of the container. "I take it you like it," he said matter-of-factly.

"That's, hands down, the best food I've had since I've been here. Can you maybe bring me the recipe next time? I'd really like to try to make it."

"You cook?" The surprise on his face was laughable.

"Sort of. I mean, I've made cookies and brownies before. And mac and cheese, of course."

"Mac and cheese. Well, that brings us to our next conversation." He pulled out his phone, very seriously cleared his throat, and said, "I have not found a Chipwich, but I did find a Nutty Buddy at a gas station. I liked it very much. So much so that I bought two boxes and didn't tell my sister about them." He glanced up at me with a grin. "Can't have her eating my American food, right?"

"Right. What about the waffles?"

"I'm sorry to say that frozen waffles are yucky."

"Yucky? Are you sure you bought the Eggo brand?"

"Yes. I tried them twice. The first one did not cook all the way through, and the second one burned in the toaster oven because I let it cook longer."

I laughed, delighted at his ridiculous assessment of frozen waffles. "Those things are a staple in my household. I'm sorry you didn't like them."

He shrugged. "What else should I try?"

"I've been thinking about it all week and have settled on pepperoni pizza Hot Pockets, Totino's Pizza Rolls, and pizza Bagel Bites. I want to see which you like the best."

"Okay. I will try them, but after the waffles, I do not have much faith in these frozen foods."

I only smiled and gave him a shrug. Then I closed the lid of the Tupperware container and handed it back. "Don't forget the recipe."

"I won't. I put it in my phone with the other foods."

"Why are you so organized? You're fifteen. And a boy."
I was super organized as a thirteen year old. I always had a
planner ready at the beginning of class. My life was sched-
uled to a T. But I didn't know many boys who did that. Most
of them shoved papers into their backpacks and forgot to
do their homework on a daily basis. "I feel really close to
you right now," I joked with a smile.

"I go to the best private school in Moscow. Also, my
father. I am first in line to inherit his business. He instilled
organizational skills in me from the moment I could put my
toys away."

"First in line? Makes it sound like you're an heir to his
throne."

A smirk curved his cheek. "You could say that."

Suddenly the hallway was filled with classical piano music drifting in from the sitting room. Misha and I listened in
silence, simply appreciating the lovely sound until he stood
and held his hand out to me. "Dance?"

My heart leapt to my throat. "Uh, no. I don't do that."
Just the thought of dancing with handsome Misha made
me want to crawl under the floorboard and hide. He was so
pretty and sweet, and I was clumsy and awkward. So... me.

"No ballet as a little girl? No school dances with boys?"

"No and definitely not! I went to dances with friends, but
we didn't actually dance!" We just flitted from one group of
friends to the next like butterflies to flowers. No one ever
danced at school dances.

"Come on, shy girl. Get out of your comfort zone." He
reached down and plucked my hand from my knee before
tugging me out from our usual spot under the stairs. We
weren't hidden from view anymore, but the only person
out there was the bouncer, and he was on his phone. I put

my free hand in Misha's and let him teach me some of the steps.

"You don't think being kidnapped and sold to a brothel in Russia is enough out of my comfort zone?" I asked with a raised brow. "How much more 'out of my comfort zone' do I need to be?"

Much to my astonishment, he leaned down and brushed his lips across the top of my head. "I know. Bad choice of words. I'm sorry." He turned us in a slow circle, quietly humming the song.

"You know this one?" I asked, surprised. "This doesn't seem like your jam, ya know?"

"It's my mother's favorite song. She plays it on the piano at home."

There was warmth in his voice when he spoke about his mom, sister, and grandmother that wasn't there when he spoke of his father, uncles, and cousins. I hadn't known Misha long, but he was sweet. My mom always told me you could tell a lot about a boy by how he treats the women in his life. My mom would have liked Misha based on that alone.

A pang of sadness squeezed my heart and choked my throat as I thought about my mom. I missed her with my entire being. I fought not to cry again in front of Misha and was able to swallow down the tears that threatened to well up and spill onto my cheeks.

"What is it, Katya?" He asked gently, pressing me closer against his slender body as we swayed.

"I want to go home. Are you sure there's nothing you can do? Can you send a letter for me? If you won't let me use your phone, could you call them for me?"

"*Niet*," he whispered against my hair. "I wish I could, but my family have been patrons of Madame Bombadine's for so many years. They would be so angry if I tried to free you and made an enemy of Madame. Also, they don't see you as their business. I hate to say it like this, but I can't think of another way. You aren't important enough for them to help." There was an apology in his voice that smoothed the rough edges of his words. "Be patient, my Katya. One day I will have the means to get you out. One day. I promise."

"Misha!" The harsh tone of his uncle's voice had us jumping apart guiltily, and I slunk back into the shadows beneath the stairs, my heart pounding. There was something about that man that made me very nervous. Something about him didn't look kind. Maybe it was the chill in his eyes as he looked me over or the way his mouth had no laugh lines. He was standing in the entry hall with one of Misha's cousins when he demanded something in Russian.

Misha shoved his hands into his pockets and gave a lazy shrug with what sounded like a flippant answer. I had no idea what they were saying in their rapid-fire Russian, but I hoped Misha's nonchalant stance was meant to not draw attention to me. I wasn't supposed to be seen by the patrons.

Misha's uncle pointed toward the stairs and gestured for Misha to bring me out. My friend reached in and snagged my arm in a way that wasn't gentle like the boy I was growing to know. I wondered if this was a show for his uncle. Even if it was, I didn't like it. No one should act one way in front of others and another way without them present. That kind of two-faced attitude was something I didn't trust, but I kept my mouth shut for the time being.

Keeping my eyes lowered to the floor, I stood before him and wrung my hands at my waist. A beefy finger slid under my chin and raised my head until my eyes lifted to meet some as dark as Misha's. I wanted to jerk my chin away from his cold touch. Wanted to push him away and run up the stairs to my little room and hide under the covers. Were all the men who frequented Madame Bombadine's this way? Were all Russian men this hard and scary? Misha wasn't, but he was still a kid. I hoped he never grew to be this cold and distant.

"*Dobre vecher*, little one. What is your name?" He asked. There was a smile on his face, but it didn't reach his eyes.

"Sveta, sir," I responded.

"And how old are you, Sveta?"

"Thirteen, sir."

"Thirteen." He sent a smile to his son who shifted a little closer before looking at me again. "She's a pretty thing, Misha. So this is the blonde you've been talking about? A lowly maid, little more than a child." There was a bit of humor in his tone I didn't like. I expected that the only reason he spoke in English this time was to be a condescending baboon's rear end. No wonder Misha wasn't a fan of this man.

He released my chin, and I took the first breath in what felt like minutes. "Off with you, little maid. We will meet again when you're older." The icky insinuation made me want to vomit as I raced up the stairs back to my room. I'd have to be more careful about staying out of sight and mind of Misha's family.

***

We went on like this for weeks. Months, even. Me challenging Misha's tastebuds with American pre-packaged food, and him bringing me homemade delicacies and recipes. Even though I had not found time—or felt brave enough to use the kitchen on my own—I treasured the recipes. I kept them in the English to Russian dictionary Misha had given me, so I wouldn't lose them. But, tonight was the night. I was finishing up the last of my chores for the day: washing dishes.

Hands deep in the frothy water, I glanced over to the head cook who was rolling out dough for tomorrow's breakfast. She and I had not spoken more than her pointing at the dishes or giving me a word or two in English, and I figured she just didn't know how to communicate with me. Lucky for her, I was ready to try out my Russian.

"Elinora," I said as I dried a plate with a dish rag.

She turned to me with raised brows which I took to mean 'go on'.

"I use oven tonight?" I asked in broken Russian.

"Why?" she gruffly responded.

"I make..." I quickly pulled the pocket dictionary out of my pocket and flipped through it while Elinora waited patiently. "Sweet. Um...dessert."

"Do you know how?" she asked slowly. I thought through her words for a moment before nodding with a smile. "I have recipe." I dug the paper out of the dictionary and offered it to Elinora who frowned down at it. "Who give you this?"

"Friend come to see me. Mother make this. I want to try," I offered in a shrug with a hopeful smile.

"As long as you clean the kitchen, you can cook in here after dinner," with a nod, she went back to her dough, leaving me beaming as I finished my dish washing.

When I was finished, I saw that Elinora had pulled out a bowl, spatula, and the ingredients I'd be needing. I'd chosen what was essentially a Russian cake pop: Kartoshka.

As I'd told Misha, I liked baking, but I didn't do it very often. I made cookies with my mom and grandmother before Christmas and a birthday cake a couple times a year. Baking for the enjoyment of it was new to me, but there was something really satisfying about being able to do this one thing that reminded me of my old life.

It gave me a sense of control that I had been missing. Sure I'd had to ask for permission to use the kitchen, but she'd given me free range in the evenings. I now had more to look forward to than Misha coming on the weekends. I now had a hobby. I'd never understood why my dad used to tell me to get a hobby. Whenever I complained about being bored, he used to quote his favorite poet, Phyllis McGinley. "A hobby a day keeps the doldrums away." I had no idea what doldrums were, but I figured they were something bad. My life now seemed to be the essence of "doldrums". Dad also used to tell me that everything happens for a reason. If that was the case, maybe all the times he'd bored me to death with that quote was a sign that I would need a hobby to see me through this piece of trash I called my current life.

Elinora kept glancing at me as I stirred the ingredients with gusto, and I knew I must have a weird smile on my face. But I couldn't help it. I chanced a glance up at her and caught her eye. She snorted a laugh at my joy, shook her head, then went back to kneading her dough.

I found myself humming as I worked. I used to hum all the time at home. Doing chores, working puzzles, taking a walk outside. I'd always been a pretty happy kid until now. So finding myself humming again in a place like this was weird. I wasn't sure whether it meant I was getting used to living here or if I was just enjoying something for once.

I frowned as I scooped some dough onto a sheet of parchment paper. I shouldn't be humming. Not here. Not in this place where women have sex for money. Not in a place that bought me from my kidnappers like I was a puppy from a puppy mill, just out to make a buck.

I plonked down another spoonful of dough a little harder than necessary.

"Sveta." Startled at the voice cutting into my thoughts, I glanced over at Elinora. She offered a tentative smile which crinkled the edges of her eyes. "It okay....ah....happy." She said in her broken English and it meant a lot to me that she tried. Then she hummed to show what she meant. I guess I'd been a little too transparent in my feelings. She gestured around her. "Not bad here."

I would keep telling myself that.

***

The Kartoshka was a hit! The next day, I let the kitchen staff have first dibs since I had used their work space, and then I took the rest to the bouncers, Madame Bombadine, and the girls.

As good food so often does, it broke the ice between the girls and me. They gushed about the rich, chocolate taste and asked me to make them some more. Madame Bombadine sat in a wingback chair in the living room, watching us all with a smile as she nibbled tiny bites of the delicacy.

"Sveta, tell us more about you," one of the girls—Maribo, a dark-skinned beauty with a mane of gorgeous black braids —demanded as she drew me to sit next to her on the sofa.

Another girl took the tray from my hands and sat on my other side, nibbling on her second Kartoshka. "Yes, tell us more. We want to get to know our baby sister better."

Baby sister? Had I understood the Russian words correctly? These girls had ignored my presence as if I was a ghost quietly haunting the place as an inconvenience instead of a human being. So this direct interest from them was surprising, to say the least.

"Um... I don't know what to say. I am thirteen. I have a brother. Older. Mom and Dad. I miss them." At least I was getting a lot of practice out of my Russian. Misha was going to be so impressed with how much better I'd gotten! The thought made me smile. "I have friends. One best friend, Lex. She call me Elsa." I giggled at the joke, but no one else seemed to get it.

"Is your real name Elsa?" Maribo asked.

"No, it's Kate," I answered with a shake of my head. "She call me Elsa because hair."

They continued to stare at me blankly.

"You see Disney Frozen movie?"

"Isn't it a cartoon?" one of the other girls, a redhead named Linea, asked, wrinkling her nose.

"Yes, but it's good!" I exclaimed.

Maribo, apparently my new best friend, smiled brightly and chucked me under the chin. "Madame," she called to the woman still sitting in her chair. "Can we have the night off to have a movie night?" At the imperious nod from

Madame, Maribo turned back to me with excitement in her eyes, "Will you make some more Kartoshka, Sveta?"

"I will!" It was so nice to have people actually have a conversation with me. Aside from Misha on the weekends, it had been a quiet life. Much too quiet.

Now I felt like I had friends.

That night after dinner, the girls kept their promise, and I kept mine. A chorus of cheers erupted from the girls as I rolled in a cart laden with Kartoshka, a humongous bowl of buttered popcorn, and a variety of drinks. The first official movie night at Madame Bombadine's was about to commence. I passed the popcorn and Kartoshka around the room, snagged a glass bottle of some sort of red soda and was pulled to sit in the middle of the sofa next to Maribo.

I was warmed by the friendly chatter of the girls who were seated on the sofa, chairs, and even on the floor with blankets they'd brought from their beds to get cozy. As I looked around, I noticed one person was missing: Madame Bombadine. I leaned in next to Maribo and whispered, "Madame?"

"She will be in soon. She had a gentleman visit with her."

I nodded and snuggled back against the plush couch pillow. One girl popped up to dim the lights and another pushed play on the remote. Everyone grew quiet as the Disney castle appeared on the screen, and I saw flashes of white teeth as girls smiled and whispered to each other excitedly like they'd never seen a movie before. But what did I know? Maybe they hadn't. I knew nothing about them.

Maybe they were all girls like me.

The thought sobered my good mood, and I found myself studying the women around me as they were absorbed in the movie. They were all fairly young, of different races, and different body types. I supposed sex wasn't a one size fits all mentality. Madame Bombadine was servicing everyone's fantasy.

What surprised me, though, was how they all seemed to get along. Not one time had I heard arguing about clothes, accessories, or men. Back home, the girl drama in my school was worse than, well, the movies. Girls fought over every-thing! Clothes, shoes, make-up, and especially boys! Lex and I tried to stay out of it, but once in a while it was in-escapable because of a misunderstanding or a dumb shared look in the hallway. Everyone was looking for something to make them unhappy just so they could find something to complain about. Drama was the universe they lived in.

Yet here, at an upscale Russian brothel, the girls seemed grateful. Happy with their lot in life, which made me think they weren't so like me, after all. Surely someone trafficked into this job wouldn't still be sitting here if they could actu-ally leave the building. It didn't make sense. I decided then and there to talk to Maribo about it later, and I settled in to watch one of my favorite movies in Russian.

An hour and a half later when the credits began to roll, the girls applauded. I had always found it annoying when people clapped when the movie ended. I mean, the actors can't hear it, so why do it? But there was something special about this. A buzz of excitement electrified the room.

They turned to each other with smiles as someone turned the lights back on, and I couldn't understand anything they said in their lightning-quick Russian. Maribo lifted a lock of my hair and called over to Madame Bombadine, who had snuck in during Elsa's big song. "Madame, can we change Sveta's name to Elsa? She really does look like her?" She twirled the long, white blonde lock in the air to show what she meant.

Madame assessed me with her eagle-eyed gaze from the top of my blonde head to my blue eyes and fair skin. "I'll think about it."

Maribo gave my hair one last tug. "Wear this in a braid tomorrow." She stood and gathered up the cozy blanket she had shared with me during the movie, and walked out of the room. The others followed, leaving me with the mess of plates, bottles, and popcorn. So. Much. Popcorn.

And so much for friendship.

With a sigh, I collected a stack of plates and set them on the cart.

"Sveta," Madame murmured as she drew a broom lightly over the popcorny floor. "How are you liking things here?"

My shoulders lifted in a shrug before I folded a throw blanket in my arms and draped it over the back of the couch. "I'm doing okay."

"Elinora was singing your praises this morning. She said you have a taste for flavor combinations. It is high praise from her. I'd like for you to work more directly with her."

My heart leapt in my chest! I'd much rather do that than wash gross sheets and dust every day!

"Yes, ma'am. I'd like that."

"Good. You are fitting in quite nicely," she said as she handed me the broom. "Elsa."

***

By the time the weekend rolled around, I had made all the recipes Misha had hidden in my English to Russian dictionary. His grandmother's dumplings were such a hit that Elinora asked for the recipe to use instead of her own.

When Misha peeked around the stairs of our usual hidey-hole, it was me who greeted him with a plastic container and a huge smile.

"What's this?" He asked with an answering grin as he pulled off the plastic lid. His eyes lit up when he spied the contents. "Sausage and peppers!" He leaned down and inhaled the aroma of garlic and paprika.

"Not just any sausage and peppers. Your grandmother's recipe," I said, pride in my voice. I offered him a fork. My fingers sizzled as they brushed against his, and I quickly put my hands behind my back.

Misha speared a slice of kielbasa, swirled it in the sauce, and with his eyes on mine, used his teeth to slide it off the fork into his mouth. He groaned and closed his eyes to savor the bite. Then he opened them again, winked at me, and devoured the whole serving as I watched with an open mouth, mesmerized as he delighted in the food I'd made him.

"That was delicious." He replaced the lid and handed the container back to me.

"Do you always eat with such..." I scrambled for the right word. "Emotion?" I was sure I'd never seen anyone enjoy eating enough to *groan*.

"Not usually, but the look on your face was reason enough," he teased, then laughed when I playfully punched his arm. "It was really good though, Katya. As good as when my mother makes it."

And that was just the praise I was looking for.

"I made you something else, too." I bent to pick up the small plate from its hiding spot, and wiggled my hand around it like Vanna White showing off the prize on Wheel of Fortune—my parents' favorite weeknight show— then ripped off the plastic wrap with a flourish.

"Honey cake!" Misha dug a finger through the frosting slathered all over the thick slab of cake and pressed it into his mouth. "Mmmm." He took the clean fork I offered and dug into the soft, golden brown cake.

There was silence between us for a moment as he savored the confection. Finally, he said around a mouthful, "You are really good at this. Are you sure you only baked around the holidays, or do I smell a lie?"

I snorted in response. "Really! I don't know why I'm good at it now. I never thought I was before. Maybe I am paying better attention now than I used to. Or I care about it more." I reached to pinch a corner off the cake, but Misha cradled the plate closer to his chest, half turning his back.

"Mine!"

"I made the thing, I think I can taste a pinch!" I made another grab for it, and he dodged me, laughing, and then took off sprinting down the hall. I followed, determined to catch him for a victory bite of cake.

The bouncer looked up from his phone as we raced into the foyer, and he pointed to the back door. "Take it to the garden, kids!" He hurried to the back door and unlocked it just in time.

Misha raced out, but I stayed there on the threshold staring out into the night. The breeze on my face felt like ambrosia of the gods. How long had it been since I had gone outside? I'd watched the world slowly pace around me from the vantage of my tiny bedroom window.

Was this a trick? I looked to the bouncer, but he was walking back toward the front door, his back to me.

"Katya, come on! What are you waiting for?" Misha's fingers linked with mine, and he pulled me out into the night with him.

The garden was little more than a walled-in rectangular patio with a few spindly chairs and a skinny round table. The garden's wall was tall for privacy. Even if I stood on a chair, I wouldn't be able to scale it.

Misha taunted me with the cake, and I gave in to the temptation to play. We ran all over the garden. Laughing. Panting. Shrieking. Yelling. Enjoying the fresh air, exercise, and rowdy company.

I was finally able to dodge the right way and grab Misha around the waist. He twisted as we fell, and grabbed me with one arm to protect me from crashing into the hard brick. As he hit the ground, the plate with the cake flew into the air, turned one somersault, and came right back down.

Splattering all over Misha's handsome face.

He blinked up at me with owlish surprise beneath frosted eyelashes. I couldn't help swiping my finger through the confectioners sugar frosting and yellow cake crumbs on his cheek and popping it into mouth.

"Best cake I've ever eaten," I said as I rolled off of him in a fit of giggles. "I'll go get you a wet towel. Luckily it landed on your face and not your clothes."

"Lucky me," he grumbled which sent me into a peal of laughter as I jogged inside.

I picked up a hand towel, thought better of it considering the amount of cake and frosting, and discarded it for a bath towel. I wet it from the sink and hurried outside where I found Misha still lying there on his back. I watched as he scraped cake from his forehead and sucked it off his finger.

With a grin and a shake of my head, I sat next to him and leaned over to peer into his face.

He smiled up at me and tapped me on the nose. "Took you long enough."

"I was gone for literally five minutes."

"Five minutes that I was out here languishing in the cold covered in sticky frosting," he gave me the puppy dog eyes that made me melt.

Luckily, I knew that trick. I waved my hand dismissively, "It's not like you didn't have food." He eyed me askance, and I laughed. "Busted."

A sheepish grin replaced the puppy dog eyes, and he sat up. "It was too good not to eat anyway."

I snorted a laugh and rose on my knees. "Hold still." I carefully scrubbed his face clean with the damp towel, trying to ignore the way he stared at me so close as I worked. His intensity made me uncomfortable. I wasn't used to being looked at—studied—like that. It made me want to fill the silence.

"Madame changed my name to Elsa. I told the girls about how my best friend used to call me that because I look like Elsa from Frozen. We had a movie night, and Maribo—she's one of the girls—asked Madame to change my name. I definitely like it better than Sveta." I cut off my rambling and met his eyes.

"You will always be Katya to me. Even when I find a way to set you free, you will still be my Katya."

His words warmed me down to my heart. "And you will always be my Misha. My new best friend." And maybe a little bit more.

Chapter 7

Misha

Past

I couldn't get Katya out of my mind. She was always there lingering like a bright angel in the deepest, darkest parts. Sometimes it was annoying, like when I was in school and couldn't focus to the point of embarrassment, and sometimes it was a blessing, like when I wasn't able to sleep.

I don't know what it was about her that attracted me so much. She wasn't the prettiest girl I'd ever seen, let alone dated. She was smart, but she wasn't going to win the Nobel Prize. Especially not since she wasn't attending school while at Madame Bombadine's. Her educational life was going to be sorely lacking by the time I was able to get her out of there.

Damn that promise.

It must have been the sad, pathetic look on her face the first time we met that made me say such a foolish thing. And once it was said, I felt like I couldn't un-say it. My father had drilled into me that a Belov always kept his promises, so despite making this promise to a future whore, I'd still have to keep it.

That made me sound like an asshole.

And worse, it made me *feel* like one, too.

Because I genuinely liked Katya. She *was* pretty, she *was* smart, and she *was* funny. All the things I liked in a girl. It was a shame I couldn't date her, couldn't bring her to meet my mother and sister. They would've liked her probably as much as I did.

A sharp pain in the back of my head snapped me out of my thoughts, and I turned from the window to frown at my twin who had both hands on her hips. "Ow, Valentina! Why'd you hit me?"

"I had an entire conversation with you before I realized you weren't even listening."

"How is that my fault?"

She stuck her tongue out at me and went to slap my head again, but I grabbed her arm and twisted it behind her back. It wasn't hard enough to really hurt her, but it was enough to get her attention. My free hand began skating over her ribs where I knew she was the most ticklish.

She squealed and thrashed against me trying to get away. This was nothing new between us. Valentina was my confidant. One of my most favorite people in the world. But she was also my pesky younger-by-six-minutes sister, and I enjoyed my fair share of brotherly torture.

"Were you really going to hit me again, Vally?"

"Yes!" she stubbornly shrieked between panicked giggles. "And I'll do it again if you ignore me!" The heel of her foot slammed against my instep, causing me to flinch and let go of her.

"You know what that means, don't you?" I asked ominously. "The Toothpaste Swirly!"

"Don't. You. Dare…" she sprinted for the door. Then, "Mama!" She called as loudly as she could before I clapped my hand over her mouth from behind.

"Just for that, you are going to get it twice!" I laughed as I hauled her into my arms and headed for the bathroom.

She viciously kicked at me and pinched my arms, but there was no way I was going to release her mouth for fear our mother would hear her shrieks. Once the door was closed behind me, I dumped her in the bathtub and held her struggling body with the flat of my foot as I grabbed the toothpaste off the counter.

"Misha, no! Please!"

"Too late. I have to say, Vally, this hurts you way worse than it hurts me." I unscrewed the cap with my teeth and used both hands to squirt the tube of peppermint goo all over her face, hair, and shirt. And then I grabbed her shaving gel.

"Misha! No, you already got me with the toothpaste. Don't do this!" She begged with large brown eyes staring up at me.

I sighed, dramatically, and lowered my hand holding the gel, before moving my foot off her stomach. "Well… I guess I can… not forgive you!" I whooped and raised the shaving gel canister like it was a weapon and let loose a stream of teal goo that turned white against Valentina's hands, face, and hair.

Grinning, I turned on the shower for her—cold water, of course—rinsed off my hands and left the room. Her shrieks were music to my ears.

"Misha, if you're done torturing your sister, your father would like to have a word," Simeon, our butler stated, stoically ignoring my sister's wails from the bathroom. "He is in his study."

Frowning, I nodded. "Is he with anyone?" It was a loaded question. If he was with my uncle and cousin or any of the other Family, it was going to be a business-related conversation. If he was alone, it was personal.

"He is alone," Simeon offered with a slight smile. He knew me too well. He knew I both hungered for and feared Father's attention. I had been born with familial pressure on my tiny shoulders, and it seemed the weight grew by the day. By the very hour. Don't get me wrong, I loved my father. But being the heir to the top Bratva boss was a lot for any teenager to handle.

"Thanks," I said before picking up my pace as I headed toward my father's study. I wondered what he wanted to talk about, but I figured it fell into one of a few categories: school (yes, Papa, I still have all top marks), relationships (no, Papa, I don't have a girlfriend. I know you probably have someone in mind for me), or family (real family, not *the* Family).

I paused in front of the tall oak door, took a breath to steady my nerves, and knocked.

"Come in," came the gruff, no-nonsense reply. I opened the door and stepped inside. "Ah, Misha. Come in, come in. Close the door behind you."

I followed his directions and sat in the wingback chair in front of his desk. I knew better than to ask what he wanted. He would tell me when he was ready. Apparently that would be after he finished typing. While I waited, I glanced around at the familiar space. The wood finish of the furniture was dark, the paint on the walls a heavy cream. It definitely wasn't my style, and I vowed to change it when

I inherited the position of Pakhan. Hopefully a very long time from now.

Finally he looked up and slipped his hated glasses from his nose, placing them on the desk. His leather chair creaked under his weight as he leaned back to survey me with his eagle-eyed gaze so much like his brother's. "Misha, how is school? What are your grades?"

I was barely able to stop myself before rolling my eyes. "Top marks in every class."

"Good. Which class is your favorite?"

This was new territory, and I pursed my lips wondering what his game was. "Mathematics."

He raised a brow at that and steepled his fingers against his chin. "Have you applied to university yet?"

"No, but I have made a list of the ones I want to apply to. Oxford and University of Amsterdam are at the top of my list." I wanted to travel more than anything, and university seemed the perfect time to do it. God knows I wouldn't be going anywhere once I took over the business from my father.

My father's brows lifted in surprise, and he laughed. He actually laughed at my response. I didn't find it funny, and I wasn't sure why he did. When he realized I wasn't laughing, he calmed, and his brows drew down in confusion. "You weren't joking? You want to go to school outside Russia?"

"Yes. I want to travel, meet new people, see new places..." I trailed off as he started shaking his head.

"No. You will go to Lomonosov Moscow State University like me and your uncles. I have already spoken with the University's president and the Dean of Students."

Anger surged through me as my dreams were once again dashed by my father's expectations. "If you already did all that, why did you ask if I had applied?" My hands were so tight around the arms of the chair that I was half afraid my nails were going to puncture the leather.

"I'm only asking to see where we are in the process. Even though you are guaranteed a spot, you still need to apply like everyone else."

"Is there anything else?" I asked, my tone frosty and formal.

"Yes. Stefano Petrovka is coming to town from St. Petersburg. I want you to take out his daughter, Galina, this weekend. Show her the most romantic sights of Moscow."

"Why romantic?" I asked, fearing that I already knew. Arranged marriage was a part of life for those in a Russian Bratva family. My parents' marriage had been arranged as had my grandparents' before them. They didn't always turn out as well as my parents who didn't exactly love each other but had an amiable relationship. My aunt and uncle, on the other hand, hated each other's guts, and they made that clear at every family function, which was why my uncle rarely brought my aunt these days.

I'm sure it was fine by her.

"Oh, you know," my father evaded with a flippant wave of his hand, his attention turning back to his computer once more. "She's a young girl out with a young boy in a beautiful city. You've been on dates before. Treat her like one of those girls."

Yeah, right. Take her out to dinner before a fumbled make out in the backseat while our driver takes a smoke outside the car. No, a Bratva princess would expect more effort. More money. Just *more*.

I was not a fan of the spoiled rich girl act. Even Valentina, who I adored as my sister, was given everything she needed in life to the point she expected it. That's what I didn't like: the expectation of being treated like royalty.

And maybe that's simply one more thing I liked about my sweet Katya. She didn't expect anyone to treat her as more than she was. She was kind and unassuming.

Refreshing.

I inwardly sighed and nodded at my father, "Okay. Tell him I will take her out Friday night. I have plans on Saturday."

He glanced up at me from his laptop. "Madame Bombadine's again? You're making an expensive habit out of that place, aren't you?"

I bristled. Why did he care? He was a frequent visitor, himself. "I don't spend money when I go, Father." He should know that since he examined the accounts every day with a fine-toothed comb. No one could get away with a single cent out of place.

"I know." He quirked his mouth in a smirk as he stared down at me.

Busted. Yet why was I feeling guilty for not spending money on women? Wasn't that what he wanted? Now that I was an initiated member of the Family—a soldier, no less—I didn't like being questioned. Especially since I wasn't doing anything wrong. I decided to look at this from a different angle. Maybe now was the time to ask about Katya *again*. The first time had been a resounding no. Maybe time had softened his stance. My heart began pounding in my veins. "Remember when I told you about the friend I made there? The girl."

Father's brows drew down as he tried to remember. Clearly, he didn't. "You don't make friends with a whore, son. It just isn't done."

I had to make him understand. Had to make him listen to me. "She's not a whore. She's a prisoner."

"The girls at Madame Bombadine's are there of their own accord. That's why we go there instead of one of the others in the city."

"I know, Papa, but Katya was bought by Madame. She's being held there until she comes of age and starts to work for Madame. I-I want to set her free." There. I finally came out with it.

Father stared at me for so long that I began to feel even more uneasy — like I needed to squirm. But I held still, barely breathing while I waited for his response.

"Whether or not what this girl says is true, it's not our business or concern."

"But Papa—" I began.

"Not. Our. Concern."

The finality in his voice made my blood boil, but I knew there would be no swaying him. I stood and headed for the door.

"Oh, and Misha..."

"Yes, Papa?" I turned to look his way.

"You will buy your sister new toothpaste, shaving gel, and pay for her clothes to be cleaned."

Damn it! How did he always know? I nodded and quietly left the room.

***

"Why are you so angry about this date, Misha?" Valentina said from her perch on my bed. "I spent the day shopping with Galina, and she's lovely."

"Lovely in appearance or personality?" God help me if she said *personality*.

"Both, actually. She's beautiful and very elegant. I think you will like her." She stood from the bed and skipped over to help me with my tie.

"I just don't want to do this. I've been dreading it all week." And I had. My obsessive thoughts of Katya had been replaced with worries over where I'd take Galina, what we'd talk about, and if we would get along. What if she was stuck up and snooty?

I could talk to almost anyone, but that didn't mean I enjoyed it if the other person was boring, rude, or just plain ignorant.

"You're going to be fine. I'll do my usual text a couple of hours in to see if you need rescuing, okay? Will that make you feel better?"

I leaned down and kissed her cheek. "Thank you, yes. You're the best wingman... woman... I could ask for."

She snorted which reminded me of Katya's laugh, and I found myself smiling down at her. "Wish she had a brother so we could double."

"Ew, that'd be weird. A brother and sister going on dates with a brother and sister? No, thank you. Better you than me."

I stuck my tongue out at her and then followed her out of my bedroom to the top of the stairs where I heard voices filtering up from below. I caught a flash of brilliant red and turned to see where the color had come from.

There she was. My date. My *stunning* date. She had the deepest red hair I'd ever seen on a human being, and she'd paired the rare color with a dark green sheath dress and white cardigan. She looked like elegance personified, and I was suddenly eager to get on with this date.

"Ah, Misha, my boy, there you are," my father stated as I came into view, pride in his voice. "This is my good friend, Stefano Petrovka, his wife, Maria Inessa, and their daughter, Galina."

I took Stefano's hand with a firm shake, sizing him up like men do when they meet for the first time. His handshake was equally as strong, but where my father was fit and stern, Stefano was portly and had smile lines around his eyes.

Then I took in his wife. Galina clearly got her looks from her mother with the same red hair and porcelain skin. She offered me her limp hand as if I was supposed to kiss the back of it. I did just that, brushing the back of her hand with my lips. And she tittered. I'd read the word 'tittered' before in novels, but I'd never really understood what it'd meant until that moment. The sound that came out of Maria Inessa's mouth was the epitome of a 'titter'.

Galina was even more stunning up close. Her eyes were the steely color of a gun barrel and held the same amount of warmth. Maybe she was as unhappy at being made to go out on a date as I was. Or maybe she was just a bitch. I knew better than to go with first impressions, so I decided to give her the benefit of the doubt until I got to know her better.

Thirty minutes into our date, I knew my gut instinct had been right. When Galina excused herself to go to the restroom, I texted my sister under the table.

Misha: Does 'lovely' mean something different to you than to the rest of the universe, or were you fucking with me?

Valentina: What do you mean?

Misha: I mean that I have yet to see anything 'lovely' about Galina Petrovka's personality. She's an iceberg.

Valentina: I swear she wasn't like that with me earlier.

Misha: Well, give me some talking points. What does she like? I'm sinking like the Titanic here.

Valentina: Don't be so dramatic. She's a girl. Talk about girl stuff. She has a dog...

I hurriedly replaced my phone in my pocket when Galina slid into her chair once again. "So, Galina, do you have any pets?" God, this conversation couldn't get any worse.

"I have a Maltese named Frou-Frou. She's the light of my life. I usually take her everywhere with me, but Daddy just wouldn't hear of it this time. He said you shouldn't take your dog, no matter how small and precious, to someone's house uninvited."

I stand corrected.

Though the date lasted only a couple of hours, each second felt like a millennia. After dinner—at a restaurant that I was sure wouldn't ask me to return considering Galina sent back her meal three times before it was "right" (it looked the same to me each time it came back)—we walked around Red Square and St. Basil's Cathedral, and we ended at my favorite creperie for dessert.

She didn't like it. Any of it. Not the dinner, not Red Square or the Cathedral—how can you not be impressed by St. Basil's Cathedral?!—nor the crepes—how can you not like dough stuffed with chocolate and strawberries?! You know who would have loved this place? Katya. She would have wanted to try one of each kind of crepe and would have been happy just for the experience.

Worst date of my life. Thank God I didn't care all that much. I'd simply tell my father it didn't go well, that I didn't like her, and we'd be done with it. Sorry, Father, she's awful.

Trust me, you wouldn't want her as a daughter-in-law. I'm saving you the trouble. You can thank me later.

Of course that conversation didn't go like that. No, that would be too easy. The next day Father called me into his office. I was hoping to find him alone, but he wasn't. He and Stefano Petrovka were sitting back in their chairs smoking cigars with huge grins on their faces.

"Sit down, my boy. Would you like a cigar?" My father had never offered one to me before, but I didn't take it. I had a feeling he would snatch it out of my mouth when I was finished explaining how I didn't want to marry Ice Princess Petrovka.

"Galina had a wonderful time with you, Misha. She told me all about your date," Stefano Petrovka said with a grand smile.

"Oh, did she?" I said noncommittally, taking a seat in the other wingback chair in the room. Must have been either a really short conversation, she lied through her teeth, or her father didn't actually listen.

"Yes. She said you were even kind enough to ask about her little doggie, Frou-Frou."

My father's eagle eyes were watching me carefully. "Stefano, would you excuse us for a moment."

"Of course. I'll go check on Maria Inessa."

As soon as he stepped outside the door, my father stood and walked around to lean against the front of his desk. It was a power move I was familiar with. In response, I leaned back and settled my hands on the arms of the chair.

"What's going through your mind, son?"

"I don't like her."

"What's there not to like? She's a beautiful girl with a large inheritance. She will bring our family wealth and new blood."

"She's also vapid and ice cold. There's nothing in here." I thumped my chest where my heart was.

"Son, you'd only need to bed her until you have children."

"Papa, I have the utmost respect for you, but I cannot marry her. I don't want to spend my life with her. I don't want to be Uncle Grigori and Auntie Luda. Please don't do that to me."

"You are being ridiculous, Misha. You've only met the girl once. You'll be fine. I had never met your mother before our wedding day, and it has been a wonderful marriage."

"Because you actually like and respect each other."

"You'll learn to do that, Misha. It's part of growing up."

Fuck. My. Life.

The only thing that got me through the rest of the day was the knowledge that I was going to see my Katya later that night. I escaped entertaining Galina by staying in my room like the bitter, pouting baby I was. At least that's what Valentina called me when she brought me my dinner. I told her she'd be doing the same thing when she met her future husband. She flipped me off when I said he'd be old, bald, and smell funny.

My cousin thought he would commiserate with me on the way to Madame Bombadine's by restating what my father had said about just having sex with her for children and coming to Madame's for real entertainment. I couldn't lie and say the idea didn't have merit, especially now that I knew for sure he wouldn't help me rescue Katya. If I couldn't help rescue her, I could at least give her comfort through the years.

***

"I brought you something," I said, finding her in our new favorite spot outside on the patio. She was bundled from head to toe. Russian winters were nothing to sneeze at, and if I didn't know her as well as I did, I'd think she was crazy for voluntarily spending time outside. Especially for someone not used to this kind of weather. She looked up, and I could see tears trailing down her cheeks. She quickly wiped them away as I approached. "What's wrong?" I frowned and touched her damp cheek.

"Nothing. Don't worry about it," she answered with a sniffle.

"You know I won't let it go. What happened?" I took her hand and drew her to one of the patio chairs. I sat down and pulled her onto my lap. "Tell me."

"Today's my birthday. I wish I was at home with a birthday cake my mom made and having a sleepover with my best friend."

"I thought I was your best friend," I pouted playfully at her trying to make her smile.

"You're my best friend here and the only thing that keeps me going besides baking. But you aren't *home*, ya know?"

"Yes, I know." Not for the first time I marveled at how quickly she was picking up my language. A few short weeks ago, she didn't speak a word, and now she had sentence structure completely down. Smart as a whip my Katya.

"So what did you bring me?" Her blue eyes gazed up into mine, and I wished I had brought her something beautiful like jewelry. Instead, I reached into my pocket and pulled out a food packet wrapped in plastic.

"You didn't!" she shrieked as she grabbed it from my hand and kissed the packet. "I thought you couldn't find one here!"

I shrugged. "I scoured the city for you, Katya. I found one in a convenience store freezer." I laughed as she ripped open the package and took a healthy bite of cookie and ice cream. "Does it taste like how you remember?"

"Yush," she said with her mouth full. She held the Chipwich to my mouth and I took a small bite, wanting her to have the majority. It was good, but nothing like the honey cake she'd made. It tasted like store bought cookies and freezer burn, but I was glad I could make her happy on her birthday.

She devoured the Chipwich in record time and then laughingly licked the package while I stared at her with my mouth open in horror. "Is that the best manners Americans have?" I asked in my snootiest voice.

"No, but it's my birthday, so I get a free pass."

"Sure. But you don't get a free tickle pass!" My fingers skated over her ribs. Nothing. Not one twitch! Slack-jawed, I looked into her face and saw her lips trembling. "You're faking it!"

She leaped off my lap and began giggling as she backed away from me.

"How?!" I demanded, my fingers outstretched, ready to tickle.

"I have a big brother! It's survival!"

"But now I know your secret," I sprinted toward her, causing her to shriek and turn tail to escape.

We ran circles around each other on the small patio. When I finally caught up with her, my arms wrapped around her waist. Our laughing breaths mingled causing steam to filter up through the space between us. I didn't follow through on tickling her, though. I simply held her until we both caught our breath in the still night. Laughter and music could be heard inside the house, but we ignored it. I bent and pressed my forehead to hers.

"Katya..." I whispered.

"Yes?"

"Can I give you another present? A birthday kiss." I couldn't believe the words coming out of my mouth, but if I was going to start something with her that was going to last through my dismal future marriage, I might as well build the foundation now.

"Okay," came her soft reply.

My hand slid up over her back and around to cup her soft, cold cheek. Though I wanted to dive down to take her mouth, I didn't rush it. Not for her first kiss. The blue of her eyes was mesmerizing as I tilted her chin upward. I wanted to make sure she was really okay with me kissing her. I drew the tip of my nose down to hers and poked her with it to make her smile. "Relax. I'm not going to bite you."

"Yeah, because you know I'll bite back," she chuckled.

"Hm... a little nibble might be nice though," I murmured as I grazed her cheek with my lips. I trailed kisses up her jaw to her ear then whispered, "Close your eyes." She shivered as my breath caressed the pale shell of her ear, and I smiled. It seemed I affected her as much as she affected me.

I pressed a kiss to one corner of her mouth and then the other. Her lips parted in surprise, and that's when I swooped in. Just a graze of breath and chilled lips, before I settled my mouth on hers.

She tasted of Chipwich and cold air. And I loved it.

Our kiss was slow, our mouths explored, tasted, taunted. I drew her closer, my hand still on her back. Her hands slid up my chest and around my neck, pulling my head down tighter against her. Sealing our lips.

When I finally parted from her, we both stood silent as the night, eyes closed, hearts beating in time with one another. It was the best kiss of my life. I couldn't wait to do it again. And again. And again.

***

The next morning, my father called me into his office. I inwardly groaned because though I loved my father, I'd dealt with him and his frustrating edicts enough lately. But I was an obedient boy, so I headed that way. I was about to knock on his office door when Valentina poked her head out of the front parlor and grinned at me.

"Dead man walking," she taunted, lifting a teacup to her lips for a sip.

I narrowed my eyes at her, though a hint of trepidation crept up my spine. What if she was right? I racked my brain to think if I'd done something wrong last night but came up empty. I finally had to ask, "Why do you say that?"

"I overheard—"

"You mean you *eavesdropped*," I interrupted. "Call a spade a spade, Vally."

Her shoulders lifted in a shrug. "Fine. I eavesdropped and heard Papa tell Uncle Yuri that some important information had been leaked, and that they were going to have to kill someone. Then they said they needed to 'get Misha in here right now'."

Shit! Had I somehow leaked some information? What information would I even have? Despite being a soldier for a year, I still knew relatively little about the business or the Family's doings. I went to school during the day and worked on homework at night. I may be a man in the Family, but in the eyes of the world, I was still just a teenager.

"Valentina!" Mama's admonishment could be heard from inside the parlor. "Stop lying to your brother." My elegant mother waltzed through the parlor door and over to me. Her presence was always a comfort. She was the essence of home to me. I kissed her cheek as she smoothed the shoulders of my shirt. "Misha, your uncle isn't even here today. Don't you know not to believe everything your sister says? She's only trying to rile you."

"It's called payback, Mother, and it almost worked," muttered Valentina as she turned and walked back into the parlor.

"Ladies don't seek revenge, darling," Mother called back to her daughter as she smiled at me. "Now go on in, Misha. Everything is fine."

It was clear to me upon entering that everything was *not* fine. Papers were scattered over Father's usually pristine desk. The gun safe was open, and Father was examining one of the semi-automatic rifles normally kept inside. Guns were an everyday occurrence in this house. Every man I knew was carrying. My mother even had a small pistol in her purse most days, despite having her own bodyguard. So the sight of my father holding a gun did not startle me. No, what caught my attention was the fact that the safe behind my great grandfather's portrait was hanging open as if left like that. It was weird. I'd never seen the inside of that safe before, and now it was open for anyone who walked in to see.

"Father, you wanted to see me?"

My father looked up and frowned. He wasn't exactly frowning *at* me, just at something he was thinking about. I guessed it had to be whatever had upset him. "It's time I teach you to shoot and give you some more responsibilities."

"Why?"

"Remember the last vow, son. Don't ask questions. Follow directions and keep your eyes open and your mouth shut."

Inwardly I sighed. I could tell something was very wrong, but Father was in the role of Pakhan, not a father.

And I was his soldier.

Chapter 8

Kate

A few years later

"Dear Katya,

Even though we are in the same city, it feels like we are oceans away. I miss visiting you every Saturday. Everyone told me university was going to be the best time of my life, but all I've found is that it's a lot of work. I study all the time because my father is nuts about my grades.

I hope you are doing well, though, and that you are practicing your Cyrillic writing and reading. When I come back, I want to make sure you've read every word I wrote to you.

Hopefully I will see you soon,

Misha"

I refolded the well-worn letter, held it to my chest for a moment, and then placed it with the others in their wooden box. This was the last letter I'd received from Misha. He used to write once a week, but the letters had stopped showing up over a year ago. It didn't stop me from hoping and dreaming I'd hear from him again. When they had first stopped coming, I held out hope and checked the mail every single day. When I realized they weren't going to show up, I felt like he had broken up with me. But it wasn't like I was actually his girlfriend.

Besides, I couldn't bring much to the table. I was un-educated, kept completely ignorant of the world, and a whore-in-training. Why would he want someone like me in his life?

A knock on my door had me scrambling to hide the letter box under my mattress. "Come in!"

The door opened and Maribo swept in to my relief. She'd come to be like a big sister to me. Even better, I had con-fided in her about Misha, which is why she took one look at my face and frowned. "Why have you not burned those letters yet? All they do is cause you heartache. There's no time for heartache in this business."

"I know, I know. I just can't do it."

"Why not? Look, Elsa, it's time I give you some tough love." She perched on the foot of my bed and took one of my hands between both of hers. I braced myself for what I knew she would say. "There's no reason to keep those let-ters. Men don't keep their promises. How many times did he promise to take you away from here?"

"Many..." I whispered.

"Exactly. And has he followed through? No. He hasn't. And he's not going to. Men are like that. They are master manipulators who tell you what you want to hear just to get under your skirt. They say they are going to bring you jewelry, they say they will take you to faraway places, they promise to marry you and take you away from all of this. But do they do it? No. They get what they want and leave."

Tears stung the corners of my eyes and burned in my throat. I gulped in a breath and held it, counting to ten to keep them from spilling over onto my cheeks.

"I don't say this to be mean," Maribo squeezed my hand then dragged me closer for a tight hug. "You're young and full of hope. I don't want you to lose that, but soon you will be a part of this underworld of satin robes and silken promises. I don't want you to be taken in by the men who come here. Not like I have. You're family, Elsa. Go into this with eyes wide open and a protected heart."

All I could do was nod as the tears finally overflowed. She held me as I cried away my fears, my hopes, my future.

***

That evening Maribo brought me to her room where I found two other girls lounging on her bed. There was an assortment of sex toys spread across the soft quilt. I quickly averted my eyes. In all my time at Madame Bombadine's, I had never seen a naked man. They were required to be clothed when they walked out of the bedroom. Had I heard sex happening in this house? Yes. All the time. But I never saw it, and I could shut myself away in my room after my chores if I wanted or needed to.

Now with the toys spread over the bed like a sordid board game, I realized my childhood was coming to a close, and other expectations were going to come up. I forced myself to look at the display.

"Oh, no," I whispered, my eyes filling with horror when I saw the large black dildo that couldn't possibly be anatomically correct for a human being. Maybe a horse, but not a person!

"Oh, yes," Maribo laughed, steering me to the bed where the other girls smiled at me. I wasn't as close to them as Maribo, but I liked them all the same. Natasha was a gorgeous red-head with peaches and cream skin, and Isabel was an exotic Asian beauty the men fell all over themselves for.

"Come on, Elsa," Isabel grabbed my hand and pulled me onto the bed beside her. "These are called 'toys' for a reason: they are fun to play with." She dangled some furry handcuffs in front of my eyes which I quickly batted away.

"Do I have to know about all of these things? Can't I just do it...*regular*?" I didn't want to do *it* at all, but if I had to, I didn't want any of these toys there with me to prolong it. This was not something I had ever worried about as a kid. I always dreamed my first time would be on my wedding night before heading somewhere tropical for the honeymoon.

The girls looked at each other and then laughed at me, making me frown. "That's called missionary position," Maribo said, "and it's boring as fuck."

"Language," I muttered, which Maribo ignored. Yes, I had learned all the Russian curse words just so I knew what not to say and when others were cursing around me. Knowledge is power.

"Elsa, men pay for the fantasy, not the act. If they just wanted a quick fuck—if you tell me to watch my language, I'm going to stuff this dildo in your mouth—" I shut my mouth with a snap. "—then they would go to a corner and pay-for-a-lay up against the wall of an alley. We," Maribo gestured to the toys and then to the closet of elegant silks and satins, "fulfill dreams."

"Like acting?" I asked hesitantly.

"Exactly. Take Natasha, for example. She looks so sweet and innocent during the day, but at night she puts on that black bodysuit and fishnet stockings, and she puts her hair in a high ponytail or braid. She turns into a dominatrix fantasy which some men crave."

"Men go gaga over Isabel's Geisha act," Natasha said, tweaking Isabel's dark hair, "and when Maribo puts on the white tunic dress and some extra heavy eyeliner, she looks like God's gift to the Nile."

Maribo snorted a laugh and picked up a pale pink glass dildo which, I was sure, was a lot prettier than an actual male part.

"What will be *my* costume?" I asked, curiously.

"You don't really have a persona except for Elsa. Maybe you could be the Ice Princess. Until you get your feet under you and some experience, you will just be innocent Elsa. Madame is letting me choose your first set of lingerie," Maribo answered with a bright smile. "You are going to be innocence personified. You already are, of course, but you will be a sexy innocence. Every man's wet dream."

"Gross!" I spluttered, indignantly. Wet dream brought me back to my 8th grade Health class where they divided us into different classrooms by gender and gave us the sex talk. Most. Embarrassing. Class. Ever.

The girls fell back on the bed laughing at me, and I hunched in on myself, uncomfortable with this discussion.

"You're going to have to get used to it, Elsa," Isabel squeezed my shoulder comfortingly. "Men are going to be a part of your life until you pay off your debts to Madame, and then maybe longer if you choose to stay. Also, it's better to have your eyes opened now than on Auction Day."

Auction Day.

Just the thought of being auctioned off to the highest bidder to do whatever he wanted to me in the privacy of a room made me want to puke. The idea was absolutely heinous! I didn't want to do it! My chest began to rise and fall rapidly, and my cheeks flushed with heat. My stomach began to roil. I had tried not to think about this part during my long years here. It was always something that was going to happen in the distant future, not right away. And then boom! It was time.

"Oh, no you don't," Maribo lifted my arms above my head and held them there by my wrists, then she bent down to look me in the eyes. "I don't want you throwing up on my new bedspread. Take a deep breath and hold it." I did as I was told, and my nausea slowly drifted away. Maribo smiled and released me. "There you go. It's going to be fine. Madame is going to invite the kindest men she knows, and it will be a private auction. You won't be up for sale to just anybody."

Thank God for small miracles! I had been so afraid that I would be brutalized for my first time. I wasn't ruling that out completely, but at least it sounded better than I had expected.

"Okay, the reason we have all these toys out is to teach you how to please a man."

"Why do I need to know that? Don't they just stick it in and swirl it around?"

"Elsa!" The girls died in laughter again. I was starting to hate how sheltered my former life had been.

"No, Elsa, just no," Natasha giggled and ruffled my hair. "You have some of the mechanics right, but here's the thing: the more pleasure you give the man, the more plea-sure he will give you back. And the more money you will earn in tips."

"And just so you know," Isabel said, "some men don't know how—"

"Or don't care—" Natasha interjected.

"To give pleasure to a woman."

"But it's still important to know how to please a man if you want to build your client list," Maribo said. "So, let's start with noises. What you say and how you sound have a lot to do with a man's pleasure. Let me hear you moan, Elsa."

With a blush as red as Natasha's hair, I moaned loudly from the bottom of my throat.

"You sound like a dying cow. Do it like this." Maribo closed her eyes, tilted her head back a bit, arched her chest out and sighed a soft, low sound that had goosebumps rising on the back of my neck. Then Isabel gave her own example. Her's was breathier and high-pitched. Natasha gave hers, it was more guttural. Visceral. "Now try it again," Maribo ordered. " Close your eyes. It'll be easier."

I closed my eyes and tried to get into the right headspace. I felt the bed shift around me as the girls moved closer. My whole body tensed at their nearness. Slowly, I tried to edge away, but gentle fingers pressed to my shoulders, kneading. I wasn't used to being touched by anyone other than Misha when he used to visit, but their touch felt nice. Thumbs rolled over my tense shoulders, easing out the kinks and tautness. When I had relaxed enough, other hands stroked my arm and across the top of my chest around my collar bone. And then someone traced the outside of my thighs. A sound I'd never heard myself utter whispered from between my parted lips.

"That's it, Elsa. Give me more," Isabel whispered, her breath tickling my ear. The hand on my shoulders slid down my back and around to my stomach. Lower to just above the danger zone. I shivered and tilted my hips for more.

My head leaned back against Isabel, and I moaned again, a touch louder. Filled with more pleasure.

"Damn," someone whispered. "She's good. That was a really good one."

"Good job, Elsa. Okay, now we are going to work on dirty talk," Maribo said. I opened my eyes and the pink dildo was in front of her mouth. "Men want women to enjoy giving them pleasure. You can do this by moaning while you're sucking them off or when they're fucking you, but dirty talk is a really good way to get them excited." She lifted the dildo to her lips, rubbing the pink glass around her lips while staring me in the eyes. She kissed the tip. "Mmm... I want you inside my mouth so bad. Want to taste you...." Her voice was soft and slightly whiny. Her words and actions made me shift as I felt a little tickle between my legs. She slid the glass between her lips and groaned as she took it as far into her mouth as possible. Ever so slowly, she drew the dildo out of her mouth keeping direct eye contact with me. She flicked the tip with her tongue. "You taste so good, baby. I can't wait to have you in my pussy. So deep and full. You're making me wet." She pulled the dildo away from her mouth and said, "Your turn, Elsa."

It took me a moment to realize she had turned off her siren's spell and was addressing me as *me*, not as a client. I looked at the assortment of penises piled on the bed and chose one that looked more like a real one instead of a fake one. Nerves danced in my stomach, but I shoved them down. If I was able to sex-moan out loud with these girls, then I could dirty talk, too. And it's not like I hadn't heard them downstairs flirting and enticing the men. I could do this.

I cleared my throat and wrapped my hand around the dildo. The "skin" felt soft and almost real as I drew my hand slowly up and then back down. "You're so big..." I murmured, shyly, flicking my eyes to Maribo for reassurance.

She gave me a thumb's up. "Good. Keep going. Tell him how much you want it."

"I love your big penis. It's so soft—"

"Stop. Men don't like their dicks to be called soft," Isabel interjected. "Try silky or smooth instead."

"And maybe... maybe call it something besides a penis. Some men like that, but others find it too... clinical. I know you don't like to cuss, but most men call it a dick or cock," Natasha said, thoughtfully.

I thought for a moment. "My mom always called it a tallywacker. Would that work?"

Isabel dug out her cell phone which I eyed with envy, "Maybe. I'm going to look up alternate words. Here's one: joystick!"

Maribo snorted, "Love muscle."

Natasha thought for a moment, "Bratwurst, jackhammer, one-eyed wonder weasel!" We all laughed until our stomach's hurt.

Isabel tossed her phone on the bed next to her. My fingers itched to snatch it up and run. To call Mom or the police. I could read Cyrillic well enough now that using the phone wouldn't be a problem, but I didn't know how to call out of the country. Misha's words from years ago came back to me. *"You don't have a passport. You don't have a reason for being here. You don't have money."* And if that wasn't bad enough, I would be in really big trouble with Madame.

"Okay, okay," Maribo said, "back to business. Try again, Elsa."

Feeling braver now that we'd all had a good laugh over it, I licked up the underside of the dildo and then sucked on the tip. In an exaggeratedly sexy, high-pitched voice, I said, "Your skin tastes so good! I need you to put your big bratwurst inside me!"

That ended the session because we couldn't get ourselves together after that.

Chapter 9

Misha

Past

I. Fucking. Hated. Political Science.

I understood why my father, the Badass Bratva Boss of Moscow, made me double major in Political Science and Business, but I detested everything to do with politics and policy. It was confusing and mind-numbing at the same time.

What I hated even more than Poli Sci, though? The lack of a social life. Wasn't college supposed to be the best time of my life? I barely graced the outside world with my presence, only going outside to walk to class. My dorm had its own workout room, and I had food delivered from a service, or was often the case, my mother sent someone over to stock my mini-fridge. Despite living in the same city, I hadn't actually been home in months.

It sucked.

The only shining star in my world of work was Valentina. Our dorm was co-ed, so we were able to share a suite. Lucky for her, Father didn't care what she majored in, so she got to enjoy Art History: the least academic of the humanities. And she got to have friends. And party.

I really wanted to party!

According to Valentina, my pity party for one was getting old. Whatever, she had her own burdens to bear. Though Father didn't care what she majored in, he refused to let her do what she really wanted out of life: to model.

My phone rang, and with my eyes trained on the textbook I'd been pouring over for the last hour, I answered it. "Yeah?"

"Is that any way to greet your father and Pakhan?"

I instantly straightened at the tone of my father's voice. "Sorry, Father. What can I do for you?"

"I need to talk with you about something important, but it can't be over the phone. Meet me at Maksim's Coffee House in an hour. I've already given your bodyguard the night off, so he won't be with you. Don't bring your sister." And then he hung up.

I frowned as I put my phone in my pocket. It wasn't like Father to need to speak in private while I was at school. The police were routinely paid to look the other way, so there was no reason to think they would tap our cell phones or listen outside in an unmarked van like in the movies. This was just weird. But like a good soldier, I didn't ask questions, followed orders. That concept had been hard to learn, but through the years, I'd come to accept it. I hardened to this life of crime my father ruled. And I knew I was lucky I hadn't been asked to kill anyone.

Yet.

The power of 'yet' held a weight no amount of hope could diminish. It was ever present. Looming over me like the heavy humidity of a storm about to break. Miserable and inevitable. But if my father—no, my Pakhan—asked it of me, I'd do it without question. It was as simple as that.

With a heavy sigh, I closed my textbook and stood. As I was shoving my arms through the heavy fabric of my winter coat, my sister's voice caught my attention.

"Where are you going?"

"Father wants to see me."

"Oh! Can I come, too? I want to talk to him about flying me and some friends to Paris for Fashion Week!" Her excitement was palpable, and I hated to break it.

"Sorry, Vally, not this time. He wants to talk business." It wasn't exactly a lie because whatever Father wanted to tell me was most likely related to his business somehow. I just didn't know the details.

Valentina's full lips curved into a pout. "Oh. Well, will you ask him about it for me when you finish your meeting?"

"I will if there's a chance. I promise." I gave her a last smile before opening the door and stepping into the dorm hallway. It was quiet at this time of day, but it wouldn't have mattered if there was a party with drunk college kids sipping booze. I had kept to myself for so long, ignored all the party and friendship invitations that no one would have even said a word to me.

Father had let me take the Maserati to school this year, and it was parked in the underground parking lot beneath the dorm. I unlocked the sleek silver car with the key fob and then slid into the buttery, black leather seat. The engine purred like a kitten, and I took a moment to appreciate the Italian leather stretched across the steering wheel. This car was my baby. I backed out and headed to the coffee house.

It felt weird not having my bodyguard following in his black SUV. Johan had been with me since I was old enough to go places on my own. He rarely left my sight. Whatever it was Father needed to talk about must be of serious privacy. In the back of my mind I wondered if he was sick. Maybe he had some sort of diagnosis that he didn't want to tell the Family about yet. Maybe he thought it would make him seem weak? I wasn't ready to take over for him. I still had a couple more years left of school and more training to do with Father before I could imagine taking over as Pakhan. I hoped it wasn't bad news.

I parked the car, got out, and locked it with a beep before jogging to the front door of the coffee house. Maksim's had been our regular place when I was growing up. Many a coming-of-age conversation happened here: puberty, the sex talk, the difference between our family and the Family. I spotted Father at our usual spot in the back corner and walked over to join him in the booth.

Two coffees were already situated on the table, their steam twining together in the still air. I warmed my cold hands around one mug and watched my father. He didn't look sick. Tired, yes, but not ill. "What's going on, Father? What couldn't you tell me over the phone?"

"We have a traitor in the Family." He placed two portfolio folders on the table between us. I recognized them instantly as business ledgers.

"Why are there two of them?"

He took a long sip of his black coffee, his eyes never wavering from mine. "Open them up, and you'll see."

I flipped open one and then the other. A frown pulled my brows down. Was I seeing what I thought I was seeing? I set my coffee over to the side and brought the ledgers closer for a deeper inspection. My finger traced the neatly written columns of numbers on each ledger, then I turned the page and did the same thing. Finally, I looked up at my Father who hadn't moved during these silent minutes.

"Well?" He asked.

"They are nearly identical."

"Nearly?"

Was this a test of some kind? "Yes, *nearly*. The second ledger has the same expenses but different amounts than the first ledger." A thought occurred to me from a discussion in one of my business classes. "This is a classic case of embezzlement."

My father sat back with a grim smile. "You are exactly right, son. And you just proved my suspicions."

My chest puffed up with my father's proud words. "Where did you find the second ledger?" Surely the culprit wouldn't have left it out in the open for Father to find. That would have been incredibly stupid.

"I was cleaning out old records in the warehouse office. The traitor stashed the real ledger in an unassuming file in the cabinet. That place hasn't been cleaned out since before you were born, so there's no telling how long this has been going on. I didn't find any past ledgers, only this one."

"Who does the accounting?" To me, the accountant had to be at fault. That's the person who recorded the ledgers in the first place. He handles the checks and day-to-day money operations.

"Your mother's brother. Anton. Yuri checks them over each month and reports to me."

Uncle Anton. That didn't seem like something he would do. He was always kind and bookish. Never took trips or made extravagant purchases, never caused waves. He was a good guy. Or was he? "Have you told Mother?"

"Of course not. She would immediately take Anton's side. You know, I have suspected someone was stealing from us for a long time, but I haven't been able to prove it until now. And I'm not sure it's Anton. Though the evidence is damning, it's not as if I plucked this ledger from his hand myself."

"Why are you talking about it with me and not Uncle Yuri?" Yuri was my father's younger brother and right hand man. I was surprised he wasn't here having this conversation with us.

"Because I don't know if this is a one person job or if this goes deeper. Anton is not only Family, but he is also family. If I can't trust my wife's brother who shares Christmases and is the godfather of my children, then who *can* I trust? Only my son."

"So what can we do about this?" I asked, feeling very small in the vast scheme of what was happening not only to our Family business but also to our family. It was as if the walls were closing in on us from all sides. "Can you contact the police? They are in our pocket, so surely they will help."

"Have you forgotten my lessons so quickly? We pay the police to look the other way, not to help us. They would draw the line at that, no matter how much we offered. Helping the enemy is too corrupt even for them." He paused, and we both stared into the dark depths of our coffee as if answers swirled inside the steaming cup. Finally, he said, "We will speak with Anton. If he doesn't reveal anything, we will look for more answers. What time is your last final exam tomorrow?"

"Three o'clock."

"Come to the house at seven. Go to the basement and knock six times. We will question Anton together."

By *question*, I knew that meant much worse. Torture. A bubble of dread rose in my throat to the point I couldn't speak, so I simply nodded my assent. I would be there.

That night was brutal. I had three finals to study for, and I'd been looking at books for so long my eyes had gone blurry. On top of that, my stomach hurt at the thought of questioning Anton with my father tomorrow night, so I hadn't eaten since the one sip of coffee I'd had at Maksim's. I sat back in my chair, rubbing my closed eyes with the heel of my hands. Music pumped outside our suite, but I could still hear my sister on the phone in the room next to mine. Her voice was muffled and raised which caught my attention. Aside from when I was getting on her nerves, Valentina was one of the most even-keeled people I knew. It wasn't like her to argue with anyone other than me.

My eyes snapped open, and I sat up straight as Valentina appeared in my doorway. Her face was pale, and her eyes looked haunted. "Vally? What's wrong?" I stood and walked to her, sliding my hands up her arms to her shoulders.

She sagged against me. Behind me, I heard my phone begin to ring, but I ignored it. "Vally, seriously, what happened?"

"Papa's dead!" she wailed.

"What? You're not making sense!" I gently pushed her away so I could look into her tear-stained face. Her features were crumpled in agony.

"Answer the damn phone, Misha," she sobbed, and slid down the door jamb to sit on the floor with her face buried in her knees.

I felt numb. In shock. I backtracked to my desk and shifted books and papers around until I found my half-buried cell phone. My mother's name was bright on the screen. I pressed the phone to my ear. "Mama, what's happened? Vally is hysterical."

"Oh, my darling, it is awful!" Mama wailed on the other end, causing me to fall back into my chair. My chest felt like it was being crushed beneath a huge weight. "There was an explosion at the warehouse! Everyone was dead when the authorities arrived!"

"What about Uncle Yuri? My cousins? Who all was there?"

"They are fine. Papa was there with some business associates."

"Where were his guards?"

"Fenkir and Runion died with him." There was a pause as she sniffled on the other end. "You and Valentina need to come home. We have arrangements to make, and I need your help. Yuri wants to talk to you, too. I'm sending a car now."

The click of a call disconnecting never felt so final.

***

The house was eerily silent when Valentina and I stepped inside. It was the somber, haunted feeling you get when watching a funeral scene in a movie. As Vally pushed past me, I surveyed the entrance hall, noticing the darkened lights and black crepe covering the windows. I peered into the front parlor to see much of the same scene with the exception of my mother sitting on the stuffed chair closest to the fireplace. The light danced over her pale, grief-stricken face. She turned and stood when Vally walked into the room. I watched their mournful embrace like an outsider peering through the window. I wanted desperately to be a part of it, and I might have been if I were younger.

But I was a man now. The son of the Pakhan, no—the *heir* of the Pakhan. I couldn't show my grief as outwardly as my sister and mother could. It wouldn't be acceptable. It would only show weakness.

"Misha."

Startled out of my thoughts, I turned to see my uncle peering out of my father's study. He motioned me over and stepped out of the room, then pulled me into a tight hug. "How are you holding up, nephew?"

"Honestly, Uncle, I'm in shock." Though my father was not in the prime shape of his life in his fifties, he hadn't been near the end of his life. His death was completely unexpected.

"We all are. Come and talk." With his strong hand on my shoulder, he guided me into the study. My father's desk chair was conspicuously empty which gave me an intense feeling of relief. At least I wasn't the only one who felt uncomfortable sitting in the Pakhan's rightful seat. But then I froze. Should I sit there? As the heir apparent, would I be taking over now? *Today*?

I wasn't ready!

Panic rolled through my stomach, warring with grief to create a nausea deep enough to make me almost vomit then and there in the entrance to Father's office. No, no, no, no. Do not throw up! You're a man. You can do this. The self-lecture seemed to help as did the huge breath I held in my throat until the ill feeling and the panic receded.

I missed my father. I attributed the fact I wasn't good with change to the way my family honored tradition and sentimentality over innovation and new direction. We ate the same stuffed pork roast and potatoes for Christmas dinner every year, celebrated birthdays at the same restaurant as the year before, and baptized children in the same baptism gown which had been in the family for a century. The Belov's didn't change things up for fun. No, we kept everything exactly the same it had always been.

Change was handled much the same way in the Family, too. And with the death of the Pakhan, especially in such a violent way, change was galloping toward us like one of those mustangs racing across the American plains.

Unstoppable.

Once my racing pulse calmed in my chest, I took a survey of the room. Luckily, no one seemed aware of my internal battle. Men stood or lounged around the large office drinking, smoking, softly talking. Cigar smoke hazed the air above our heads. The sweet scent was a comfort to my battered heart.

I leaned against the wall by the window and took the cigar my cousin offered from Father's expensive cigar box used only on special occasions. If this wasn't the perfect time to take up smoking cigars, when was? I snipped the end and lit the cigar from the match my cousin held, then took a bracing inhale. Cigars weren't new to me. Ever since I was initiated into the Family, my father offered me a cigar when the men gathered for meetings. They weren't normally these fancy Cubans, though. These had a nicer finish and a cleaner taste.

My uncle walked to my father's desk, and I tensed until I realized he wasn't going to sit down. He simply leaned against the front of the desk. His dark eyes—like my father's, like my own—bored into each man's face. He stopped on mine and held my gaze. I straightened my shoulders and didn't look away. Everything with these people was a test of strength. Through the years, I'd found myself doing the same to my friends. Testing their loyalty. Testing their strength of will. Of character. It had become ingrained whether I liked it or not.

"Now that Misha has joined us, tell us what happened, exactly," muttered Anton, my mother's brother.

Father's words from yesterday rippled through my mind, and I narrowed suspicious eyes on Anton. He wasn't one you could look at and say *Bratva*. He was bookish with glasses and a shiny bald head. He looked exactly like what he was: an accountant. He didn't look like a murderer. But what did a murderer look like? Almost every man in this room had killed someone at some point. Death was a part of our family tree as much as any person here.

"Alright," Uncle Yuri said, "I'll share what I know. Constantine received a call from the warehouse that the latest shipment had come in. You know how he checks each shipment. He was always paranoid that the Americans would short us or send bad products. When he jimmied open the crate, it exploded killing him, his two bodyguards, and the warehouse worker who had taken in the shipment."

"What caused the explosion?" I asked, my focus still on Anton for any speck or sign of guilt.

"The police report said it was a bomb." Uncle Yuri pinched the bridge of his nose, and I knew that one of his headaches must be coming on, either from the grief over losing his brother or the upheaval it was causing. "It reacted with the ammunition in the crate. That's why it was so deadly."

"Do you think it was the Americans?" Anton asked with a frown. "We've done business with them for many years. I don't know why they would suddenly turn on us."

"It could have been. Constantine had confided in me a few weeks ago that he felt the quality of the product wasn't as high grade as it used to be. He had been considering ending the relationship with the Americans and using the Saudis instead."

That was news to me. Despite being a Russian loyalist, Father loved the Americans. They had a good relationship. I chewed on the end of the cigar, mulling over Yuri's words. If he really was going to sever the contract with the Americans, they definitely could have planted the bomb. But how would they know he would open it? I decided to ask that very question.

Uncle Yuri turned his gaze to me and shrugged. "I'm sure they were simply conveying a message to Constantine. I doubt they knew he would be the one to open the box. An unhappy coincidence."

An unhappy coincidence? Seriously? My cheeks flushed in anger at my uncle's words. How could he phrase it like that? Like my father's death was as trivial as the McDonald's worker forgetting to put the apple pie you paid for in your to-go bag. "It was murder, Uncle, not an *'unhappy coincidence.'*"

"You're right, nephew. I apologize for my word choice. I haven't slept since your mother called me with the news last night."

My anger melted away. Damn, I hadn't considered all he had been through. As the senior member of the Family and the Pakhan's brother, everything fell on his shoulders more heavily than on mine. I dipped my head in acknowledgement and tapped the ash of my cigar into an ashtray. The cigar suddenly tasted like it was made of ashes, but I stuck it back in my mouth anyway.

"Everyone is dismissed. I'll send word of the funeral arrangements soon. Misha, stay." We waited while everyone filed out, and then my uncle sat down in one of the vacated chairs and gestured to the chair next to it. "Come sit with me, nephew."

Nerves fluttered to life inside my stomach once more, and I rubbed the flat plane as if I could iron out the awkward feeling. I sat in the chair and studied my uncle's hard, weathered face.

"Nephew, I know that you probably think you are ready to take over for your father as Pakhan, but I feel he would want you to stay in school and get your degree. You know how much education mattered to him."

Relief settled my nerves. I hadn't realized how desperately I wanted to stay in school. I wasn't ready to take over, and I was so glad my uncle realized that. "Thank you, Uncle." A cloud passed over my eyes as I remembered Father telling me about the embezzlement. Was Uncle Yuri the culprit? Or Anton? I couldn't imagine either of them hurting my father. Maybe I should tell them about it? Let Uncle handle the situation so I could finish school. Something stopped me from voicing my thoughts, and I held them close to my heart as if saying them out loud would betray my father's confidence.

"Of course. Now that Constantine is gone, I can say this out loud. You haven't been able to live your life. University is supposed to be the best time of your life, and from what I've observed, you're killing yourself over your academics. You do not have to be the very best, nephew, you just have to get good grades. So, listen. I contacted the university and told them of your father's death. They are granting you and Valentina a delay of your finals. Today is Thursday. You have a full week until you need to take them."

"Thank you, Uncle!" With my mind reeling from chaos and grief, I'd completely forgotten about my finals.

"Of course, of course. I also have an idea for how to lighten your mood." He opened his suit jacket and pulled a large piece of cream card stock from the interior pocket which he held out to me.

I took the card stock and my eyebrows nearly rose to my hairline. The front of the card was a glossy picture of my beautiful Katya. Beautiful didn't do her justice. She was stunning! Radiant, even. The writing across the top said, "You're Invited". I flipped the card—invitation—over and read what this was all about. I glanced up at my uncle with a crinkle of confusion in my voice, "You want me to buy her virginity?"

The room echoed with my uncle's laughter. I watched him patiently with a raised eyebrow as he calmed down and wiped his eyes. "Not exactly. Buy *her*. Isn't she your little friend from Madame Bombadine's? Buy her freedom and take her with you to college."

"Why? Every time I asked Father about saving her from that life, he blew me off."

"It wasn't Con's style to save prostitutes." I almost said it wasn't Yuri's either, but I held my tongue at the last second. "You are like a son to me, Misha. I want you to be happy, and this is something I can do for you."

"Thank you, Uncle. But what about Galina Petrovka?" My upper lip curled into a sneer. I didn't want to marry her. I was glad to have a reprieve from that until I at least finished school. But I did have to think about her in this instance. I knew she would hate me fraternizing with another woman if she found out.

"I'll handle the Petrovkas. You just focus on your education and livening up your life a little. You're only young once."

True. All of this was sounding better and better. "What am I supposed to do with Ka...*Elsa* at university? Hide her in my dorm room like a live sex doll?" That idea gave me the creeps.

"No, nephew. I will enroll her in school with you. So tell me. In all your time together, did you find out anything she might be interested in? She clearly doesn't have a classical education, so business, political science, or communications may not be the best fit. Surely there is something she can do, though. Or you could just use her as a bed buddy. I don't care. She would be a pleasant diversion for you."

I couldn't use Katya as a bed buddy. She was my friend. A little more than a friend, if I was honest with myself. Instinctively, I knew what she would want to do. "Enroll her in the pastry school program."

"I will. Get me all her information, and it will be done before the next term begins."

For the first time in what felt like years, I had something to look forward to. Maybe my mother was right, that there is always a bit of light in the darkness.

Chapter 10

Misha

Past

Tonight was the night. Everything was planned out for every eventuality that I could dream up. I was going to buy my girl on her 18th birthday, and make good on my promise to set her free. Sort of. At least I was going to help further that goal for her. I knew this would take a bit of finagling and convincing, but I could do it. She was going to want to go home right away, but she wasn't ready for it. I hadn't seen her in a long time, but I'd taken a psychology class last semester, and one topic from that class made me think of Katya: learned helplessness. It's a condition in which a person faces a negative, uncontrollable situation and gives up all control. They learn to obey, to stop thinking for themselves. I just knew Katya had started down that path before I left for university. It had to be worse now.

I was ready to sweep her out of this situation like a knight with his princess. Just the thought—the hope—of this night got me through my father's funeral and the final exams the week after. Now I was ready to have some fun. It was about time.

I dressed in my favorite Armani suit with a light blue shirt that matched Katya's gorgeous eyes. I styled my dark hair, slicking it back with gel. It was a look I rarely used because the 'wet look', as my sister called it, made me feel like some sort of Italian used car salesman. But I wanted to look mature and elegant.

I tossed my keys into the air and bent to kiss my mother's cheek on my way to the front door.

Mother caught my hand and linked her fingers through mine like she used to do to keep me still as a child. "You look nice, darling. Where are you off to?"

"I have a surprise for you, Mother."

My mother always managed to see through me when I was at my sneakiest. Maybe it was the grin I couldn't keep off my face? "What kind of surprise?"

"The female kind." I disentangled myself from her before she could think of a reply, and I raced for the door with a laugh on my lips.

My silver Maserati gleamed in the overhead light of the garage, making my smile broaden. I wasn't really a car-guy, but I did appreciate sleek, pretty things, and this had also been a gift from my father for my sixteenth birthday. She was still in pristine condition even four years later. I slipped into the driver's seat and pushed the start button. The Maserati purred to life, rumbling under me. The garage door opened with another push of a button, and I zoomed out of the compound and into the night.

Madame Bombadine's looked the same as it always did, huddled against an alleyway with warm lights welcoming strangers off the streets. It was already busy which made me wonder how many invitations Madame B. had sent out for this intimate affair. I had hoped for fewer people.

I found a parking spot down the street and slid into it with ease then headed for the front steps. I was greeted by a bored-looking bouncer who I sort of recognized for all the attention I'd paid him the times I'd come when I was younger. And he didn't seem to recognize me, either. Wordlessly, I flashed the invitation at him.

"Mask?" He asked, offering one from the basket by his feet. The mask was mandatory for secrecy. Madame Bombadine's was the most popular brothel among Russia's elite, catering to everything from the wholesome to the exotic. Usually no one cared about appearances as business was often conducted here, but tonight was different. Buying a girl's virginity was... special. And also risky. This wasn't your usual fuck-and-pay.

I picked up one of the simple black masks and tied it behind my head. It covered my forehead, eyes, and nose, leaving only my mouth and chin bare. Like Batman. I stepped into the house and made my way to the living room. The transformation was astounding. Gone were the myriad sofas and loveseats. No one was playing piano. Girls were not sitting on laps or draped over men's shoulders from behind to whisper in their ears.

No. This place was the exact opposite. A small, round stage with a tail toward the far door had been placed in the center of the room, and a white gossamer curtain adorned with fairy lights hung from the ceiling around it. Chairs had been formed in a semi-circle around the stage, and some men were already seated. Waiting. Others were chatting quietly in groups. A few more were smoking cigars or pouring drinks for themselves. The thought of Katya beneath one of these perverted assholes made me see red. I had half a mind to go find Madame, buy Katya right then and skip all this bullshit. But I figured Madame wouldn't go for that since all these men had showed up to her Perv Party.

After taking a cursory glance around, I decided to stay sober. I needed my wits about me to make the best deal possible. Uncle Yuri had given me carte blanche to buy her. Money was really no object in my family, but I definitely wasn't used to spending so much money in one sitting. It was uncomfortable but also exciting. I felt like I was gambling at a casino in Monte Carlo or Las Vegas.

I was going to win. I had to!

***

Kate

The day I had been dreading for five years had finally come, and I was sick to my very core. I didn't want to be here. I didn't want to do this. This wasn't right in any shape or form. My 18th birthday was supposed to be one of the best birthdays because I was finally an adult, but adulthood brought problems in this instance.

From sun-up to sun-down today, I'd been groomed within an inch of my life. Waxed. Plucked. Scrubbed. Buffed. Lotioned. Until my body was practically hairless—and skinless—and my long, white-blonde hair shone like the moon. I smelled like a freaking rose garden which made my nose twitch, and my finger and toe nails had been lacquered a shell pink. My hair had been curled into long, gleaming spirals down my back.

With all of this grooming, it felt like this should be my wedding day. In fact, this was very much how I'd always imagined my wedding day to be: a lot of sitting and pampering. But there was no sweet champagne and bevy of close bridesmaids. No mother to squeeze me tight and make sure I knew I could back out if I wanted to. No, I just had Maribo and the girls and Madame. It was cold comfort.

Finally, after hours of primping, I stood in front of the full-length mirror in Maribo's room. I looked like a wedding cake. A sexy wedding cake, to be exact. The heart-shaped bodice was made of pure white lace which covered my nipples but left the rest of my small breasts on display. From there, sheer fabric draped from beneath my breasts to my upper thighs, where a hint of my white thong could be seen. I wore sheer white thigh-high stockings and a garter belt. Silver stilettos finished off the look.

Sexy wedding cake, indeed. Or a sexy Goldilocks.

And I was about to meet all the ferocious bears in the forest.

Maribo smiled at me as she draped the white satin robe around my shoulders and belted it at my waist. "You look scrumptious."

"That's what I'm afraid of."

She laughed and turned me to face her. "We've prepared you for this. You know what to do to make him want you. Tonight is the hardest part. After tonight, it will get easier."

I nodded and let her lead me from her room and down the back staircase only employees used, so I wouldn't be on display quite yet. She put me into position behind the closed door.

I could hear Madame B. speaking on my behalf, and I waited for my cue. "Gentleman, thank you for coming tonight. Each of you was chosen by me to attend tonight's affair based on your reputation both in—and out—of the bedroom." There were some deep chuckles at her joke. "I have known Elsa for five years, and she has grown into a stunning young woman, and I know you will agree. Now, gentleman, I don't need to tell you that I am expecting you to do well by her tonight." I knew she meant kindness to me as well as money. She was hoping to make bank, and so was I. The sooner I could pay off my debt to her, the better. "It is my greatest delight, gentleman, to present my ward, Elsa."

There was applause as the door opened, and I walked up the steps to the stage. Then the applause ceased. It was as if the collective room was holding its breath. I continued to walk, my eyes trained forward on the back wall to keep me from shivering in fear.

Why weren't they saying anything?

Why were they so dang quiet?

The silence made me finally begin to shake. My eyes darted to Madame B., standing behind the last row of chairs, who had a huge smile on her face for some reason. She gestured for me to remove the robe. My fingers plucked at the satin tie until it unraveled, and then I raised my fingers to my shoulders and slowly parted the robe, letting it flutter ever so slowly down my arms to pool at my feet.

A soft, shuddering sigh sounded around the room.

"Let's start the bidding at 70,000 rubles," Madame B. intoned. I knew that was nearly the equivalent of a thousand American dollars. And that got the bidding going.

During the rapid-fire bidding, I was asked to turn around this way and that. Bend over. Lift the fabric so my stomach could be seen.

And the rubles kept rising.

Until there were only two voices chiming in. Competing. For me. Suddenly the humiliation I'd been feeling gave way to fascination. I wondered who these two powerful men could be. Mafia? Businessmen? Were they even Russian or did they live somewhere else in the world and came for just this one opportunity?

"One million rubles." The soft chatter that had been accompanying the escalating bids died down to silence. I held my breath. With the bright light shining in my face and the masks I couldn't tell who had made the bid.

"Too rich for my blood," the other man—black devil mask—said and crossed his arms. Relief flooded me. There was something about the deep voice of the man who won that settled my nerves a bit. There was something I recognized in the man who lost...his voice, maybe? His attitude? I'd been silently praying for him to lose.

I picked up the satin robe, placed it around my shoulders once more and turned to leave the way I'd come. I stepped into the hallway and Maribo bounced as she hugged me tightly. "One million rubles! No one has ever gone for more than five hundred thousand! Elsa, this is amazing!"

I struggled to feel her excitement through my nervous energy, but I smiled all the same and shrugged. Then I walked to the designated room. There was a queen size bed with a white duvet and sheets. The same gossamer fabric with fairy lights lit the dim room around the bed. I busied myself by turning down the bed and then making vodka on the rocks in case my client wanted one. Then I settled myself on the bed to wait as I had been instructed.

What I really wanted to do was pace, but I'd been told not to. I'd been doing what I'd been told for five long— really long—years that merely the thought of disobeying didn't cross my mind. I pulled my knees up to my chest and wrapped my arms around them. The cold air against my inner thighs had me remembering I was wearing nothing under this dress except a thong. My legs dropped and I looked longingly at the duvet, wanting to wrap it around myself to hide my nearly nude body.

It didn't take long for there to be a knock at the door. "*Prikhodit*," come. The door opened and the man who bought me stood in the doorway. His eyes immediately zeroed in on me. His face was mostly hidden behind his simple black mask, but his eyes were penetrating through the eye holes anyway, or maybe more so because I couldn't see them fully.

He stepped in and closed the door, turning the lock with a snick. He walked toward me, and I sat up a bit straighter, unsure why he wasn't speaking. "I made you a vodka... if you want it," I spoke in Russian and gestured to the table by the door where the decanter and glasses were situated.

He paused beside the glass and lifted it to his lips. His eyes never left mine as he swallowed the clear liquor in its entirety before sauntering closer and placing the glass down on the bedside table. And then he did something wholly unexpected: he removed the mask.

It felt like my eyes were too large for my face as I watched him push the mask up and over his head. Those familiar dark eyes. The playful smile.

"Misha!" My shriek rang in my ears as I jumped to my feet on the bed and ran along the mattress toward him.

He laughed as he swept me up into his arms and twirled me around in a tight hug. When he set me on my feet once more, I stared up at him in wonder. "You spent a million rubles on me."

"Of course I did, Katya. I couldn't let some fucker take your virginity for a mere one million rubles. Plus, you belong to me." He chucked me under the chin with a gentle knuckle. "I've missed you." He bent his head, and I knew he wanted to kiss me. My hand flew up to cover his mouth.

"Language. And if you missed me so much, you could have continued to write." My pointed tone was punctuated by one raised eyebrow as I eyed him askance. Now that he was in front of me, I was downright angry with him! How dare he show up out of the blue and buy me like it was his right?! At least I didn't have history with the others. This guy, friend that he was, stopped speaking to me a year ago! My own letters went unanswered.

Misha kissed my palm and drew my hand away from his mouth. "Yeah, I'm sorry about that. I took to university like a worker bee takes to making honey. Once I got started, I didn't come up for air. My father," a shadow I didn't understand crossed his face, "demanded I be the best. It's a hard expectation to live up to. He's dead now. He died last week."

Rats! I felt horrible for him. From what I remembered, Misha hadn't really spoken much about his family other than he had a twin sister and parents, so I didn't know if he was close to his father. Still, losing him had to be hard. "I'm so sorry, Misha!" I linked my fingers with his and squeezed his hand for added support. "Are you doing okay?" Aside from the dark expression which had briefly shown itself on his face, he did not appear emotional about losing his father. If my father passed away, I would be a wreck! Like, I'm pretty sure I wouldn't leave my bed for at *least* a week! As I studied Misha's face, I saw a hardness that hadn't been there when he used to come visit me.

"Yes, I'm okay." When I narrowed my eyes at him, he continued, "Really, Katya. I'm dealing with it."

Dealing with it? What did that mean? But I decided to drop it. This wasn't exactly the time and place to have this discussion. "So... are you here to... to...." Goodness, it was hard to say this in front of him! My eyes begged him to take pity on me.

The smile returned to Misha's eyes, and he leaned down to press his forehead against mine. "No, I'm not here for that. I wouldn't do that to you. I'm here to fulfill the promise I made you as a child."

My heart flip-flopped in my chest. Was he for real?! Was I finally going to make it out of this place and go home? But then a thought had my heart sinking, and I shook my head at him. "One million rubles isn't enough to buy my freedom." My voice dropped to a whisper, "It's not even close."

"I know, and I don't care. I have the money to buy your freedom. I want you to go upstairs and pack a suitcase with whatever you want to bring." He pulled away and slid his dark gaze down my body. My nipples puckered under his stare, and I felt an awkward dampness between my thighs. "As much as I love how sexy you look in that outfit, I need you to change into something normal."

"Are you sure about this?" I asked, doubt entering my tone. I knew Misha's family was rich. He'd proved it to me over and over again through the years, but who had this kind of money just lying around? Maybe now that his father was out of the picture, Misha had more freedom to do what he wanted.

"Of course I'm sure. I made a promise to you, and I always keep my word. Now, go pack. I'm going to settle up with Madame."

We exited the room together, and gave each other a last look before I darted upstairs. The hall was dark and quiet because all the girls were downstairs soothing the egos of the men who lost the auction. I stepped into my room and froze with a frown. How was I supposed to pack? I didn't have a suitcase. Were these clothes even mine? I hadn't bought them myself. They were hand-me-downs from the other girls. My eyes filled with tears as I stood in the doorway of my prison, not sure how to follow Misha's directions. Not sure how to even leave this place.

***

Misha

It was easy to find Madame Bombadine. She was fluttering around the common room like a butterfly, laughing, chatting, flirting. Now that the auction was over, everyone had removed their masks. The wine and liquor were free-flowing, and apparently so were the breasts. The room looked like a bacchanalia with so many half-dressed, drunk people rubbing up against each other. It was enough to make a young man really uncomfortable in tight-fitting trousers. I adjusted myself before walking in.

I really hated to interrupt the revelry, but I had business to conduct. My eyes trained on Madame as she offered a drink to an older, liver-spotted gentleman I didn't know. Lifting my fingers in a slight wave, I caught her attention. Her smile slipped when she realized who I was—and who I was not with.

A hand clapped on my shoulder, and I glanced around to see my cousin's annoying smirk as he lifted a glass of dark liquid to his mouth. "That was quick. Was it your first time?"

Fucking Pavel. I stepped away, forcing him to remove his hand or be dragged with me. "Of course not. I just want to get the business paid for before I go back to her." That wasn't a lie, but I still felt like a douchebag for saying it because I knew what Pavel would think.

"Paying up front is always appreciated in my house," Madame cut in smoothly, linking her hand through my arm.

Pavel lifted his glass in a salute before turning to join the crowd once more. When he was gone, Madame turned me toward her and raised a brow, "What is this really about, Mr. Belov? Did Elsa put you out in some way?"

"Of course not. She's perfect. Always has been." I could tell by her less-than-surprised reaction that she had known about my friendship with her ward. "I want to buy her."

This statement gained a reaction, though not the greedy excitement I was expecting. It was confusion from the wrinkled brow to the puckered lips. "You already did that, Mr. Belov, with a sum I am extremely happy about."

"No, no. I want to buy her freedom." I waited a bit, and when she didn't respond quickly enough, I continued, "Completely."

"Let's step into my office." I followed Madame through the room of revelry and into the quiet stillness of the hallway. The difference in sound was jarring to the senses, and it took a moment for my ears to stop ringing. Madame's office was just across the hall. It was as small as a closet, and I wondered if maybe it actually was a coat or linen closet she turned into an office. There was a small desk and two chairs on either side. She sat in one and gestured for me to sit in the other.

I sat and tried to cross my legs but gave up after turning several directions in the tiny space. I was immensely glad

I wasn't bothered by enclosed spaces or this conversation might have had to happen where any ear could overhear.

"You said you want to buy Elsa's freedom." She rummaged in a stack of documents and placed a piece of paper in front of me. "That's the price."

Leaning forward, I perused the document. It was a contract of service. Katya's contract, to be exact. And the sum for which she owed was enormous. Way more than I had anticipated to the point that I wavered in my resolve. Could I spend this much money? Would Uncle Yuri allow it? I pulled my phone from my pocket and smiled sheepishly at Madame. "Let me just check the bank before I decide for sure." Yeah, the bank of Yuri Belov. I texted him the amount and waited.

"Tell me, Mr. Belov, why do you want to buy Elsa when you can visit her at any time? She will always be here."

My gaze steady on the three dots which told me Yuri was typing, I answered truthfully, "I love her. She's my best friend, and I want to do this for her. I made a promise years ago that I would help her, and now I can."

My phone pinged with Uncle Yuri's response. Relief flooded me. With a wide smile I couldn't dim even if I wanted to, I placed the Family bank card on the table between us. "Charge it."

Minutes later and a fortune lighter than I had been when I walked into this place an hour ago, I took the stairs two at a time. I found my girl standing in the doorway of a tiny bedroom. My enthusiasm dimmed when the soft sound of crying entered my consciousness. Why the hell was she crying? Shouldn't she be celebrating? Dancing? And most of all, packing?

"Katya?" I called to her softly as I approached her from behind.

She startled at my voice and whirled to face me. Tears coursed down her pale cheeks. She didn't even try to hide them.

"What are you doing? Do you need help?"

She nodded but simply stood there. Unmoving. I approached her slowly and cupped her damp cheeks. Then I lowered my forehead to hers. "Shh, Katya. Everything is going to be okay now. Can you tell me what's going on in this pretty head of yours?"

She sniffled then pulled away enough to finally wipe her cheeks with her hands and then dry them on the white silk of her babydoll dress. Valentina would have had a fit if she'd seen that. "I don't know what to do."

Confusion had me gnawing on the inside of my cheek. What was she talking about? "You don't know what to do about what? You just pack and then we go. It's that simple."

"But it's not that simple!" She shouted and clenched the sides of her hair with both hands. My eyes widened in shock. Never in all my years of knowing Katya, had I seen her get angry about anything... other than yelling at me for not writing. And she should be the furthest from angry at this moment. She should be elated. Something was definitely off.

I raised my hands and backed off a bit. "Alright. Tell me about it." If I was a better man, I might have ignored the way her breasts rose and fell with each breath beneath her sexy outfit. But I wasn't a better man. It made it damn hard to concentrate. But I needed to. I made myself look into her eyes and wait for her explanation.

"I...." She turned to look in the tiny room again as she hesitated. "I don't have a suitcase or bag. And I don't know what to take with me. What is mine? What stays here?" Then in the softest, loneliest voice I've ever heard someone speak, she said, "I'm so lost."

That did it. That sweet, strong girl I befriended and fell in love with had become a woman who didn't know who she was anymore. I was going to change all of that. Starting right now. If it were up to me, I'd throw her over my shoulder in that babydoll dress and leave, but I didn't want the men downstairs to see her like that. They'd already seen enough of her. I pushed past her and rummaged through the clothes sitting haphazardly on a chair. "Jeans, shirt, underwear. Put them on." I tossed the clothes on the bed then averted my eyes.

It took several seconds for her to act, but soon I could hear the rustle of clothes and knew she was following directions. Good. Now I knew for sure that what I was going to do with her would be the best thing for her in the long run. I would heal her.

"I'm ready," she said, and I looked at her with a smile. And without another word, I took her hand and led her away from her personal hell of the last five years.

Chapter 11

Kate

Past

Warmth like I haven't felt in years surrounded me. The pillow under my head felt like a cloud, and I wanted to burrow myself deeper into its softness. A soft knock had me inwardly groaning. "Ten more minutes, Mom," came my muffled voice from beneath the covers.

"Mom?"

The deep voice on the other side of the door had me sitting up straight. My eyes blinked blearily in the dimness. Where the heck was I? I managed to pull the covers up to my chin before the door opened and Misha stood in the doorway with a half-smile on his handsome face.

"Must have been having some happy dreams. I take it you slept well?" He moved aside and gestured to a person in the hallway. A woman wearing a light gray uniform walked in and set a tray on the bed. Deja vu nearly turned my blood cold as I was suddenly reminded of waking up in Madame Bombadine's house that first night. A similar tray of food, placed on the bed much in this same manner.

"*Spasibo*," Misha and I said in unison, and the maid smiled in response before leaving. I lifted the domed lid on the tray, and my eyes widened. Whatever similarities there were to my first day in Russia evaporated with the smell of hot chocolate, fresh fruit, scrambled eggs, and hot toast. This wasn't hell anymore, it was heaven!

"I did sleep well," I answered Misha, reaching for the hot chocolate, "and I could have slept longer."

"I'm sure you could have, but you have a busy day." When I looked at him curiously over the rim of the mug warming my hands, he continued, "Mama and Valentina are taking you shopping. So eat up because you will need your strength to keep up with those two."

I snorted into my mug. Surely it couldn't be that bad. I shifted my legs as he walked over to sit next to me on the bed. "Thank you for keeping your word on getting me out of there. I'm not going to lie, I didn't think I would ever see you again once you stopped writing."

Misha's warm gaze traveled over my face, and he reached up to smooth a lock of white-blonde hair from my forehead. Not able to help myself, I leaned into his touch like a puppy wanting affection. "I know. I shouldn't have let anything else distract me from my promise. I'm sorry."

"It's okay. Heck, everything is going to be okay now. And your mother and sister don't need to take me shopping. No reason you can't send me home in the same clothes I wore yesterday. Plus, I'd really like to call my parents." I dug my fork into an egg and plopped it into my mouth. Salty and buttery goodness.

There was a pause long enough that I glanced up at my friend. "Katya, listen, now isn't a good time. How about I put some stationary in your room, and you can write them a letter? I'm not s—"

"There she is!" A voice cried from the still-open doorway. A tall, statuesque woman bustled inside and over to my bed, sitting on the opposite side from Misha. Her black hair was in an elegant bun on the back of her head. She looked so much like Misha but older with strands of gray and lines webbing the outsides of her eyes. She had to be his mother. "Hello, Katya, I'm Larissa, Misha's mother. I am so happy to have you here with us." She glanced at her son. "I can see why Misha is so taken with you. You are quite lovely. We are going to have so much fun today!" She clapped her hands in a show of childish excitement.

I didn't have the heart to tell her I was ready to go home. My heart sank at the thought, taking away her excitement. Surely one more day here wouldn't hurt? I would just convince them not to spend a fortune on me. A new pair of jeans, a sweater, and underwear would be good enough to send me home tomorrow. Then I'd look presentable when I saw my parents again.

"Mrs. Belov, thank you for letting me stay here last night. I don't think I've ever slept so well."

A sadness crept into Mrs. Belov's eyes, and she took my free hand, patting it gently with her warm, soft fingers. "When I heard what you have been through and that my Misha was determined to set you up in a better life, I knew Valentina and I needed to be a part of it." Before I could speak, she called out, "Valentina! Darling, are you ready?"

"Of course I am!" Came the prompt reply as a woman, who looked like a female version of Misha, marched into the room, her arms full of clothes. "I just wasn't sure what to pick out for her." The young woman—Misha's twin—smiled brightly at me before she grabbed Misha by the arm and tried to yank him off the bed. "Move, brother. I want to sit next to her."

Misha grinned, grabbed hold of his sister's hands and shoved her hard enough to make her fall. My mouth dropped open in shock.

"Ow!" Valentina stared up at her brother while rubbing her bottom, then her frown wobbled into a smile. She giggled! Right there on the floor!

A loud clap sounded from my right where Mrs. Belov was sitting next to me. "Children!"

"Sorry, Mama," they both said, but despite the words, I could tell they were anything but apologetic.

Misha hoisted his sister off the floor, and she immediately began laying out clothes on the foot of the bed. Once they were arranged, she bounced over to me and wrapped her arms tight around my shoulders in a hug. "Oh, Katya, we are going to have so much fun together! I've always wanted a sister!"

What the heck was she talking about? I was leaving tomorrow and probably wouldn't see any of them again. Ever. As much as I might want to see Misha in the future, I'd honestly like to put this entire episode of my life into a safe and throw away the key.

Confusion must have been written all over my face because Misha carefully extricated his sister's arms from around me and took his seat once again. "Katya, we aren't sending you home. At least not immediately."

My heart dropped to my toes.

***

An hour later, I was still searching for answers. Plenty had been given to me as Mrs. Belov and Valentina dressed me like their little personal dolly before we left (I felt weird wearing a long-sleeved, red dress while both Belov women were wearing black). But none of the answers were satisfying.

I knew nothing of the world.

Legality issues.

I didn't have a passport.

And the most infuriating of them all, apparently I was a victim of 'learned helplessness'. *Seriously?!* Just because I was startled and confused last night and couldn't pick out my own clothes to dress in and take with me, I supposedly couldn't make decisions. To make matters worse, to prove his point, Misha fired a series of questions at me that I couldn't answer.

What would I say to my family if I just showed up out of nowhere?

What's my favorite color?

Did I want to go to college?

What kind of job did I want?

How in the ever-loving world was I supposed to answer those questions? I hadn't known my own mind since being kidnapped. My whole day was planned out from the time I woke up to the second my head hit the pillow.

And my favorite color was blue...

I think.

Pink?

Well, who cares what color I liked the most? That didn't mean a thing! Right?

I tilted my head against the cold window of the limousine as it sped through the wintery white streets of Moscow. Luckily Valentina lent me a heavy coat and some nicer clothes than the old ones I'd worn last night. I was comfortable and stylish.

"We're here!" Valentina, who I was finding out had to have inherited all of the boisterousness in the womb instead of her brother, bounced in her seat as the car came to a stop in front of a building. "You are going to love this place, Katya. Mama and I have a spa day every Christmas break."

"Spa day? I thought we were shopping." Another surprise. What did one do at a spa?

"We will do that after," Mrs. Belov answered. "We felt you could use some pampering. And a haircut. Not that your hair isn't beautiful. I swear I've never seen a color that pure before. Simply gorgeous. But a trim will make it healthier."

Cut my hair? Thank God! I'd been wanting to do that for ages, but Madame B. had forbidden it. She said men loved long hair. The longer, the better. And she said it made me look young. I wasn't exactly sure that was the compliment she meant it to sound.

A blast of icy wind cut into our conversation as the driver opened the car door, and the three of us quickly walked into the large building. The lobby was actually very small. And thankfully heated. A fountain trickled in the corner. A large desk stood at the far end with two receptionists. One was on the phone, but the other glanced up and beamed a red-lipped smile at us.

"*Dobro pashalovat.*" Welcome. The woman clicked a few keys on her computer before walking around to hand us each a soft terry cloth robe. "Mrs. and Miss Belov, so happy to see you again," she gushed. "Let me get you three a glass of champagne as you wait."

And that was just the beginning.

Two hours later, I had been massaged, wrapped, masked, and buffed within an inch of my life... for the second day in a row. I was pretty sure my skin color was brighter than when I was born! My toenails and fingernails were stripped of yesterday's polish and repainted to a shine. Now I was sitting in a black chair staring into the mirror at a very unusual man who was fluffing and fussing with my hair.

"Darling, darling. You have split ends for days. *Days*! But no fear, Oleg will fix you right up. Inga!" He screeched, and a harassed-looking assistant hurried to his side. "Mix up my special Starlight cocktail."

"Oh, that sounds delicious," I said, licking my lips. I hadn't realized how hungry I was.

"Oh, no. It's not for *you*, darling. It's for your hair!"

Inga returned after a few minutes and handed a suspicious black bowl with what looked like a small paintbrush and tin foil to my stylist who grinned in a way that made me doubt his sanity. "We are going to keep your base color but add some highlights!"

"Isn't my hair already too pale for that?"

"Darling, shush. You know nothing about hair. Shush, shush." He clucked his lips, tweaked one side of his mustache, and then began to work.

Valentina's eyes found mine in the mirror, and she grinned at me. "Don't stress about it. Oleg is the best in the biz. He does mine, and doesn't it look great?" She tipped her head so a thick swathe of midnight fell over one shoulder.

"Yes, it's gorgeous." That did put me at ease. I could do this.

It didn't take long before I was sitting beneath what looked like a rotating heat lamp, a magazine filled with different styles of haircuts in my lap. Long curls, sleek bobs, and short caps of tousled locks. What was I supposed to choose? At least I knew I wasn't ready to go too short. A chin-length bob? Would that fit my face? Or a layered medium-length style? Did I *like* layers? I was starting to see why Misha thought I couldn't make decisions. I gave my head a shake.

Learned helplessness.

It took a solid thirty minutes for my hair to be cut, dried, and styled, and from what I could see, it looked like Oleg had sheared an entire sheep by the amount of white-blonde hair all over the floor. When everything was finished, Oleg's hands massaged my shoulders, and he bent down to murmur in my ear, "Are you ready for the reveal, darling?" When I gave a nod of agreement, he slowly turned the chair to face the mirror he had denied me the entire time.

I looked... different.

My hair had been lightened with almost silvery-white highlights and cut to right above my shoulders. It was straight and bouncy, and I had bangs—bangs!—swooped off to the side. I looked more mature. More elegant. This was someone I wanted to become. I found Valentina's eyes in the mirror, and we shared matching smiles. I wasn't Kate the kidnapping victim anymore.

I was Katya.

Chapter 12

Misha

Past

She took it better than I'd expected. I was expecting hurled insults and crying. A *lot* of crying. But I should have known better. My little Katya would never be so unsophisticated as to shout, scream, and cry about not getting her way. Did she look confused as hell? Yes. But that was to be expected. Luckily she'd been quickly distracted by my mother and sister, and I'd been able to escape.

She'd asked so many questions and had probably come up with more while she was out. I needed to figure out the best way to answer them before she came home. How was I supposed to get her on board with not going home immediately? I felt kind of stupid thinking about how excited she was going to be to go to university with me. Dumbass. Of course she wanted to go home instead. Not that I had a chance to tell her about university before I ran away like a coward.

The door downstairs opened and closed, and the cacophony of female voices and laughter echoed in the halls darkened by mourning. Katya was already breathing life back into my family. I closed the book in my hands and set it aside before wandering to the large front staircase. I was halfway down before my eyes met hers and my heart nearly stopped beating.

"Katya... fuck, look at you!" The long train of hair was gone, replaced by an elegant layered bob the color of starlight. It looked so soft that I wanted to run my fingers through it. Her clothes were vastly different from what she'd come home in and a universe different than what she'd been wearing at the auction. I liked her in every single item from sexy to grunge, but this elegant woman standing before me had confidence that I found incredibly sexy.

"Language!" All three women said together before sweeping past me with their heads held high. When they turned a corner, I heard them giggling which made me smile and shake my head. This was either really good that they had bonded or really, really bad. For me. Either way, it was good to see my mother smiling and happy. She had been like a somber, sad waif every day since Father died. Maybe, with Katya in the house, she would be inspired to take down the heavy black mourning curtains from the windows.

The door behind them opened again, and my brows rose as bags and boxes were carried inside by the driver and one of the bodyguards who had ridden with the ladies. They placed them on the floor before heading out again. With another shake of the head, I followed the laughter down the hallway to my mother's favorite parlor. Apparently she had called ahead for tea as she was already pouring the fragrant brew into three steaming porcelain cups.

"Tea, Misha, dear?" She called when she glanced up to see me enter.

"No, thank you, Mother." I had a feeling I was going to need something stronger for this conversation. Explaining

Katya's future to her was going to be a delicate process. The cold smell of vodka burned my nose when I unscrewed the lid on the bottle and poured it over some ice.

Liquid courage. I could do this.

I wandered to the sofa and sat. Uncomfortably. This room was incredibly feminine from the floral wallpaper to the fancy, cushioned sofas on spindly legs. Why anyone would want to sit on something that looked like an overgrown pin-cushion without the pins, I would never understand. But Mother liked it, so I pretended to like it, too.

"Did you all have a good time? It looks like you broke the bank with all your shopping," I said as I lifted the glass to my lips for a sip.

"We had the best time, Misha," replied my sister, kicking off her shoes and crossing her legs on the chair across from me. "And your bank account should feel lucky to be so used. It was probably feeling neglected."

"Probably not after his large purchase last night."

All of our eyes went to Katya who was now staring blankly into her teacup as if it held answers to the world's prob-lems. Or even just her own. Her mood shifted so quickly. I met the eyes of my sister and mother who both seemed as concerned as I felt.

"Maybe, but it was worth it," I said gently. "*You* are worth it. You were a great friend to me growing up, and I'm keep-ing my promise."

Her head jerked up, and I was caught in her icy blue stare. "But are you? Are you keeping your promise?"

I dipped my head in a slow nod. "I know it doesn't seem like it right now, but I am. Before you go home, I want to make sure you have every advantage."

"My family will help me." There was fire behind her words.

Calmly I breathed air in through my nose and slowly out so I didn't speak too hastily. "I know that, but there are things I can help you with here so you aren't at such a disadvantage due to your circumstances."

"Like my 'learned helplessness'?"

"Yes, like that. But also getting a degree from a university. Real world training."

"I can't go to college, Misha. I didn't graduate high school. I didn't even *go* to high school."

The pain in her words kicked me in the solar plexus. How had I not realized how much it pained her not to have an education? I knew she wanted to learn Russian and Cyrillic, and I'd helped her with that, but I didn't help her learn anything else. But I could. "You like to bake, right?"

"You know I do."

"My university has a great culinary program. You don't really need a high school education to cook, right? I know plenty of chefs who don't have degrees."

"That doesn't help me get accepted into the program, though," she fumed, setting down her cup on the end table. "No one is going to say, 'You don't really need a diploma to cook, so you don't need one for university, either'." The way she said it in a deep voice and in a way my sister would call "mansplaining" made my mouth twitch. I barely contained my smile. She was already annoyed. I didn't want to make her downright angry.

"My uncle has contacts in the university, Katya. You have already been accepted." I finally beamed at her. Problem solved! I had an answer to every question!

She stared at me, dewy pink lips parted in a way that made me want to kiss her. And I might have if my mother and sister weren't watching our every move like we were in an episode of Gossip Girl.

"You have it all figured out then."

My smile faded at Katya's tone. Why wasn't she happy? "Yes?" I said and cleared my throat. "Yes. We wanted it all figured out for you before you got here. To give you hope. Plus, if we hadn't tried to get you into classes, you might not have been accepted in time. And you will get to be with Valentina and me! We have a suite with an extra bedroom. It will all work out perfectly. And once you have your degree and can be self-sufficient, you can go home."

Though I hoped by then she would be too attached to me—us—that she might want to stay. After all, she'd spent half of her life here. What did she really have left back in the United States? She wasn't the same person she was when she was brought here. The whole experience of going home might actually be... disappointing.

She continued to stare at me as if I had grown another head. At this point I didn't know if she was happy, disappointed, or pissed the fuck off. But what I did know was I didn't like her reaction or lack thereof.

"Why are you not excited?" I finally burst out. "You're free from your servitude, you get to follow your dream, and then you get to go home!"

A touch on my shoulder had me turning to look at my mother. "Misha, darling, Katya has a lot to process. All of this has happened at once."

"Yeah, Misha, give the girl a break. Her life has been flipped over twice. She needs a breather. Katya, do you want to go for a walk?" Valentina set her cup aside and stood.

Katya nodded and stood, quickly moving away from me and linking her arm with my twin's. I watched them leave, my heart in my throat.

"Misha, look at me."

I turned to look at my mother once again. Her dark eyes studied my face intently. I'm not sure what she saw in my expression, but she sank onto the sofa next to me and took one of my hands between hers. "You have lived a unique but privileged life, my son. Everything you ever needed or wanted was handed to you. You cannot treat this girl like one of your sister's dolls to play with and abandon at your will—"

"Who said anything about abandoning her?!" I almost shouted in exasperation. Why wasn't anyone listening to me? I should be congratulated on my clever thinking at the least!

"Bad choice of words. Let me rephrase. Katya has trauma you will never understand no matter how well or how long you know her. She has not yet owned that trauma. Only time can do that. You can be her friend. Help her. Encourage her. But you cannot save her from her experiences. Give her time to adjust."

With those final words, she returned to her chair, lifted her tea cup, and sat back against the sofa cushion in silence.

Chapter 13

Kate

Past

I was shocked to find out that Christmas was two days away. I felt like it was my birthday and then all of a sudden, it was Christmas. That wasn't unusual since my birthday was the first of December, but time felt different in the Belov household. The Belovs were overwhelming but in a fun way. They were all so kind as was their extended family. There were always people in and out of the house. Mostly uncles, Misha explained, visiting his father's brother who had taken over the business while Misha finished his education. It was a little weird to me knowing that every man I met was part of the Russian mafia... er... Bratva, as they called it. And it was even weirder knowing I had seen most of them at Madame Bombadine's. None of us mentioned it, though. I had a hard time wrapping my head around the fact that my sweet and funny friend was part of an organization that dealt in who knew what... guns, drugs, even trafficking. I didn't want to ask. Ignorance is bliss, right?

But I couldn't overlook the fact that Misha's family were so good to me. Not only did they buy me a year's worth of clothing, but they took me horseback riding and included me in their daily lives. They didn't have to do any of that. And I wanted to give back to them, but how? I didn't have money of my own to buy gifts. I only existed on their charity. However, an idea came to me in the form of my favorite nosh: a sticky bun.

The chef of the Belov estate was talented, but she did not often deviate from a set of her favorite recipes. Which was why I found myself forcefully pounding dough into the wooden counter while trying to convince her to let me contribute to the Christmas breakfast. She'd welcomed me into her kitchen sanctuary with a kind smile. Being the Belov's guest didn't faze her at all. When I told her I loved to bake, she plopped a blob of dough in front of me, as if saying, show me what you got.

She eyed my technique as we kneaded our individual dough balls, giving me tips and showing me alternate methods for when my hands tired. I even taught her a thing or two when I rolled the ball of dough into a length and looped it several times to form a decorative knot. Once the bread was proofing with a towel over it, she sat me down at the freshly cleaned counter with a bottle of water. *This* was when I confessed my plan to bake for the Belov family Christmas breakfast.

Thank God I waited to ask instead of barging in here asking favors. The chef raised a brow at me, but I could see her mulling it over. Her eyes flickered to the proofing dough. She knew I knew what I was doing. Chefs are notoriously protective of their kitchens and ingredients. I was only a guest here. I didn't know her well at all, and she might have sent me out with a smack to the bottom with the rolling pin, or she might have complained about me to Mrs. Belov. Neither would be wanted.

"I promise I'm not coming in making changes to your menu. One day only."

"But it is an important day."

"It is. This is the only gift I can give them, Chef. The circumstances of why I'm here... I don't have money to buy them anything. And you and I both know the best gifts are homemade." That sold it. I could read it all over her face. "We can plan a menu together."

"You have a deal."

Two days later, I found myself in the kitchen at four o'clock in the morning wearing an apron with my hair tied back from my face. People bustled around me. Chef, sous chef, preps. I ignored them all and did my thing. Soon I was lost in the now-familiar process of baking. The scents of flour, baking powder, cinnamon, and sugar were like a warm hug to my senses. They comforted me like nothing else.

I rolled the dough into a flat surface, slathered it with a mouth-watering mixture of butter, cinnamon, and sugar, and then rolled the dough into a tight log. Then I used a thread to slice the log into even coils, setting each one lovingly on a sheet pan and popped the pan into the oven.

While the rolls were cooking, I made a fruit salad with fresh mandarin oranges, strawberries, apples, blackberries, and pomegranate seeds. It looked fresh and festive. While I chopped, Chef mixed a yogurt sauce for the fruit.

The sun rose, adding extra natural light through the kitchen windows. But I only had eyes for the window of the oven as I watched the dough rise into the round, plump pillows of cinnamon rolls. When they were a delicate, flaky golden brown, I slid an oven mitt on each hand and opened the oven door. Damp heat assailed my face. I took the hot pan into my mittened hands and closed the oven door with my shoulder. Then I deposited the hot pan onto the counter.

While the cinnamon rolls cooled, I mixed the icing in a bowl. Then I slathered it all over every single roll. I didn't skimp on the icing because it's the best part. When I was a kid, I always hated when the cinnamon roll didn't have enough icing to cover the entire thing, so I made sure to drench each one. Then I placed all but four hand-sized rolls on a large platter. One was for Chef and the others went onto plates I left out for her assistants. They smiled appreciatively before digging in, their moans of approval fueled my love of baking.

After tossing my apron into a laundry bin reserved for kitchen items that needed washing, I hefted the cinnamon roll-laden tray and headed toward the dining room. Chef followed me wheeling a cart filled with the bowl of fruit, an egg dish, and a plate of pickled fish which I would never get used to eating in the morning no matter how many years I lived in Russia, and a tureen of sweet oatmeal.

Nerves fluttered in my stomach at the sound of voices coming from the dining room. What if they didn't like what I made? What if they didn't like that I went against their traditions? I paused outside the double doors and took a deep breath in before exhaling slowly. Pasting a bright, cheerful smile on my face, I pushed the door open with a hip.

The table was long, but the family all sat together at the very end with Misha at the head. They glanced toward me at the sound of the door opening. All three family members smiled, and Misha stood. He rounded the table and approached, his hands outstretched to take the heavy tray.

"What do we have here, love?" He bent to press a kiss to my cheek. "Looks like you got up very early for this surprise. Here I was thinking I was going to have to wake you up and you've been awake since dawn." He placed the tray on the sideboard and smiled at Chef who was filling the rest of the space with the food from the cart.

I took a seat next to Valentina who leaned over to put her arm around me in a tight hug. "You are so sweet to help make breakfast, Katya, but you didn't have to do that."

"Oh, I know. Baking is life to me, and I'm a firm believer in handmade gifts. So... Merry Christmas, Belov family! I am so thankful for how you all took me in as one of your own. You didn't have to do that." Tears clogged my throat, and I had to swallow them down several times. "The best way I can show my gratitude is to bake something for you with all the love I have in my heart."

"Darling...." Mrs. Belov—Larissa, as she insisted I begin calling her—rounded the long table and knelt in front of me. "We are so happy to have you here. Thank you for baking us this gift. We can't wait to try it."

"Shpeak fur yurshelf," came a mumbled reply from the sideboard. When Larissa, Valentina, and I glanced over, Misha was shoving bite after bite of cinnamon roll into his icing-coated mouth.

"Misha Belov!" Screeched Larissa in shock. "I know I taught you better than this! Where are your manners?"

"I think he ate them, Mama," Valentina laughed, aiming her phone at her brother with a wide, devilish grin.

Misha ignored his sister and took a napkin offered by the chef to wipe his sticky hands and face. "Sorry. They smelled so good! I couldn't resist."

"Well, leave some for the rest of us," Larissa said, coming to her feet again. "Ladies first. You can serve your plate when we have gone through. Come, ladies."

Valentina and I grinned at each other before following her to the sideboard for the best Christmas breakfast I'd had since my last Christmas at home. Though the cinnamon rolls reminded me of my own Christmas mornings, I still missed the usual traditions. Opening Santa's presents. Baking Christmas cookies with my grandmother. Sledding with my best friend and brother at a park outside of town.

After breakfast, we gathered around the main Christmas tree—the house had at least six!—in the largest parlor to open presents. Because the family had spent so much money on me with the spa day and wardrobe shopping, I was not expecting to receive any gifts. So I was shocked when Valentina approached me with a colorfully-wrapped, weirdly misshapen gift. It was squishy, and I smiled at her. "What is this?"

"A present, duh. Open it!"

I tore off the paper and gasped at the pink and black Kate Spade backpack in my hands. I had never owned a backpack this expensive in my life! I had used the same trusty Jansport from 6th grade through 8th grade. Mom always said if it wasn't damaged, it was still good to use. She bought us shiny new pencil boxes, binders, and notebooks, but the backpack was always the same. During our shopping excursion, I'd found a love of Kate Spade *everything*. "Valentina!" I squealed, "I love it! Thank you!" I threw my free hand around her and hugged her tight.

After that, more gifts were dropped at my feet. The cooking utensils I'd need for class, a hand-written cookbook of Larissa's family recipes with some included from the chef, a set of Kate Spade bed sheets and comforter for my dorm room, and a delicate gold bracelet with a tiny K charm.

This was the happiest I had been in a very, *very* long time.

Whether it was the excitement of the day or the rich food eaten at a later hour than I was used to, and the nervousness of being around Misha's extended family for dinner, I found it hard to sleep. I went about my nightly routine. I brushed my hair, washed my face, and dressed in a lavender satin nightgown. Then I lay in bed and tossed and turned, unable to get comfortable. The queen-sized bed was softer than a cloud, but I still couldn't fall asleep.

Finally, I gave up and rolled out of the comfy bed. I stretched before digging in the closet to find my new robe and swished it around my shoulders. Then I padded barefoot into the darkness of the hallway on my way to the kitchen.

It was easy to find all the ingredients I needed in the large, well-organized kitchen. Such organization was the mark of a trained chef as all staff needed to be able to find the spices and ingredients quickly when cooking for many people. Though the immediate Belov family was small, I'd observed that extended family was often here for meals.

I pulled out sugar, flour, chocolate chips, butter, eggs, baking powder, and salt from the cupboard and refrigerator as well as small and large glass bowls and a sheet pan. I prepped the pan first by laying a strip of parchment paper over the metal and set it aside. As I measured and scooped, I lost myself in the smells of chocolate and dough to the point I didn't notice the sound of the kitchen door opening behind me.

Two strong arms slid around my waist, and I jumped with a stifled shriek. His scent of cologne and musk helped me identify the intruder. "Misha! You can't sneak up on a kidnapping victim!" I playfully reached around and swatted him on the back of the head.

A chuckle warmed my skin before he nuzzled his nose against the side of my neck. "Sorry. Damn, you smell good. Like cookies."

Chills raced over my rapidly-heating skin. And when the nuzzling turned to soft, slow kisses, my eyes closed in bliss. "Language," my voice sounded breathy in my ears. "And that makes sense considering I'm *making* cookies." There was an unsaid duh in my tone. Misha hadn't shown me more than brotherly affection since he installed me in his household, but I caught him watching when he thought I didn't know. Long looks. The kind that make you hold your breath to see how long they last. The tension of our quiet knowledge of romance building between us made this moment a scattering of emotion. Excitement, nervousness, and relief. Excitement and nervousness from the building desire and the relief from a coiled tension which made the skin feel a little too tight every time we were together around his family. I was looking forward to our time at university where we might be able to explore this budding awareness of each other.

"What kind?" Misha pressed against my back to peer over my shoulder into the bowl.

"Chocolate chip."

"Your grandmother's recipe? Please say yes!"

I giggled at the eagerness in his voice and nodded. "Yes! Of course it is."

"Yes!" Misha pulled away from me and punched the air extravagantly while I just shook my head and laughed at his antics.

"You are a nut, Misha, I swear," I giggled while rolling a ball of dough between my hands before placing it carefully on the parchment-covered sheet pan.

"I'm your nut, so what does that make you?" He grinned, leaning over to swipe a finger through the dough, scooping up a chocolate chip.

"A nutcracker!" I smacked his hand with the wooden spoon.

"My little nutcracker," he cooed, sliding his finger into his mouth and sucking off the dough.

My eyes tracked his finger to his lips. If it was wrong for me to envy that digit, then I didn't want to be right. I squeezed my thighs together to ease the ache growing there. Ugh, I needed to switch my attention to something else before this got out of hand.

Roll the dough.

Pan the dough.

Do it again. And again. And again.

The repetitive nature of preparing the cookies settled my mind once more, and I took a deep breath before finally looking up at my friend. My best friend, if I was honest with myself. He was watching my every move as if I was his favorite movie. I smiled at him, "What?"

He lifted his shoulders and shrugged. "Nothing. Just watching the master at work."

I snorted, picked up the pan of cookie dough and headed for the oven. I set them in the middle of the rack, closed the door, and set the timer. When I turned around, Misha had circled the counter and was right in front of me.

There must have been questions in my eyes because he touched my cheek with careful fingers and murmured, "I've missed you. Missed *us*. It's not the same with my family around is it?"

"No, but they are truly amazing, Misha. You should count yourself very lucky to have a mom and sister like them.

Your life would have been much different without their support." Not that I had my own experiences to gauge that, but the girls at Madame B.'s had told me stories of their upbringing. Even I found myself thanking my lucky stars that, though this whole kidnapping thing happened, at least my life before was filled with happiness and warm memories.

"Trust me, I know. But that's cold comfort when all I've wanted to do for weeks is kiss you."

I blinked up at him, a small smile curling one edge of my mouth, "What's stopping you now?"

He closed the meager distance between us until we were breathing each other's air. I leaned into his hand on my cheek and sighed as his fingers slid back into my hair. Slowly he wrapped my hair around his fist and pulled until my head tilted at just the right angle for his lips to settle perfectly on mine.

He sipped at my lips, taking his time to warm me up to his touch. It had really been so long. Years of missing his friendship. His love. I leaned into him, parting my lips and his tongue sank into my mouth. He tasted of vodka and something sweet that was unquestionably him. My arms slid around his neck and held him tightly against my body. I wondered if he could feel my heart beat because it felt wild within my own chest.

Misha pulled away enough for us to catch our breaths and he pressed his forehead against mine, his eyes still closed. I studied the sinfully unfair length of his dusky eyelashes. So unfair.

"You taste just as I remember," he murmured against me.

"Yeah?" The words this man said! He could make me tingle in places I didn't know existed!

"Yeah. Like snow and vanilla."

I pulled my head back and cocked an eyebrow at him. "Isn't that just vanilla ice cream?"

"No... I mean, maybe? But better. Imagine the ozone scent of snow mixed with vanilla and sugar. Haven't you made snow cream before?"

Snow cream. A distant memory of Dad, Derek, and I scooping snow off the deck into disposable cups. My dad made a corny joke about not eating yellow snow. Then he and Derek helped me scoop sugar and vanilla into the cup and mix it up.

Snow cream.

"Actually, yes. I do remember that." But the memory was all I had. I didn't remember what it actually tasted like or its texture on my tongue. But the memory warmed me from the inside out. "Thank you."

Misha's dark brow quirked in question. "For what?"

"For helping me remember."

The oven timer shattered our quiet interlude. Misha stepped back and allowed me to work. I peered into the oven to check the cookies, hoping they weren't burned. They didn't smell burned, but you couldn't be sure without taking a peek. Normally I liked my cookies on the gooey side, but for what I had planned, these cookies needed to be a bit tougher. So the extra time in the oven actually did the trick. Using a pair of oven mitts, I pulled the hot pan out and set it on the counter before lifting the cookies one-by-one to a cooling rack.

A hand shot out and snatched a piping hot cookie from the rack. I stared in rapt amusement as Misha tossed the cookie from hand-to-hand before dropping it to smash on the counter.

Pointing to the remnants of cookie scattered over the counter, I accused—a bit over-dramatically, but I mean, they were cookies!—, "how dare you take one of my cookies? Now I don't have equal pairs!"

"What about my poor, burnt hands?" he asked with a pout, holding out his red hands where a tiny blister was forming. A boiling hot chocolate chip must have touched his skin.

"You deserved that. Why in the world did you think it was okay to pick up a cookie hot out of the oven?"

"I didn't think it would be *that* hot!"

I rolled my eyes at him, then took his hand and led him to the sink. While I ran some cold water and pushed his hand under it, I studied his pinched expression. I suddenly felt bad for giving him such a hard time about it. Gently, I asked, "Haven't you ever made cookies with your mom or grandmother?"

"No, I've never made cookies with anyone before. I've just watched it on television."

"Okay, well, now you know better." I lifted his hand from the water and kissed the cold, reddened skin before pushing it back under the water. "Keep your hand here for another ten minutes. That should do the trick."

With a sympathetic smile for him, I walked back to the counter to clean up the broken cookie. "Anyway, these aren't your usual chocolate chip cookies. They are a little bit hard—"

Misha's lips twitched, but before he could open his mouth to say something probably raunchy, I cut in, "Keep it to yourself, Casanova."

He snorted in reply. "Okay, I'll bite. Why did you bake these differently than you normally would?"

"These are for homemade Chipwiches."

Misha scrunched up his face.

Offended, I asked, "What is *that* look for?"

"I hate to tell you this, Katya, but the Chipwich you love so much... is gross."

My gasp nearly knocked me over. "How dare you disparage the Chipwich! It is the best thing to hit stores since sliced bread!"

The dry look he gave me could wither leaves. "No. It's really not."

I carefully patted the cookies to test their warmth and then walked to the freezer. I dug out a huge jug of ice cream and brought it back to the counter. After setting out four cookies, I scooped a large dollop of frozen ambrosia— aka vanilla bean ice cream—onto two of the cookies then topped them with the other cookie. I was going to prove him wrong. "What food would you say is better than sliced bread?"

Misha turned off the water and walked toward me with a wicked grin on his face. "The best thing since sliced bread is fresh pasta. But the best tasting thing I've tasted lately is y—"

I shoved one of the cookie sandwiches into his mouth. "That should shut your mouth for a while," I snarked, but I couldn't help the way my lips wanted to twitch up in a smile.

"I thought you liked my mouth," he replied after removing the Chipwich and eyeing it dubiously.

"Eat your Chipwich before it melts. No need to look at it like that. I promise you'll like one that's homemade better than the store bought.

I watched as he sank his teeth into the cookie sandwich. His eyes rolled back until they closed, and he shook his head as he chewed. A soft, "Damn..." was whispered into the air between us.

"Language, Misha," I gently chided for what felt like the millionth time. I took a bite out of my own Chipwich and sighed in happiness.

"Why are you so against curse words? They're just words. I don't think I've ever met anyone who hasn't ever said a curse word before."

"I never told you that. I mean, I have said curse words before when I was back home in Chicago."

"Then what changed? Why are you so offended by them now? If anything, you deserve to say them daily after the hand life has dealt you."

"I didn't used to be so against them. But my grandmother was very proper and hated what she called 'ignorant language'. She said that curse words were for people who had too limited a vocabulary. One day she caught my brother and his best friend cussing at each other while playing Call of Duty. Before they knew what she was doing, she had unplugged their game. Then she dragged them to the bathroom by their earlobes and stuck a bar of soap in each of their mouths! My brother's friend never came over again while my grandmother was visiting."

"Harsh! How old were they?"

"Eleven. But that's not the worst experience with cussing. When I was nine, I was really angry with my dad because he grounded me for getting an F on a Science test I forgot to study for because I wrote it on the wrong week in my planner. I yelled, 'Screw you!' at him. I don't think I have ever seen him that mad. He said, 'Do you even know what that means?!' I shook my head because of course I didn't have the faintest clue. I thought it had to do with using a screwdriver." Misha chuckled. "Anyway, he said, 'It means to have sex with!' Now, imagine being a nine year old girl, and your father says that to you! I was mortified! Stop laughing! It's not that funny!"

I whacked Misha on the arm with the flat of my hand. It only made him laugh harder. After a moment of gaping at him while he lost all control, I let go of my own. We both laughed until our sides hurt and Chipwiches had melted all over the counter.

Finally, Misha was able to say, "Your dad has balls, Katya. That's a great story."

"Gross! Don't ever mention my dad and balls ever again."

Leaning against the counter, we ate and laughed until our stomachs were full and our worries of the day faded away. When we'd eaten our fill, we cleaned the kitchen together before heading up to our respective bedrooms. Like in a fairytale, Misha leaned in and pressed his lips to mine in the sweetest kiss of my life before heading to his own room. I slept like the dead the rest of the night with dreams of snow cream kisses making me smile in my sleep.

Chapter 14

Misha

Past

Leaving the comfort of home and leaving my mother alone to head back to school was bittersweet because I was excited to have Katya all to myself, but I also didn't want my mother to be sad. It felt unfair to be moving on from the funeral while she was still at home in that huge, dark house with only the servants to keep her company.

As a positive to the situation, at least things were finally happening the way they were supposed to. My mother and sister loved Katya and already saw her as part of our family. Katya, herself, was finally ensconced in my dorm suite, and I could continue life as I knew it for the foreseeable future until I graduated.

Life. Was. Good.

I mean, there were still some issues—small things—that arose, like the yearning glances I saw Katya giving me when I hugged my mother. She wanted to go home. Desperately. And every time I explained why she couldn't, she gave me a sad smile and shrugged her shoulders. I didn't want to feel like another prison for her. Another person who took away her basic human rights. But it couldn't be helped—at least not right now.

I still hadn't quite figured out how to get her back to the United States without a passport or basic identification. It was something I was going to have to work through, though, because she would want to go at some point. My hope was that once classes started up, she'd be so interested in learning her passion that she'd temporarily forget about going back home. Right now, Katya was unpacking in her room.

"Misha," Katya's sweet voice had me blinking out of my thoughts.

"Hm?" I smiled at her standing in the doorway of the third room in my college suite. It had been empty since Valentina and I got it. We never wanted a roommate and paid enough not to have one. Until now. "Are you all settled in?"

"Yes."

"Good. Grab your coat. I'm going to take you somewhere special."

"Already? We just got here."

I could tell she really didn't mind. My girl loved the freedom of coming and going whenever she wanted. It was something I'd taken for granted my whole life. "I've been wanting to take you to this place for ages, but there wasn't a time when we were home. Come, hurry."

I helped her with her coat, going so far as to zip it up for her. Her sweet blue eyes stared up at me so innocently that I couldn't help myself, I had to kiss her. My mouth swooped down and brushed against her own. Once. Twice. Before settling onto a pair of pink lips that tasted of home and the peppermint stick she'd eaten on the way here. Her tongue tentatively touched mine, and I stroked it with my own, delving into her mouth with a soft groan.

"Gross! Already making out? We've only been here an hour!"

Katya pulled away from me with a pretty blush staining her cheeks. "Sorry, Valentina."

My twin snorted a laugh as she opened the fridge and pulled out a protein shake. "Where are you going?"

"The Creperie, and no, you can't come."

She stuck her tongue out at me, "Didn't say I wanted to, brother. After all of that delicious, heavy Christmas food, it's going to be diet shakes for me for a while."

This was no surprise to me. The life of a budding model was rife with body image issues and fad diets. Valentina wasn't new to any of it. She had been prepping to model for years by reading autobiographies and watching as many modeling competitions and fashion shows she could get her hands on. Now that Father was out of the picture, she had a much clearer path to her passion.

"Valentina, I've been meaning to ask. Why are you in school if you want to be a model?" Katya asked, making me sigh as I knew this was going to potentially be a twenty minute conversation. "I mean, it's not like a degree is in the requirements."

The sound of the aluminum can cracking open filled the room. Valentina lifted the thick drink to her lips for a sip before answering. "Father didn't want me to be a model. Plus, it's good to have something to fall back on if modeling doesn't work out."

That went quicker than I thought! Not wanting to push my luck, I grabbed Katya's hand and pulled her out the door with me.

"That was rude, Misha," she murmured.

I swung her around and grabbed hold of the lapels of her puffy coat, bringing us nearly nose to nose. "She's my sister." That was all the explanation I felt I needed. If you couldn't be mean to your sister, who could you be mean to?

Katya raised a golden eyebrow, and I met her look with a smile. "You may be cute with those dimples, Misha Belov, but they won't get you out of trouble with me."

Her sass made me laugh, and I had to smack a kiss to those sassy lips. Then I took her hand once more and led her out the door and into the world. "I hope you're hungry."

"You told Valentina you are taking me to a creperie? What is that?"

"Not *a* creperie, *The* Creperie." I didn't mention that I'd taken Galina there on our one and only date, which I'd dubbed Date of the Damned because it was so terrible and boring. "Do you like crepes?"

"I don't think I've ever had one."

That... that was surprising. But maybe it shouldn't have been? She'd been so sheltered. I guess I thought maybe she'd tried crepes back in Chicago. Guess not. "Then we are going to remedy that today. You're going to love them. They are like very thin pancakes filled with all sorts of savory or sweet fillings."

"Oh! Like a Russian blini?"

"Yes! Very similar. Now come on!" I sped up to a near trot, tugging her with me. I couldn't wait to feed her at one of my favorite restaurants, take her ice skating near the Kremlin, and visit the museum to see the crown jewels. I was going to make up for all the time she'd missed being in captivity.

It didn't take us long to get there, but I must have been walking too fast because Katya was huffing and puffing by the time we stopped. I gave her an apologetic smile and helped her out of the coat when we walked inside the warm restaurant.

We were swiftly seated, and I ordered wine for the table. I watched her struggle through the Cyrillic writing. I knew she could do it, but she was slow-going. "Would you like me to read it to you?"

Her baby blues flicked up to me. I'm not sure what she saw in my face, but she clearly didn't find what she was looking for. Derision? Loftiness? If that's what it was, I'm glad she didn't see it. I would never make fun of her for taking her time after learning to read Cyrillic. "Yes, please," she stated primly and lowered the menu.

I carefully read her every single item and description while she listened attentively. I also threw in a few suggestions of my favorites. She was ready by the time we ordered. We made small talk like the old friends we were, but the romantic ambience of the restaurant soon got to me. I wanted to hold her hand. Let me rephrase. I wanted the right and freedom to hold her hand in public, but right then I didn't know how to bridge the chasm that gaped between friendship and lovers.

Sure, we'd kissed. A lot.

We flirted more than a lot.

But neither of those was the basis for a relationship, right? Where did I begin with that? And did she even want it? Was I man enough to accept a reality where she didn't really want me? I was man enough to admit I didn't know. And I didn't like it.

"Why does your face look like that?" Katya asked, a wrinkle scrunching her nose as she stared at me across the table.

"Like what? I haven't used any new products...." I scraped my hand over my jaw and chin to see if anything was amiss. Heaven forbid I have a pimple!

"No. You were obviously thinking about something you didn't like because your eyes were all dark, and you sort of looked like you were going to throw up for a minute."

Damn. This woman could read my expressions which was kind of nice but also kind of not. A man needed a little mystery. Since she caught me, I decided to be honest. It was now or never. "I was thinking about you, actually."

"*I* put that awful look on your face?" Her offense was written all over her face from the pinched bow of her full lips to the furrow between her brows.

"Kind of... no, I mean no. Of course not. Fuck, I'm bungling this."

"Language, Misha," she whispered with a half glance around her as if the people seated nearby would care about the words I used.

"Sorry. It's just... I want you to be mine, Katya. Fully mine."

Silence engulfed the table. Not the kind of silence that was peaceful and gave you insight and energy. No... this was the kind of silence that wound you up like a bow string until you snapped. I may have said a prayer to not snap in such a public location.

Katya's small hands slid across the white table cloth and settled over mine. Her fingers curled until she linked our hands together. "I'm not immune to you, either."

Well, that was not the love letter I was hoping for. Immune? Who uses that word when talking about someone's feelings? Immune, like you are catching a disease. Many in my family may think love is a disease, but I definitely did not.

Apparently my expression now was hilarious as Katya began laughing. When my lip poked out in a pout, it made her laugh harder until she had to wipe away tears from her cheeks. "I'm sorry. I'm sorry!" She said emphatically when I continued to pout at her laughter. "Bad choice of words. I meant to say that I like you, too. Always have. You know that. And I wouldn't let you kiss me if I didn't like you."

Like. Like. Like.

I didn't *like* where this conversation was going.

"But I want to eventually go home," she continued softly and reached across the table to slide her soft fingers over mine. I turned my hand over and linked our fingers together. I'd been waiting for this moment, but definitely not in this context. I didn't want pity hand-holding. "What would happen to us if we pursued this relationship, and then I left? You have duties here. You can't go back with me, and I wouldn't ask you to leave your family. Are you asking me to leave mine?" There was a sad earnestness in her tone like she was begging me to understand her point of view.

And now that she put it that way, I guess I did. "Katya, I more than like you." Damn it, this sounded like a school yard crush. "I'm in love with you. And I will make this work any way that I can. Can't you trust me to do that?"

There was that silence again, but this time it was punctuated by our plates being placed in front of us. We both ignored the steaming food, our eyes locked across the table. "I don't know, Misha. I still feel like you lied about setting me free."

"Katya, we've been—"

"Over this. I know."

"At least allow me the opportunity to change your mind."

"Okay, but don't get your hopes up."

"Deal."

We both dug into our dinner with gusto. This was everything my date with Galina was not. Katya thoroughly enjoyed every bite. And she even let me feed her a few bites of my food and of the strawberry cream cheese crepe we ate for dessert.

Though she sort of shot down my advances, I still had hope. I was going to show her that I was the best thing that ever happened to her. And I was going to find a way to make her stay.

Chapter 15

Kate

Past

The next two years were pure heaven. Misha made good on his threat to woo me. When I wasn't in class or studying, he was taking me around Moscow. We visited museums of art and Russian culture, we shopped, we ice skated. And every time, he was a perfect gentleman.

I was ashamed to admit it, but I was getting bored. Not bored of being with Misha. He was always fun and funny. The life of the party. But I wanted more. After every date, he'd walk me to my bedroom door, give me a chaste kiss on the lips, and go to his own room. What the heck was that?! Where were the searing kisses he'd given me before? I wanted them. I *yearned* for them! But I wasn't about to give him the satisfaction of telling him that after I'd con-fessed—*lied*—that I didn't want to be with him.

I was a liar, liar, pants on fire because the truth was that I wanted to be with him. Desperately! He was not only my best friend, but my savior, my constant, and hot as a frying pan in the fire. And those dimples... I wasn't kidding when I'd called them cute. But they were more than that. They were *devastating*. How the man was single was beyond my understanding. But I was going to capitalize on it eventually... when I put my big girl panties on and told him the truth about how I felt.

The words on the pretty stationary I'd brought from Misha's house blurred as I read them for what felt like the millionth time. I'd restarted the letter at least four times, but I just didn't know what to say to my parents. And honestly, I didn't know if they would even believe it was from me. Before I knew what was happening, I was standing outside his door with my hand poised to knock. Apparently, tonight was the night. I sucked in a deep breath and knocked.

"Come in."

His deep voice was soft, distracted. I turned the knob and pushed the door open. Misha was sprawled on his bed, one leg bent the other foot touching the floor. But what I noticed more than anything was his bare chest gleaming in the lamplight. Did the man slather himself in oil or was the lamplight worshiping his body the way I wanted to right now? And even more tempting than his chest— as if anything could tempt me more than that!—was the pencil stuck between his teeth as he poured over a textbook spread on the bed in front of him. He flicked his eyes up to meet mine and smiled toothily around the pencil. He dropped it from his mouth and placed it in the book to save his page. "You okay?"

Anxiety must have been written all over my face. I instantly tried to smooth it away with a deep breath and a silent prayer. "No... I mean yes. I'm okay, but I wanted to talk to you about something."

Misha's cheerful smile softened, and he quickly gathered up his textbook and binder, tossing both onto a nearby chair, then patted the space on the bed next to him. I stared at the spot as if there was a snake hiding beneath the covers. But I perched there anyway and tried to look everywhere but at Misha's muscled chest. The lankiness of his youth was far gone. He had filled out nicely but wasn't overly muscular like a bodybuilder.

"Misha... I thought you were going to woo me." There. I said it. My fingers tangled together as I anxiously awaited his response.

Misha's dark brows knitted in confusion. "I am. Haven't you liked going to the museums and restaurants? I chose them specifically for you."

"Of course I have. I love going to those places, and I wouldn't want to visit them with anyone else. But why haven't you... you know...." My tongue felt like it was stuck to the roof of my mouth.

A warm hand rested on mine and squeezed. He untangled my fingers from each other and linked our hands together. I looked up into his warm, dark eyes. "Because I want to date you properly. And I don't want you to feel like I'm forcing myself on you after all you've been through."

God, he could be the sweetest man sometimes. And an idiot. "I want more," I said decisively. "The entire dating experience. The whole shebang."

"Shebang?"

There wasn't a Russian word for shebang, so I'd used English for that. And it was clearly a miss. "Nevermind. I want real kisses starting now. And more, but not all at once. I'm not totally ready for...."

"The shebang?" Misha waggled his eyebrows at me causing me to snort a laugh.

"Yes, the shebang."

"You got it." With that, he gave my hand one forceful tug until I was wrenched up and sprawled over his magnificent chest. Fingers speared into my hair and cupped the back of my neck. He drew me in until our breaths mingled. "What's a safe word you can use when we reach your limit?"

I thought about it for a moment before saying, "Russia."

Then his lips were on mine and all talking ceased. His kisses were sweet and gentle at first. Tasting me. Tempting me. But when I nipped his lower lip, it must have set something off in his mind because he growled low in his throat, his hand firmed on the back of my neck, and his tongue thrust into my mouth.

That growl sent a trickle of wetness slipping between my thighs, and I shifted on his lap to ease the tickling pressure. I answered his growl with a soft moan to let him know I liked the way he was kissing me. The world tilted and swirled around me, and I realized he'd rolled us over so he was on top smiling down at me.

"Pretty Katya. I've been wanting you beneath me like this for a very long time. You're like an angel with your white blonde hair spread out on my pillow." His smile widened, and he dipped down and nudged the tip of my nose with his. "My naughty angel."

I snorted and shoved his shoulder, not moving him an inch. Then my hands slid into his thick, dark hair, pulling him down for more sultry kisses. I wasn't through with that filthy mouth of his.

A large hand slid beneath the back of my knee and hiked my leg up so Misha's trim hips were settled between my thighs. He was hard already, the bulge between his legs nearly unconstrained in his loose sweatpants. The pressure felt so good that I couldn't help myself and wantonly rubbed

my center against him. Misha pulled away with one lingering bite to my lower lip, and he trailed his lips down to my
ear. Hot breath sent chills racing over my arms and neck.

"I can feel your heat through your jeans, baby."

Baby? He'd never called me that before, but I was too far
gone right now to examine how I felt about the nickname.
I gasped as he sent a nip to the sensitive spot beneath my
earlobe. God, why did something so sinful feel so good? My
body felt like it was on fire. And I liked it! No, I *loved* it.
I was also loving the hot, open-mouthed kisses sweeping
down my neck. I felt a tug on my shirt. With a glance down I
gaped realizing my shirt had already been unbuttoned. How
the heck had he done that without me realizing? Sneaky
Misha!

I suddenly wished I'd worn a different bra. Something
sexier than the innocent white cotton number currently
cupping my breasts. Apparently I didn't need to worry because the bra didn't stay on much longer. Misha's clever
fingers flicked the front clasp, and the bra slithered to both
sides of my body, baring me to the cool air and Misha's
hungry gaze.

"Fuck, baby... your breasts are gorgeous."

Before I could admonish him for his language, he had
caught one pink nipple between his lips and was sucking
like his life depended on it. I'd never really wanted to cuss
before, but now I couldn't think of any other words that
might be good enough to describe the heat of his mouth on
my sensitive flesh. My back arched. My hips ground against
his. And I felt like I couldn't breathe but in the best way
possible.

Misha's cheeks hollowed as he sucked hard and then pulled off with an audible pop. He studied my face before asking, "You okay, baby?"

My fingers stroked the dark stubble on his cheeks, and I nodded in response.

"I need the words, Katya. Should we stop or keep going?"

"I'm good. Let's keep going." There was no way I was stopping right now. We'd barely started and my body hummed with want.

Misha's smile lit up his eyes, and he held my gaze as he slowly drew the tip of his tongue across the valley between my breasts to the other pink-tipped peak. His teeth scored my sensitive nipple. Then he laved the pain away with a slow lick of his tongue.

At Misha's quiet urging, I lifted my hips enough for him to slide my leggings down and off my legs. The chilly air caused goosebumps to rise, and I shivered in response. As if sensing my distress, Misha rubbed my legs until the friction warmed me up. I hated being cold, and for so long as I had been in Russia, it seemed this country was just a lump of ice three out of the four seasons. Chicago had its frigid winters but it didn't compare to Russia.

With heavy-lidded eyes, I watched as Misha bent to press a kiss to the soft white cotton covering my center. He stuck out his tongue and drew the flat of it slowly from my core up to my clit. And then he sucked until the cotton was wet and clinging. I could feel the heat of his mouth through my panties, and suddenly I wasn't sure if the wetness coating them was from his mouth or from me.

He hooked a finger against the sodden material and pulled it away, baring me to his gaze. And gaze he did. Embarrassment heated my cheeks, and I shoved my hand down to hide my most private place from him. The last time someone had actually looked there was the day before my auction when Madame had hired a woman to wax me from what felt like head to toe. That person was a professional, so though it was awkward, I felt comfortable knowing she did this all the time. And though I knew Misha probably wasn't a virgin (I mean, look at the man! No woman could withstand that dark hair, dark eyes, bad boy combination! And his dimples?!), his level of professionalism was null and void in this instance.

"Are you okay?" He murmured, his eyes rising to mine again. When I nodded, he said, "Then don't hide yourself from me." The growl in his voice made my center quake, and I'm pretty sure more wetness seeped out of me. His teeth grasped my middle finger and lifted my hand away. I could have kept it in place just fine, but I let him move me to see what he would do next.

The hot swipe of his tongue across my clit made me jump, and a sound I'd sure never heard before erupted into the room. It was me. *I'd* made that sound! It was somewhere between a yelp and a groan. Embarrassment flushed my skin, and I covered my face with both of my hands. "Sorry."

"Don't be sorry. Baby, that was the sexiest sound I've ever heard a woman make. Do it again." He sucked my clit into his mouth and flickered his tongue all around it like an erotic butterfly kiss.

I continued to cover my face, but the sounds of my desire echoed around us. In the far back of my mind, I hoped Valentina couldn't hear me, but I couldn't bring myself to care enough to stop. Misha's mouth on my clit felt too good to care about anything else.

Strong hands pushed my knees up to my chest, baring me entirely to Misha's ministrations. His tongue slithered through my drenched folds until he reached my center and plunged inside. The heat melted away as he raised his head to smile at me. "You taste like heaven, Katya."

Another intrusion caused me to shift uncomfortably, and I realized it was his finger. He brought it to a rhythm, slowly moving in and out. My hips wriggled, searching for the right spot to make this building urgency go away. And that's when he curled his finger inside me. Fire engulfed me, and I fractured in bliss. My core tightened rhythmically around Misha's still plunging finger which he didn't remove until my bones turned to jelly.

I relaxed back into the mattress, my breaths panting in and out of me like I'd just run a race. I felt Misha's weight as he shifted on the bed next to me, and I opened my eyes to his smiling face. "You look like the cat who caught the canary."

"And you tasted delicious." He slid his finger into his mouth and sucked before slowly sliding it out.

I snorted at his silliness and lightly shoved his shoulder. He felt like a boulder and didn't move. "Well, that was... that was...."

"Phenomenal? Outstanding? Tremendous?"

"You can stop now," I giggled with a shake of my head. The man was incorrigible.

"And you didn't even use your safe word. You okay?" The silly Misha of before had sobered up and was checking me over to make sure I was good.

His worry touched me in a way I wasn't used to. Before Misha took me away from Madame's, it had been a long time since anyone truly cared about my well-being. "I didn't need to use it. Trust me, if I'd wanted to, I would have."

Misha's head dipped down into a nod, and he leaned in to press a tender, soft kiss to my lips. I kissed him back, simply savoring his gentleness and warmth. Lucky wasn't strong enough a word to describe how I felt about Misha coming into my life when I most needed him.

It was unsettling to realize I was starting to want him as a constant in my life. What was I going to do—how was I going to choose—when the time came for me to finally go home?

Chapter 16

Misha

Past

I skimmed my fingers through Katya's white gold hair, pushing it off her face. She'd fallen asleep during the movie, and she'd been sleeping like the dead ever since. A pang of guilt zinged inside my chest at the thought that I might have exhausted her. Between her classes, practicing baking techniques in our dorm room, date nights, and our new late night activities, it was no wonder she couldn't keep her eyes open.

She looked like an angel. *My* angel. My free hand picked up a cookie from the plate on the end table. I was so going to get fat by eating all these sweets, but I was going to relish every bite because Katya's baking was my fucking kryptonite. I sank my teeth into the crisp cookie and smiled at how it shattered against my teeth and tongue. Katya assured me shortbread is an easy recipe, but I'd never tasted shortbread like this. Sweet, buttery, and exploding into a zillion pieces as soon as it hit my tongue. And she added a dollop of marmalade right in the center. If I wasn't already in love with my baking angel, I would've gladly given her my heart after eating just one of these cookies.

I looked down at my angel and realized crumbs had fallen onto Katya's pale cheek like fairy dust. I took a moment to admire it, then gently brushed my fingers over her skin to remove the crumbs.

Katya shifted and opened her eyes. Her nose wrinkled as she smiled up at me. "Sorry for falling asleep. I'm just so tired today."

"Hey, no worries. You clearly need it. Why don't you turn over and go back to sleep?" I had something special planned for her that weekend, so I definitely wanted her to rest up before then. I watched as she turned over and snuggled into my pillow, and I brought the coverlet up and over her shoulders to keep her warm and help her doze off again.

My pocket buzzed, and I shifted to reach for my phone then glanced at the screen. Mother. It wasn't like her to call at this time of night. I rolled out of the bed and left my bedroom, closing the door with a soft click behind me. I pressed the accept button and said, "Mother. You okay?" The quick beat of my heart in my throat was difficult to ignore. Something had to be wrong for her to call this late, and it made me purely uneasy.

"I don't think so, Misha." Her voice was soft on the other end, almost like she was far away from the phone.

"Mother, why are you whispering?" I whispered and then gave myself a shake. Just because she was whispering didn't mean I had to.

"Because the walls have ears, son."

"What are you talking about?"

"Misha Nickolai Belov."

I winced at the use of my full name. That normally meant I was in trouble or about to be. Clearly I wasn't taking her seriously enough. "Sorry, Mother. Tell me what's happened."

"I think your Uncle Yuri has been stealing from us. The maid is on maternity leave, so I took it upon myself to do some cleaning. When your uncle left, I did some light dusting in your father's office. I tripped on the carpet and knocked into the side of the desk and several ledgers fell to the floor. I picked them up and started straightening the receipts that had fallen out, but when I was putting it all back together I realized both ledgers were for the same year. They were mirror copies of each other except that when I looked closely, some of the numbers were wrong."

I felt the blood drain from my face. With Father's death, I completely forgot about his suspicions about the ledgers. The weight of failing my father settled heavily on my shoulders. Slowly, I asked, "Mother, what did you do with the ledgers?" The ramifications of her finding this could be potentially damning for her in Bratva law. She was now at extreme risk. If Yuri found out she suspected him of embezzlement, she could meet with an unfortunate "accident". I'd heard about it and seen it in action. Fear for my mother that I'd never felt before began clawing its way up my throat, and I had to take deep breaths to settle it back down.

"I put them back on the desk, of course, but I didn't know which ledger the receipts were supposed to go in, and I hadn't even been looking at the desk when I bumped into it. I don't know if I put it back in a way Yuri will know or not."

Shit!

Fuck!

"Fucking shit!"

"Language," my mother parroted Katya which made me roll my eyes.

"Mother, listen very carefully. I wish you could pack up and come stay with us, but it would look suspicious since you've never done that before. You are going to have to pretend like nothing happened. Treat Uncle Yuri the same way you always have or he is going to know something is up. Has he said anything about the ledgers?"

"Not yet, but he hasn't been in the office, yet. He just got here and is smoking a cigar while on the phone outside."

"Okay. Keep me posted."

When I hung up, I realized my hands were shaking. Shit! How was I going to keep my mother safe? She had her own bodyguard, but he was part of the Family and therefore is owned by Yuri right now.

Yuri.

Pieces of the puzzle were clacking corners in my mind as I tried to work it out. But it wasn't making sense.

Yet.

Chapter 17

Kate

Past

The box was perfect. Large, rectangular, pristine white. The only color came from the black silk ribbon tied in a perfect bow with a card and a perfect white rose. The box had been sitting in the middle of my bed at the Belov's estate when I arrived after having afternoon tea with Larissa and Valentina. Larissa had invited all of us over for tea, and I had just gone upstairs to look for a hair clip I'd left in my old bedroom. I hadn't been expecting such a surprise.

I lifted the rose to my nose and inhaled its heady perfume. I found a water glass in the bathroom and plonked the rose's stem inside before setting it on the bedside table. Then I reached for the card. *"My dear Cinderella, join me at the ballet tonight."* Only Misha would write something that romantic.

I untied the ribbon and carefully lifted the lid of the box and set it aside on the bed. Buried under layers of scented pale pink tissue paper sat a ballgown of shimmering teal crepe. My fingers cascaded over the satiny folds of fabric before delicately wrapping around the bodice and lifting it out of its scented nest. I draped it over the bedspread. The cut of the gown was simple—just a one-shoulder drape with a tiny seed pearl encrusted belt. I had never seen—let alone owned—something so ethereal. So spectacular. I felt giddy! Something sparkly in the box caught my eye. I rummaged in the tissue paper until I found a sheer hair ribbon that matched the belt. I had never seen anything so gorgeous in my life. And it was all mine. I couldn't wait to put it on and feel like the princess I used to pretend to be when I was a little girl.

"Do you like it?"

The shock of Misha's voice in the stillness and privacy of my old room made me jump, and I whirled to face him. "Make a sound, why don't you?"

His laugh told me he wasn't offended by my words. He stepped into the room and closed the door behind him. "Not my fault you're so jumpy." A finger stroked the silk of the teal gown. "Do you like it, though?" I wanted that finger stroking me just as tenderly. I had gotten used to his touch in our last few weeks together, and I always seemed to hunger for more.

"It's perfect! I don't think I've ever seen such a beautiful gown except for what movie stars wear on the red carpet." In my downtime at Madame Bombadine's, I'd often read the girls' magazines from cover-to-cover to practice my Russian reading and find out what was going on in the world around me. "Did Valentina pick it out?" Misha's twin had an eye for fashion, especially haute couture. I suppose it was the model in her.

"No, I picked it out, myself," Misha stated proudly, his chest puffing up. "I was driving when I saw it in a designer's window. I bought it right away before anyone could snatch it up. I knew it would be a hot commodity. And I also knew it would suit you perfectly."

Touched that he picked out a gown for me without his mother or sister, I couldn't help but lean up and kiss him.

He hummed against my lips and squeezed my waist with his strong hands. He pulled away just enough to say, "I like this kind of thank you."

"I can do better." I smiled up at him as I slid down his body to my knees. In all the time we had spent together intimately, I had never gone down on him. And I wanted to. I *really* wanted to. He stopped my hand when I reached for his belt.

"Baby, I'm not expecting anything for the dress. You don't have to do this."

I gazed up into his dark, earnest eyes. For a mobster, he was the sweetest man. And the sexiest. "I know, but I want to do this." I pushed his hands away then dove for his belt once more. Making quick work of it, I dipped into the opening of his pants and pulled out his rapidly hardening member. He was thick and long with a smooth, pink head shining with a bead of liquid. Leaning forward, I lapped it up with my tongue. He tasted of salt and musk, but the taste wasn't unpleasant.

A groan rumbled above me. When he spoke, his voice was gravelly with need. "Damn, baby. Take me in your hot mouth. Oh, God, just like that."

I sank slowly down, my tongue flat against the thick vein on the underside until the tip of my nose touched his pelvis at the apex of that luscious V of stomach muscles. The girls at Madame Bombadine's had taught me to take a man this way. We'd practiced on different shapes and lengths of dildos and even cucumbers, much to the annoyance of the kitchen staff. After all that practice, taking Misha this way wasn't too difficult. I breathed slowly through my nose then slid him down my throat. I held there a beat while he cursed a blue streak above me. I pinched his thigh in retaliation.

He didn't allow me to have control for long. Strong fingers sank into my hair and curled to grip at the root. I loved it when he pulled my hair. He pulled his hips back until the head of his shaft popped free of my mouth.

"Open."

I parted my lips eagerly and stared up into his eyes dark with passion. He swiveled his hips so his head smeared my saliva all over my lips and tongue. Then he pushed forward and sank deep into my mouth. My hands clenched his bottom through the fabric of his designer dress pants. And he began to piston in and out of mouth, holding me steady with a tight grip on my hair. My scalp burned. And I liked it. In all of our intimate interactions, he had been gentle and sweet. I liked this side of him, too.

"God, baby, your mouth feels so good on my cock. Suck, baby. Mmm… just like that. Reach down and touch yourself while you suck me. I want you good and wet when I return the favor." I slid my hands beneath my skirt and dipped them into my panties to rub my throbbing clit. Sucking him had made me so hot that I was already wet. "Damn, I'm going to come so good in this sweet mouth." He kept up this litany of dirty talk as he stroked himself harder inside my mouth.The sight of me touching myself must have set Misha off because he thrust one more time deep in my mouth and came. I swallowed every drop. Then he made good on his promise to eat me out.

***

"Stunning," Larissa said from her seat on a small, padded vanity stool where she was putting on her makeup. "Simply stunning." She smiled at me in the mirror before putting the finishing touches on her lipstick.

Valentina and I had gathered in Larissa's suite to dress for the ballet. What I thought was going to be a date between Misha and me was actually a family affair. But I wasn't disappointed. Larissa was excited to show me off to her friends and acquaintances, and I loved spending time with both of her and Valentina like they were my own family.

Valentina wore a vibrant red gown which complimented her olive skin and dark hair. She'd left her hair free down her back in a sleek sheet of black with the exception of a gold and ruby barrette sweeping up one side.

Larissa was still in mourning, so her gown was a dark plum color. Demure and sophisticated, just like her. Her only adornment other than her wedding ring was a pair of diamond earrings she said Constantine gave her on their first wedding anniversary. "Hmm. I think something is missing," she said from her seat.

Turning this way and that in front of the tall, standing mirror, I couldn't imagine what was missing. I had attached the seed pearl belt in place beneath my breasts and wound the matching hair ribbon through my hair in a pretty updo circa 1920s. "What's missing?"

"This." Larissa opened her cherry wood jewelry box and removed a black velvet bag. She dumped the contents into her hand and walked up behind me. She draped a gorgeous pearl necklace over my collar bone. "These pearls belonged to my grandmother. She was so beautiful that every man who met her instantly fell in love with her. Including a certain sheik from Iran who had business with my grandfather. The sheik told my grandmother that her skin was as flawless as these pearls." She clipped the clasp behind my neck and placed her hands on my shoulders. "They suit you."

I stared at my reflection, taking in the creamy pearls glistening against my pale skin above the shimmering teal of my gown. "She must have really been something!"

"Oh, she was! She also liked to play cards and gambled a small fortune away from that very same sheik."

"Are you sure you want me to wear these?" I asked. Larissa was becoming more and more like a mother to me, but I would never presume to wear something as special as those pearls.

"Of course I do! You are like a second daughter, especially since my son is so taken with you. I am hoping you will become my daughter in reality soon."

Her words both warmed and guilted me. Once again I felt the dilemma of what was going to happen when I eventually graduated and was allowed to go home for good. Luckily the culinary program wasn't as long as a normal degree but there was still quite a bit of time left. Looking back at Larissa, I smiled and said simply, "Thank you."

It wasn't long before we were standing at the top of the stairs staring down at Misha who looked incredibly handsome in his tuxedo. He placed his hand over his heart and pretended to stagger dramatically. "Do my eyes deceive me? I must be the luckiest man in all of Moscow to escort such beautiful ladies to the ballet tonight."

The three of us giggled like little girls before starting down the stairs. Larissa was the first to reach her Misha and reached up to cup his cheek. "Such a flatterer. You should save that for your Katya." She pinched his cheek then swept past him out the front door with a grinning Valentina behind her.

"She's right," Misha said as he took my hands and kissed the back of each one. He lifted one hand and turned me in a circle as his eyes stroked down my body and then back up. "That dress suits you even better than I'd hoped. I can't wait to peel it off you later tonight." He leaned in and pressed a kiss to my cheek then brushed his lips down to my neck. His tongue flicked out to tickle my skin.

I giggled and smacked his arm lightly before pulling away. He caught my hand before I could get too far and touched the pearl necklace at my throat. "Great-grandmother's pearls." His expression was unreadable for a moment, but then he smiled and guided me to the door. "They suit you, too. Skin as flawless as a pearl. And a heart just as pure."

***

The Bolshoi Theatre was everything I'd heard and imagined. All the girls at Madame's talked about going. Once in a while a gentleman would bring a date from the house to see the ballet, and she would come home with stars in her eyes and tales of live orchestras and sparkling costumes. I was so excited to experience it myself!

Light illuminated the Grecian columns and statue on the roof. "Who is that?" I asked Misha as he helped me out of the car.

"That, dear Katya, is Apollo in his Chariot of the Sun. It is the symbol of the Bolshoi." He led the way to the door and offered his phone to be scanned by the doorman who soon waved us through.

If I thought the outside was arresting, the inside stole my breath. The theatre oozed elegance from the black and white floor tiles to the twin marble staircases on either side of the entrance hall. I was in awe.

"Come, my darlings, let us introduce our Katya to our friends," Larissa stated, grandly sweeping ahead of us. I had met many of the family friends at the wake, but that was such a somber affair that most introductions were simply that. Now, however, Larissa's bosom buddies swarmed us and reintroduced themselves. They asked about my background, my interests, even who my gown designer was. This wasn't just a trip to the theater, it was a social event. You were meant to see and be seen.

Not once did Misha leave my side, my hand on his arm, his hand covering mine protectively. Though I was overwhelmed by the number of people vying for my attention, I felt safe with Misha. He helped me field questions when I floundered for answers and kept me on track.

When it was time to find our seats, Misha led us up one of the staircases to the first balcony. The elegantly curved wall was lined in red velvet drapes which parted and were tied off at each numbered box seat. Misha gestured to one of the open entrances, and I stepped inside, much to the annoyance of the couple making out inside.

"What's wrong?" Misha asked when I stopped in my tracks. He stepped in next to me and growled, "Pavel. What are you doing here?"

The young man in question, not much older than Misha, looked up with a frown. "Enjoying our family's box with my intended."

Intended? It was then that I looked at the woman he'd been kissing. She smiled at us and flashed a sparkly engagement ring with a wriggle of her fingers. "Pavel met with my father and signed the agreement this morning. Looks like I will be a Belov after all."

"Congratulations, Pavel and Galina," Larissa skirted around me and bent to give each of them an air kiss. "This gives us something to look forward to and celebrate." She took my hand and led me to the front set of padded chairs. She and Valentina bracketed me on either side, and Misha sat behind his mother to my back right.

Galina. It had to be the same Galina Misha had told me about on one of our dates. I looked back and met Misha's gaze. I raised my brows as if to ask if this was going to be a problem, and he shook his head. I remembered Pavel from Madame Bombadine's and had seen him at the Belov's Christmas dinner, but we hadn't interacted. Thank God. He gave me the heebee jeebees. I was not happy to find him here, especially with Misha's ex-intended.

I turned back to gaze out at the central part of the theatre. It was spectacular, just as opulent as the lobby. Thick red curtains. Painted ceiling. Curved balconies. The orchestra in the pit began to warm up, the lights dimmed, and all else was forgotten as the curtains rose on the first scene of Cinderella cleaning the cinders from the fireplace.

At intermission, I turned a beaming smile on Misha who stood and leaned in to press a kiss to the corner of my mouth. "Are you enjoying the ballet, Katya?"

"I love it!" I gushed. "The music, the dancing, the sets... it's all so magical!"

He smiled. "We will have to get tickets to the next one. According to the program it's about Valentina."

Hearing her name, his sister turned around to look at us. "About me?" Her brow furrowed in confusion.

"Mhmm. Taming of the Shrew."

"Misha!" She rolled her program into a scroll and reached around me to try to whack him with it.

"Children, we do not behave like wild animals in the theatre!" It sounded like Larissa had used that line many times before. "Especially as we are adults and not unruly children."

"Yes, Mother," the twins said, grinning at each other.

"Would you like some champagne, Katya?" Misha trailed his fingers over my cheek, and I nodded. I was parched.

After he left, Valentina pouted at her mother, "Why didn't he offer us champagne?"

"Because he only has eyes for his Katya, and he is trying to make this night extra special for her. We can get our own like the independent ladies we are. Escort me to the powder room, Valentina. Katya, would you like to come?"

"No, thank you." I didn't want to be bombarded again by all those people so soon.

"Galina?"

"Yes, I need to touch up my lipstick." I just bet she did after that make-out session from earlier. The three left, and I soaked up the quiet stillness of the private box even though the theater's main floor buzzed beneath me.

A shift in the air and the scent of cigarette smoke and patchouli oil invaded my senses. "Hello, little Katya."

"Pavel," I sighed. Why was he bothering to talk to me? I hadn't the pleasure—or lack thereof—of speaking with him directly, but there was something off-putting about him. And I thought it was just plain weird that he and Galina were engaged. Even though Galina and Misha hadn't actually been *together*, the whole thing about dating your cousin's ex gave me a certain *ick* factor.

"Tell me, Katya," I didn't like his sneaky tone, "do Valentina and my aunt know who—or should I say *what*—you are?"

I finally turned in my seat to face him. The sneer on his thin lips and the glint in his eyes told me more than his words. He was trying to intimidate me. Between classes and date nights, Misha had been working with me on building my self-confidence. Poise and Assertiveness Training was actually what he called it, but that was a mouthful to me. We mostly did this through discussion and a series of challenges related to my school work. He would ask me how I felt I performed that day in my classes, what was the feedback from my instructors, and then he asked me to bake exactly what I was taught in class before asking me to jazz it up with my own ideas and decorations. Through my love of baking, he was teaching me that what I liked and wanted mattered.

Using that same technique, I examined what was happening right now with Pavel. The old me wanted to excuse myself and run away or cower in the corner. But the new me, the slightly more confident me, didn't want to take the dish Pavel was offering. I wanted to change it up and send *him* on his way with a sour flavor on his palette.

Firming my spine and resolve, I narrowed my eyes on him and quietly, but firmly stated, "Just because I am lower status in your eyes does not mean you may speak to me that way. It is absolutely none of your business, but of course Larissa and Valentina know what I used to be. And just so *you* are clear on what that was, let me enlighten you. I was a baker and a housekeeper. I may have been learning the ropes of seduction, but they were never put into play.

So maybe before you cast judgment on someone else, be sure to have all your facts straight."

There was a mountain of silence between us then. I wanted to break eye contact and turn around, but Misha had told me that would be losing the battle. I had come this far, I wasn't going to lose this small fight. Determination filled me. Self-advocating for the first time since I was a child was a heady sensation. Part terror, part fire.

Don't back down.

Don't back down.

I chanted quietly in my head, and then the unthinkable happened. Pavel looked away first. He stood up and buttoned his suit jacket. As he turned away, he shot over his shoulder, "My mistake. But be warned, little Katya, my family won't have a simple housekeeper living under the same roof unless she's an employee." With that obscure remark, he left me in the dark box alone with my glowing pride and a lot of questions.

***

Misha

The concession line felt forever long. Why did it take so long to pour someone a Coca Cola, wine, or champagne? As Mother liked to point out, patience was not my greatest attribute. And right now, it was wearing thin because all I wanted to do was go back to my girl. After I'd left, I'd realized she'd been alone with Pavel. Despite his father being my favorite uncle, I couldn't stand Pavel. Never could. He was the kid who always picked on others smaller than him. I wouldn't be surprised if he kicked puppies, honestly.

Warning Galina was on the tip of my tongue, but they would probably get along great and make annoying, pretentious babies together. I didn't want to get in the middle of that, especially since Uncle Yuri had done so much for me with Katya.

Uncle Yuri. I had tried to talk to Mother today before tea was served, to see if anything had happened with the ledger situation. I wanted to get my hands on both of them, but I wasn't going to put Mother in danger. And Yuri had been there all day. The timing was off.

I could feel something building though. Something wasn't right in my sphere of the world. I could admit that I wasn't exactly a man in tune with his surroundings. I'd grown up in this Bratva life, I was a made man, I was the heir. And because of that, I felt pressured to uncover Yuri's embezzling plot. Without him finding out. And making sure my takeover happens seamlessly.

But my role in the Family itched. Chafed. Didn't fit the person I was inside. Not that I could do anything about it, though. This was my life, and right now I was feeling the world around me simmer like a pot starting to boil.

"Still in line? I would've thought you'd be at the front by now."

My nerves nearly had me jumping out of my skin! "Valentina! Don't sneak up on a man." Especially one who's armed. To her credit, she didn't know I was carrying. I didn't usually, but with the way I felt lately, the gun made sense.

"I don't see any men, just a brother who is daydreaming about something that doesn't seem too good by the way your eyebrows were caterpillared together."

"Caterpillared?! They aren't that bad, are they?" My fingers swept over each brow, attempting to smooth them.

"Nothing a little tweezer work won't fix."

"I'm not letting you near my face with any pointy metal objects."

Valentina scoffed and crossed her arms. "I'm going to be a model, Misha, I know what I'm doing with tweezers."

"About that. When are you going to get started on that modeling? You keep talking about it, but I'm not seeing any actual modeling happening." I leaned in and scrutinized her face. "Maybe you aren't plucking or moisturizing correctly. I think I see a wrinkle right there!" I poke her right in the middle of the forehead.

"Misha! That was so rude! I don't have wrinkles!"

"Was it ruder than telling me I have caterpillar eyebrows?" I grinned at my twin as the line shifted forward. Almost there!

"Children, no arguing in the line," Mother stated as she joined us.

"Yes, Mother," we both said, chuckling.

Soon enough, we headed back to our family box with our champagne and one for my girl. Happily, Pavel and Galina had not returned, and Katya was smiling that sweet smile she reserved just for me. We all took our seats once more for the second act. Cinderella got her prince.

And I couldn't keep my eyes off my own princess.

Chapter 18

Misha

Past

"Are you going to answer that, Mr. Belov, or are you going to continue letting it disrupt my lecture?"

Only Professor Ninkasha would speak to a Belov that way. It was why she was my favorite. No special treatment.

"My apologies." I snatched the vibrating phone off the table and excused myself to the hallway. The damn thing had been buzzing in my pocket all morning. I had just set it on the table so I could turn it off when it started up again. What's the point of vibrate when it still annoys the hell out of you? "Hello?" I answered with a sigh, not even looking to see who was calling. This had better be life or death. I hated being called out in a class.

"Misha, thank God I finally reached you!"

I perked up instantly. "Mother? What's going on?"

"Your uncle is taking the house!"

"What do you mean? It's in our name. He can't just *take* it." What the fuck was going on? Anxiety skittered over my nerve endings like tiny ants, making it difficult to stand still.

"He says it belongs to the Family and the person who is the head of the Family gets to live there. They are kicking me out!"

Never had I heard that level of panic from my normally cool-headed mother. Not when my sister fell off her horse during a riding lesson. Not when the leader of a rival Bratva surrounded us at a dinner party, weapons drawn. And not when my father passed away, and she was left alone to tell her children their father was gone. I didn't know whether it was because she was still able to be in control in those situations, whereas in this one, her control had been stripped from her. Whatever it was, I never wanted my mother to feel this way again.

"Hang tight. I'm on my way."

I debated for half a second about calling a Family car to pick me up so I could keep up with what was happening at home via text or call, but right now I didn't feel like I could trust anyone in the Family, not even a driver. I headed down to the parking lot to get my own car. I entered the classroom again, grabbed my satchel and quietly excused myself, stating a family emergency. Then I left. A text was sent to my sister and Katya, and both were waiting at the corner by the time I got to the end of the block. Thank God for dependable people. As much shit as I gave Valentina, she really was the best sister and friend I could ever ask for. My anxiety lessened as Katya leaned up with concern in her eyes and kissed me gently.

"Everything okay?" Valentina asked, opening the door and sliding in after Katya.

"No. I'll fill you in on the way." We piled into the car and were on our way to save my mother and home.

By the time we arrived, you could cut the tension in the car with a knife. After I told Katya and Valentina what Mother had said, they had bombarded me with questions I had no answers to. Silence finally reigned between us which made the tension ten times worse. Questions filled me, like why would my uncle do this to my mother? His own sister-in-law. Was this some sort of punishment for her going into his office? I had no doubt he figured out what happened. I didn't tell my mother because it would've just worried her, but there was a security camera in the office.

As we pulled into the long driveway, Katya slid her small hand into mine and squeezed her strength into me. She got a smacking kiss on the head for that, and then I opened the car door. My eyes zeroed in on the moving van backed up to the walkway and my aunt standing outside directing the movers.

"Aunt Petra!" I shouted, rushing up to the pinch-faced woman. I'd never been fond of her. She found fault with everyone and everything. "What the hell do you think you're doing?"

She only gave me a side-long glance before turning her back and ignoring me completely. I was two seconds away from grabbing her by the shoulders and forcing her to talk to me, and I would have if I wasn't interrupted.

"Misha!" Mother's voice cut through my anger, and I turned to jog up the stairs to find her in the doorway with Katya and Valentina on either side of her. "Leave Petra alone and come inside. She's not the one in charge, anyway." She said that last part extra loud for my aunt's benefit which made me smile. *Good job, Mother! Don't lose your spirit!*

"Misha's here?" My uncle's gruff voice echoed in the entryway, and I saw him walk out of his office with a smug smile. "Welcome, my boy. No doubt your mother called you."

"Of course she did. And no need to welcome me to *my own home*," I all but snarled at him, stepping in front of my mother, sister, and girlfriend. He wasn't going to get *near* them.

"And that's where you're wrong, dear boy. This house belongs to the Belov Family, not your immediate family. The head of the Family is dead, and I am current acting head—"

"Just while I am finishing school," I ground out. How dare he come into my mother's house and just take over everything. He was fucking moving in!

"That may be, but you have several years left of schooling. This is where the Pakhan lives, and I am currently the Pakhan. As I told your mother, I am not forcing her to leave the premises. I am simply moving her to the dowager cottage."

"You are not the Pakhan, Uncle Yuri. You have to be voted in to be..." I froze, eyes assessing him. Did he call for a vote while I was at school? What is the saying...*while the cat's away, the mice will play*. Looks like quite a few of them have been playing while I've been away at school.

"The dowager cottage is all the way on the other side of the property!" Valentina shrieked behind me. "She'll be lonely out there. Not to mention that place hasn't been cleaned in who knows how long!"

"Hmm. It is a long way from the main house, isn't it? Maybe on the long walks back and forth, your mother will think about what a bad idea it was to go into my office while I wasn't there. She might also consider herself lucky that I have such a forgiving heart." He leveled a stern look around my shoulder at her before looking at me once more. "I need to speak with you. Come."

I followed my uncle into the office and sat in the chair he indicated. My mouth stayed shut because I knew if I opened it, something not-so-nice would come out. So, I just watched and waited like the good Bratva soldier Father trained me to be.

"Misha, I didn't want to bring this up in front of the women, but I've found out someone has been embezzling from our accounts. Moving in to "take over" is just a front for me being able to have more eyes and ears to the ground here to find out what is happening. You understand?"

My eyes widened, and I nodded in understanding. "Yes, Uncle. I confess I'm glad you are looking into it. Before he died, Father mentioned suspecting the same thing, but I forgot about it until now. I'll help Mother move out to give you room to investigate sooner."

"I knew I could count on you, Misha."

I stood and shook his hand before exiting the office. With my mind on Yuri's efforts, I approached my mother and squeezed her shoulder reassuringly. Her face was as pale as a ghost's. "Come, Mother, let's start packing everything of value before it's either stolen or tossed. Valentina and Katya, why don't you help her? I'll locate the housekeeper and see if she can head over and start cleaning the cottage before we get there."

With all our duties laid out before us, we went our separate ways. None of this felt right. That pot that was simmering before was building pressure to a boil every minute. Things were already starting to go downhill. I couldn't help but wonder when the pressure would finally explode?

We spent the rest of the day and into the evening moving Mother into the small cottage on the edge of the property. The housekeeper had rallied a few of her friends, and they had spruced the place up nicely while we packed. Luckily the cottage was already furnished, if outdated, but Mother didn't care as long as it was clean. She had all her memories in the boxes we'd brought over, and that was all that truly mattered.

After the girls had said their goodbyes to Mother, I lingered in the doorway. "I hate leaving you like this. I wish I could have been able to change Uncle Yuri's mind."

She smiled and raised her hand to cup my cheek. "I know, my son. But I am okay here. I have enough to keep me busy with redecorating this old place. And I have my pictures and mementos with me. I'll be fine."

I studied her tired but smiling face and realized that yes, she really would be fine. Another thought slid into place, then, too. "I think this will be a safer spot, actually. You know, away from whatever is going on at the main house. Maybe you being out of sight, out of mind will keep them away from you until we figure out what is going on. I'll make sure the chef stocks your refrigerator and pantry, so you don't need to join Aunt and Uncle for meals." And I would also make sure they sent meals her way, too. I knew Mother could cook for herself, but she'd chosen the family's chef herself and loved her cuisine.

"You are such a good boy, Misha. Now go home and get some rest." And then she closed the door in my face.

Rolling my eyes, I dragged my hand through my hair and turned. I made my way down the drive to my car to take us back to university.

The ride was silent with the exception of Valentina softly snoring against the window. Katya was on my other side, gazing out at the passing landscape. Soon enough we arrived in the parking garage of our dormitory. I gently shook Valentina awake, and once we exited the car, I led both women up the stairs to our suite. The normally boisterous halls were mostly quiet at this time of night with music wafting from only a few of the rooms as people studied, burning the midnight oil.

Valentina immediately took off to her room and closed the door. I expected Katya to do the same, but she surprised me by taking my hand and leading me to my room. She leaned against the door, closing it behind her. What was she doing? I knew she had to be as exhausted as Valentina and me. I scratched my bristly cheeks with both hands and sat on the end of the bed. A yawn cracked my jaw, and I rubbed my eyes. Damn, I was tired. "Ready for bed?" I opened my eyes and glanced over to the door and froze.

"You could say that." Katya, my shy girl, had stripped down to her underwear in seconds! Her rosy pink nipples pressed against the black lace of her bra, and all I wanted to do was play hide and seek with her nipple and my tongue through the delicate webbing of lace.

"Fuck. Me." I murmured, stunned, as she turned and snicked the lock, then started walking my way like every woman in every porn movie I'd ever watched. She was my walking wet dream.

She frowned at me and murmured, "Language, Misha. But yeah, that's the idea." She did a little twirl, and I saw that the back of her lace panties was actually a thong. I'd died and gone straight to heaven. Surely hell wouldn't be this sexy.

I reached for my girl and smoothed my hands down the sides of her torso, my thumbs venturing out to lightly graze her nipples. Her back arched and a soft sigh escaped her parted lips at my touch. She was so sensitive everywhere, and I drank in every reaction she gave me. My fingers slid down her arms now pebbled with goosebumps. When I reached her hands, I linked our fingers and brought her hands up to kiss the back of each one. I was falling so hard for this girl. I released her hands and spanned them around the indentation of her waist to grasp her hips.

She settled her hands on my shoulders and leaned up on her toes so her breasts were level with my face. I breathed in her vanilla perfume and the scent that was uniquely her. She tilted her head back as I captured a nipple in my mouth and swirled my tongue over the lace, tasting and teasing the pink flesh into a tight bud. I kissed my way across her chest to give the same attention to her other nipple, sucking it until it matched the first in rosy color and aroused tautness.

Sliding my hands behind her back, I worked the clasp of her bra until it parted in my hands. I tossed it to the side and cupped both of her breasts, lapping at each one until they shimmered in the low lamplight. Grasping her waist, I rolled us both onto the bed, her back pressed to the blankets and me on top of her.

I smiled at her shocked expression and then nipped her nose. "Didn't think you were going to run this game, did you?" I liked being in charge. And based on her reaction to me taking control when she gave me a blow job before the ballet, I knew she liked it too. So I dove down and took her mouth with mine. She was so sweet! I could kiss her for days without stopping—just sipping the nectar of the gods from her lips. But who had time for that when there was so much more of her to taste?

I traveled from her lips down the side of her neck, over to the center of her chest and the flat plane of her stomach until I reached the band of her black lace thong. My teeth scraped against the lace as I slid lower. Her little clit pressed tight against the flimsy fabric, and I couldn't help but dip down and swirl my tongue over it. Katya moaned and pushed her hips into my mouth. Such a pretty pussy. I wanted to make out with it, but most of all, I wanted to plunge my hard dick inside it, like it was the home I'd never known. Her taste bloomed on my tongue, so I swirled again and again. The soft moans above and the restlessness of Katya's legs told me I was doing a good job. Grasping the sides of her thong, I pulled it off and tossed it to the floor. Then I settled in to feast. My baby was going to feel so good tonight. Tongue, teeth, and lips all worked in tandem to make her wet and ready for me. I slid one finger inside my girl's hot pussy, and she exploded. Fuck, I wished that was my dick she was pulsing around instead of my finger. I pulled it out and sucked her essence from my finger.

"Feel better, baby?" I asked with a smile, stroking her leg as she panted softly.

"Yes, but I still want you."

My hands froze and my brows drew down in confusion. Did mine ears deceive me? Was she asking for what I thought she was? My heart quickened its drum in my chest. "What do you mean?" *Please, please, please...* I silently begged for sex like a fresh-faced teenager in the first bloom of lust.

She met my eyes over the swells of her breasts and smiled as she turned beet red. "I'm ready to take us to the next step, Misha. I want to have sex with you."

Yes! It was as if the pearly gates of Heaven, themselves, opened up for me instead of Katya's pearly white thighs. I couldn't get out of my clothes fast enough. Where the hell was my finesse? I was so much better than this! Instead, I was floundering with my head, arm, and shoulder stuck in my shirt which I'd forgotten to unbutton. I finally ripped it, scattering buttons while my girl laughed her ass off.

Grinning like a loon, I set on taking off my pants. This was a lot easier because I didn't even bother with removing the belt completely. Just unbuckled, unfastened the button and zipper, and shimmied out of the pants, taking my underwear with them. I snagged a condom from my bedside table drawer, ripped the foil and rolled the latex down my hard length. Finished with that unsexy task, I turned back to more pleasurable things.

I pounced on my girl, making her giggle. My fingers skated over her sides which I knew were ticklish, and she gasped for breath, begging me to stop as she laughed and thrashed beneath me. . And then I nestled down on top of her and smiled down into her flushed face. She smiled back then leaned up to kiss and nibble my lower lip. The kiss soon deepened, and I swept my tongue inside her mouth. My hips shifted, fitting my cock snugly between her damp lips. I rocked slowly, my cock rubbing against her clit, until Katya's breathing deepened, and her cheeks turned pink with the flush of arousal once more.

"I love you, Katya," I murmured, not able to keep it to myself any longer. And it wasn't just because we were about to have sex. This love had been building since we were kids playing in Madama Bombadine's fenced-in patio. It built from every smile, every morsel of food she made me, every memory we shared. It was pure, and nothing could taint how I felt about her.

"I love you, too, Misha," she said with a soft smile, and I bent down to kiss her. Arching my hips back, I reached between us and guided the head of my cock to her entrance and slowly pushed.

I felt her tense beneath me, her hands squeezed my shoulders till her nails pricked the skin. I pulled back to give her some air. "You okay?" She nodded but didn't say anything. Her eyes were closed, and there was a frown in her brow. I couldn't tell if that frown was concentration or pain.

"Keep going, Misha. I knew it was going to hurt." She eased her nails from my skin and smoothed her hands over my shoulders.

Hurting her was the last thing I wanted to do. Carefully, I shifted to reach into my drawer for the bottle of lube I'd bought recently for this occasion if it ever came. I opened the bottle and shivered as the cold gel slid over my hot skin. And then I kept going. I tried to distract her by pressing hot, open-mouthed kisses along her sensitive neck and skating my fingers over her nipples. I ran my hand down her stomach and rolled her clit in gentle circles with my thumb. Gently easing in, pulling out. It became a process. A rhythm. And when she was less tense and her legs fell open, I surged forward, pressing deep inside.

"Ow!" She slapped me on the arm but not enough to really hurt. I looked down into her pain-filled eyes. Tears were leaking down the sides of her face into her hair.

"I'm sorry. Shh... it's okay. It'll feel a little better in a minute." I didn't actually know if it would, but I hoped so. Damn, she was so hot and tight around me. All I wanted to do was thrust until I came. I carefully wiped away her tears and gave her soft kisses while telling her how sweet, beautiful, and sexy she was. And when she relaxed again, I began to move once more.

This time she didn't cry, thank God. I would have felt like the biggest dick (and not in a good way) because I don't think I could've stopped if she'd started crying again. My hand snaked down between us, and I used my thumb to rub tiny circles around her clit. Her hips began moving beneath me, meeting my thrusts with her own.

I groaned and buried my head against her neck, my body not my own anymore. A tingle began in my spine and started to trickle down to my balls. With a cry, Katya tensed under me. Her legs snapped around my hips and drew me deep inside.

And that was my undoing. With a groan, I came, my hips thrusting hard against hers until my body was spent.

Carefully I pulled out of her, removed the condom and tossed it into the wastebasket before gathering her into my arms. We shared sweet kisses there in the dark until she fell asleep. I curled up with her to sleep the rest of the night.

Chapter 19

Katya

Past

Time seemed to pass like normal for a few weeks. I attended class, and as much as I argued with Misha about his choice of enrolling me in university versus sending me home, I'm glad he did. I absolutely loved everything about it. My professors were intelligent, and I had learned so much about the culinary arts. Of course baking was my favorite, but learning the chemistry involved in the other types of cooking had upped my baking game. I was making things I'd only dreamed about! French macarons, a variety of breads, Russian classics like Bird's Milk Cake that Misha almost swooned over.

Even Larissa was enjoying living in the dowager's cottage. We had been to visit her a couple of times for tea. I'd even made a special cake for her, and she declared it was better than her grandmother's recipe!

Everyone was happy. Everyone except Misha. I could feel the tension in him a mile away. He just couldn't relax. When we were watching TV or out on a date, he was constantly checking his phone. When he wasn't on his phone, his attention felt a million miles away. Something was wrong. And what was worse, he wouldn't confide in me. I pestered him with questions.

"Is one of your classes giving you trouble?"

"No."

"Are you sick?"

"No."

"Are you missing your dad?"

"Yes, but that's not what's bothering me."

"Then what is bothering you?"

"Nothing for you to worry about, Katya."

I couldn't weasel it out of him, and it was starting to drive me crazy. When I mentioned it to Vally, she shrugged and said it must be Family business. I guess that was the difference between growing up normal versus growing up Bratva.

And then we received an invitation to Galina and Pavel's wedding.

"We aren't going," Misha said when Valentina and I descended upon him with the invitation.

"We have to go, Misha. Pavel is family, whether we like him or not. Plus, the Petrovkas are allies. We need to keep them that way," Larissa stated from Valentina's phone. She'd called in reinforcements.

"Mama's right, Misha. Maybe our attendance will help solidify Petrovka to us and show there are no hard feelings since you dumped his daughter," Valentina urged.

Misha snorted and leaned back in his chair to stare at his sister. "I didn't 'dump his daughter', Valentina. Yuri handled it by setting her up with Pavel."

"Can we go? It's been so long since I've been to a wedding. Galina might have some handsome cousins I can dance with. You know how much I love to dance." Valentina was nearly on her knees.

Misha's frown deepened, and I quickly took Valentina's arm, guiding her to the door. "Maybe it isn't a good idea to talk to your brother about boys. He's really protective of you."

"I heard that, Katya," he growled from his seat. "But you are right. I don't want to think of my younger sister dating."

"I'm only younger by a few minutes," she stuck her tongue out at her brother.

"But acting like that makes you seem *much* younger," he chuckled. "I'll think about it okay?"

We both nodded and left him alone with his thoughts.

***

In the end, we won. We were all going to attend the wedding. Luckily it was months away, so we had plenty of time to find appropriate—and fashionable, thanks to Valentina— dresses to wear and a gift for the couple. Which was why I found myself, two weeks later, trying on what had to be the fiftieth dress in a row. Is this what my Barbie felt like when I dressed and re-dressed her for every event my six year old self could imagine? I was hot from all the changing, and my stomach was growling. I hadn't eaten since this morning, and it was long past lunchtime.

I wasn't sold on this antique gold dress, but I would wear it if it got me to food faster. A hopeful peek at Valentina dashed my hopes. The frown on her pretty mouth was the same with each dress. I knew better than to tell her I didn't care what I wore to the wedding. It wasn't my wedding, after all, and I distinctly disliked Pavel and Galina. Wearing a paper bag was as much care as I gave about what those two thought. But I couldn't say that to Valentina. Just like baking for someone was my love language, dressing me in high fashion was hers. So, I sucked it up and walked back into the dressing room to try on something else.

The last dress in the pile was a pink so pale it was almost white. I'd saved it for last because I wasn't sure the color would look right on me. Between my hair, my fair skin, and the dress, it would be pale on pale on pale. I held it up against my body and rubbed the feathery, raw silk edges between my fingertips. Such a unique design.

In minutes, I had removed the gold dress and pulled this one on. The side zipper was easy to fasten, and I liked that it was hidden beneath my arm. I stepped out of the dressing room and gazed at myself in the mirror. The dress was simple and elegant. A sweetheart neckline, fitted bodice to my waist, and then a gently flared tea-length skirt. I piled my white gold hair atop my head in a mock updo and turned to glance at the back. My heart sped up as I gave a twirl and the skirt belled out around me. The pale pink added roses to my cheeks and a blush to my skin. This was the one. It had to be.

I risked a glance at Valentina in the mirror. Instead of that frown, there was a soft smile. She turned to the store clerk and handed him her credit card. "We'll buy it."

"Thanks, Vally!" I twirled again and then danced over to her for a hug.

"Of course! Misha is going to lose his mind when he sees you in this! Especially with how low cut this neckline is."

A heated blush swam up my body, and I knocked her hand away from where her finger was gliding along the edge of the sweetheart neckline.

A cleared throat caught our attention, and we both turned to the clerk who was standing stiffly nearby. "Miss Belov, I'm sorry to say this, but...your card has been declined."

"*Declined?*" She nearly shrieked the word. "Did you try it again? Maybe the strip is worn out or damaged. Did you type in the number?"

"Yes, miss. I ran it three times and tried the number. Declined." He offered her the card back and walked into the dressing room to snag an armful of discarded dresses. He paused to look at me. "Miss, I'm going to need you to return that garment to its hanger, please." And then he swept off to put the dresses back on the racks.

With a worried look at Valentina who was staring at her card as if she'd never seen it before, I walked into the dressing room to change.

The Uber ride back to the dorm was quiet as Valentina concentrated on her texting with Misha, and I stared out the window. I felt helpless as to how to help her. Somehow I didn't think a batch of pink thumbprint cookies would suffice in this instance. Luckily the ride was short, and we were soon walking through the door of our suite.

Misha's voice could be heard from his room. The intermittent pauses showed he was talking on the phone. Valentina walked into his room to find out what was going on. That was not my business, so I went to my room and sat at the desk to stare at my half-written letter. But I couldn't concentrate. Misha and Valentina's conversation had dissolved into a fight.

"Vally, I can't tell you exactly what Uncle Yuri said. It's Family business." That was Misha.

"It's more than Family business when it involves the actual *family*, Misha. He cut me off!"

There was a long sigh from Misha. "He cut off the whole family. Even Mother. Even me. Just wear one of the dresses you already have."

"Wear something I already have?"

I winced at her screech. You'd think it was the end of the world.

"You sound like a spoiled brat, Valentina. Just...deal with it."

I winced again, this time at Misha's words. Not cool. I tried to stay out of their sibling squabbling. My brother was a lot older than me, so we didn't fight like this. Part of me thought it was funny, the other part not so much.

"*Deal with it*?!"

The slam of Valentina's door was my cue to come out. I walked across the hall to Misha's room and stood in his doorway. "You okay?"

He looked raw and tired. His hair was mussed as if he'd been running his hands through it. He rubbed the spot between his dark brows, and I knew he had a headache coming on. "Not really. I always say the wrong thing to her when we fight like this. And the worst part...I can absolutely understand where she is coming from. I hate that Yuri cut us off without telling us. It's a really shitty—don't correct me—thing to do."

I couldn't argue with that. "I think it really embarrassed her to have her card declined in the store."

"Of course it did. Valentina is proud and is accustomed to the lifestyle she grew up in. I imagine she felt humiliated, which makes it even worse what I said to her." He paused for a moment. When he spoke next, his words were soft and filled with remorse. "*I* made it worse."

"She will forgive you if you apologize. She always does. Is Yuri going to unblock the cards anytime soon?"

"I don't know. He's dealing with something having to do with our finances. I can't say what it is. We just have to be patient."

I nodded and went to him, wrapping my arms around him in a tight hug. "Then patient we will be."

Chapter 20

Kate

Past

Misha and I observed the hustle and bustle of Galina's family and Pavel's mother in the church from our comfortable position in the sidelines. "Is this the type of wedding you want, Katya? Large with a thousand people, white doves and swans, and a twenty-tiered cake?"

I considered Misha's question for a moment, then shook my head. "I used to think this was what I wanted, but now I'd love something quiet and simple with just our loved ones. Who wants all this chaos on their special day when all you need are the people you love?"

"I'll drink to that," Valentina said, sidling up to us.

Misha frowned at her. "There is no alcohol here in the church."

Valentina snorted. "Just wishful thinking. Or was it?" She opened her clutch and pulled out a shiny tube of lipstick. My brows rose as she flicked the cap up and I realized it was actually a tiny flask. She downed it like a shot.

"Valentina Ekaterina Belov!"

"Now you've done it," Misha stated with brotherly glee at his sister getting into trouble.

Larissa marched over to us and pointed a finger at her daughter. "You better put that away right now. I don't want to see it again in church. Ever."

"Yes, Mama," Valentina sighed, re-capped the flask, and dropped it back into her clutch.

"Now, let us all go take our seats," Larissa took her son's arm, and Valentina and I walked behind them down the aisle to the family's seats in the front.

The wedding was beautiful. The bride was beautiful. The ceremony was beautiful. And super boring and long. Really long. It was made worse by not understanding the archaic form of Russian the priest was using to perform the blessings.

I must have dozed off because the clapping startled me awake, and I stood with everyone as the bride and groom made their smiling way down the aisle. The couple was going to take a traditional tour around the city with their immediate family and wedding party, stopping to take pictures along the way, so Larissa, Valentina, Misha, and I had time to get to the house with the rest of the guests before the couple and their families arrived.

Everything was cream roses, red silk, and gold accents. Very pretty; very traditional. Even the food was traditional. Whole roasted chickens, potato dumplings in rich sauce, tureens of soup, and lots of crusty bread. I had been enlisted to help bake the bread. Pavel had called me a week ago to demand—not ask—that I make the bread. I knew I was asked to do it as part of a joke. I wasn't part of the Belov family. Misha was mad enough to charge over to his house and beat his cousin to a pulp—his words. But I stopped him and agreed to bake the bread because I love baking, and this type of bread was a new recipe to me. I also loved what it stood for in the traditional sense. Apparently bread was a symbol of prosperity and fertility for the couple, so there were loaves of round bread, braided bread, and any other kind of bread you could imagine. It pushed my culinary skills to the limit for several days before the wedding.

Bread in place, the guests filed in and sat down at the long dining table. Petra had ordered the extra leaves be placed to elongate the table, so everyone could have a seat. Misha sat at the head which was his due. I sat on his right, Larissa and Valentina on his left. The happy couple was in the middle with Yuri and his wife on the other end with Galina's family.

As I ladled soup into my bowl, I curiously glanced around at all the guests. I had never seen so many people in this dining room before, but it looked like someone was missing. I scanned the faces, trying to determine who I wasn't seeing. My hand froze and I carefully replaced the ladle back in the tureen before leaning over to Misha and whispering, "Is it normal for the bridesmaids not to be here?"

Misha lowered his spoon to his bowl and scanned the assembled group. There were six empty chairs together with empty plates. "Maybe they stepped out to take pictures together. I'm sure they will be back soon."

Once I started thinking about it, I couldn't let the thought go. Why would they step out? It was one thing to go to the restroom with your bestie, but it was another for the entire group to go. And now that I thought about it, I didn't remember seeing them come in with the bride and groom. And there were others missing, too. Wives. Petra, Mrs. Petrovka, Galina, Larissa, Valentina, and I were the only women present.

"Stop thinking so hard and eat. Your soup will get cold," Misha chided with a smile. "It's a happy day for them." Why couldn't he see what I was pointing out? Why was he ignoring the fact that the bridesmaids *still* hadn't joined us?

After a few more minutes, Misha stood and clinked a spoon against his wine glass to get everyone's attention. "Good evening, everyone. As the heir of the Belov family, I wanted to take a moment to congratulate my cousin and his beautiful bride. May you live long and be blessed in many wonderful ways. *Za zda ro vye!*"

"*Za zda ro vye!*" The assembled repeated, and we all drank to the bride and groom's good health.

When Misha sat down, Yuri stood, a wide smile on his face. "I have been waiting a long, long time for this day. My only son, Pavel, is married. You have done your duty like a good son," his eyes flickered to Misha which made me grind my teeth in annoyance, "and have made me incredibly proud. Such a lovely wife will bring you much happiness. And her connections bring us even more." What a weird speech, but maybe this was normal for a Bratva wedding? I didn't have anything to compare it to, but I was still uneasy. "When you were a tiny baby, I promised you that I would do all in my power to make you happy, rich, and powerful. Today is the day I fulfill that promise."

A horrendous bang deafened my ears and something sprayed across my face. Had someone knocked over a water glass that shattered? I glanced around and blanched. Red was sprayed across the table! Screams filled the air, and I whipped my head around trying to figure out what was happening. The only people reacting were those at my end. And then I saw him. Misha was hunched over on himself, blood poured from a wound in his shoulder.

"Misha!" I cried. I reached for him, but I was snatched up in someone's arms and carried from the room at a dead sprint. "Misha! Misha!" I screamed until I was hoarse. "Take me back!" I shouted at the man who had grabbed me. He had his cell to his ear and was speaking in rapid-fire Russian to someone on the other end.

A car swerved into view and stopped at the edge of the drive. The man tossed me into the back, then got in and pushed me against the back of the seat as the car lurched forward. He peered into my panicked face. "Shut up and listen."

"But I need to go back! He's hurt! He could be dying!" I began to smack his shoulders, his face, anything I could with my open palms. He simply grabbed my wrists and pressed them to my sides.

"Listen!" He roared, cutting through my hysteria until I was simply a shaking mess. "I am not going to hurt you unless you make this difficult. Understand?" I gave a shaky nod. "Good. Mr. Belov has a plane ready to take you back to Chicago. You are to leave here and never come back. Do you understand?"

Again, I nodded. Tears pooled on my lower lashes, spilling over onto my bloody cheeks. Cheeks red with Misha's blood.

Chapter 21

Misha

Past

Through the haze of burning pain, I watched as Katya was plucked from her seat. "Katya..." Fury like I have never known gave me an adrenaline rush to stand. I tried to whirl around. To follow. But the hot blood running in rivulets down my arm gave me pause. As did my mother and sister who were still in the room. Still in danger. Katya would have to wait. My eyes zeroed in on Yuri, but before I could utter another word, he spoke.

"Sit down, Larissa," my uncle said jovially when she ran to my other side to check my wound. It felt like fire. When I was a kid, I wondered what it would feel like to be shot. Such an idiotic kid thing to think about. But now I knew. It felt like flaming lava was poured into a hole in your body.

"No! What do you think you're doing, Yuri? Misha is your nephew! Your own blood!" I hissed through my teeth as she pressed a linen napkin to the burning wound in my shoulder.

"So was Constantine."

The implication of that statement had me raising my head to stare in disbelieving horror at my uncle. No. No!

He wouldn't do that! "You killed my father?! Your own brother?!"

"Yes. He was weak. We needed stronger leadership and he would never have stepped down as head of the family. Now, sit. Down. Larissa. I won't ask again."

"It's okay, Mother." I slowly sat back in my chair and leveled my gaze at my conniving uncle. Mother kissed my cheek and took her seat once more. I reached over and linked my fingers with hers. One glance at Valentina showed me that she was very close to doing something stupid with that temper of hers. Her face was drained of all color, but there was fire in her eyes. Her fingers slowly stretched to take the knife next to her plate. "Vally, stand down," I commanded, and she turned to look at me with a frown, but she did drop her hands into her lap.

My eyes tracked down one side of the table and back up the other. "Looks like we have a whole Family of traitors. Mr. Petrovka, I'm curious now as to how my uncle handled this arrangement between Pavel and your daughter."

"He said you reneged on our arrangement, you arrogant son-of-a-bitch. When Yuri said Galina could still be the wife of the head of the Belov family, I listened. Like your uncle said, you are weak and need to be removed."

"What about the rest of you?" I glanced at the others.

My mother's eldest brother shrugged. "Weak does not look good on a leader. You are young and inexperienced. Yuri knows how to bring the Family back to its glory days before your grandfather." He looked at my mother. "Sorry, Larissa, but Constantine was not good enough for you. Yuri promised to set up marriages for you and Valentina that are worthy and will truly benefit the Family."

My mother's eyes flashed defiance. "I am not remarrying!"

"Calm yourself, Larissa. We will discuss it later when you feel better. We have more pressing things to do." Yuri nodded at one of his bodyguards, several of which were stationed around the room, and the man zip-tied each of us to our chair and gagged us with a piece of duct tape across the mouth. Then, as if nothing had happened, they all began to eat once more.

I stared at the spot where my sweet Katya had been sitting. I hadn't recognized the man who had taken her. He was obviously a new hire by Yuri which meant Katya could be in a great deal of danger. A cold sweat broke out on my skin, and the hairs rose on the back of my neck.

"Don't worry about your little sex toy, my boy. She's on her way back home to Chicago. I even gave her a little money, so she won't be living on the streets. See? I'm not a monster. I don't kill unless I need to. I don't need her DNA tipping off anyone who might connect her to a missing person from the States. Best just to send her home with enough cash and fear to keep her mouth shut."

I rolled my eyes and snorted, but secretly I was relieved he'd sent her away. I wanted her far, far away from what was going to happen to me here. I had no illusions that I was going to come out of this alive.

We sat like this for hours while the group ate, drank, and were merry. My shoulder had stopped burning and it and my arm had gone completely numb. A glance at my mother and sister showed they were nearing the end of their patience and stamina. Both were strong women, but this was very far outside the borders of their tolerance. Not to mention, pain. The zip ties were tight and sharply dug into the skin. The wrist of my uninjured arm was busy trying to stretch out the hard plastic which was cutting into my flesh until it was slippery. Luckily, once all the food was eaten and the wine was drunk, everyone... left. Everyone except Yuri, that is.

"Take the women upstairs and lock them in one of the bedrooms. Station someone outside the door and below the window," my uncle said to one of his goons. I narrowed my eyes at the man as he untied first my mother and then my sister. He grabbed each roughly by the elbow and pushed them ahead of him as he walked out of the room.

Now it was just me and him.

Or so I thought. He walked out of the room without a word, leaving me alone and bleeding all over the place. Maybe it was his idea to have me bleed out? I wasn't sure a gunshot wound to the shoulder would do that. He hadn't hit a vital organ. Or maybe he was letting me stew. I was left like that while the servants came in to clean up after the guests. They gave me frightened looks as they cleared the dishes and mopped up messes on the table. I tried to catch the attention of the servants I knew best, but they each ducked their heads to avoid meeting my eyes. It was clear they had been threatened not to help me.

I sighed and rolled my head backward against the chair to stare at the ceiling. This was going to be fucking long as hell. A tug on the linen napkin covering my wound caught my attention, and I turned my head to see one of the servants trying to gently remove it from my shoulder. I winced in pain, and her startled doe eyes flicked up to mine. I gave her a nod of encouragement, and she poured water over the wound to loosen the dried blood attaching the linen to the wound. She carefully cleaned the blood with more water from the glass.

The door opened, startling her, and she quickly stepped away. "Go," Yuri said, making a shooing motion with his hands. The servant quickly filed out under his watch. And then Yuri walked to me and took the chair my mother had vacated. He grabbed the edge of the duct tape and ripped it viciously from my mouth.

Fuck, that hurt! I refused to give him the satisfaction of a response, though, so I made no sound. Was he was going to kill me now? I was surprised he didn't do it during the dinner as a statement in front of everyone. "So, tell me the truth, Uncle. Why did you kill my father?"

Yuri watched me for a moment then leaned forward and dug his finger into my wound causing me to actually cringe away and scream in pain. He dug around in there until he removed the bullet and showed it to me. My body shuddered, and I felt bile gather in my mouth. I spat at his shiny, black shoes hoping the stomach acid would be enough to ruin them. He only tsked and cleaned them with a linen napkin. "I'll be keeping this bullet as a souvenir of this special day." He dropped it into the glass of water to wash it off, and then he pocketed the clean bullet.

"Are you going to answer me?" I demanded.

Yuri's hand fidgeted in his pocket, and I knew he was fiddling with that damn bullet. His bushy brows drew down, hooding his eyes as he watched me. Bastard was trying to decide if it was worth it or not to tell me. I was testing him. If he told me, he was planning on killing me, and if he didn't, I might have a fighting chance to live.

"I think you already know," he finally said. He walked to the sideboard and poured himself some vodka, then he turned and propped himself against the banquet. He lifted the glass to me in some kind of fucked up salute before taking a sip.

"The ledgers." My heart sank. That meant I was in deep shit.

He nodded and sipped again. "Your Uncle Anton and I had been doing the books for the Family for thirty years before my idiot brother discovered something was off. I made one tiny error, and he found it."

"Not so much an idiot then, was he?" That's right, I liked to poke the bear once in a while. It wasn't always a smart thing to do, but in this case, I needed to get him to keep talking and drinking. A steak knife had been left on the table, forgotten by one of the servants cleaning up after dinner. I was desperate to get my bound hands on it.

My uncle's gaze hardened on me, and he downed his vodka like a shot, slammed the glass on the banquet, and filled it again. Instead of drinking it this time, he stomped his way to me and poured the alcohol over my gun shot wound. Fuck! It burned like chilled liquid fire! I clenched my jaw and my eyes shut tight and breathed through the pain. *This is worth it. This is worth it. This is worth it.*

"You are just like your father: mouthy, dumb, and too good for this line of work. While Constantine was attempting to legalize and legitimize some of his operations, I was paying off police to look the other way and taking a little bit here and there to buy the loyalty of his men. Not one of them batted an eye when I gunned him down in that warehouse. Before setting it on fire to cover my tracks, of course."

I couldn't help the snarl that curled my lips at his words. *Gunned down.* And he'd pretended to mourn his brother for months.

"Then I convinced you to go back to school with your little toy, and I've been running the show ever since. I had no intention of handing the Family over to you. Idiot son like idiot father." He laughed and turned his back on me as he walked back to the sideboard for more vodka.

His mistake.

Watching him for any sign he was about to turn around, I scooted my chair back from the table. I rocked forward until I was able to stand on my feet like the Hunchback of Notre Dame. My hands were zip-tied to the back of the chair, so this next part was going to be damn difficult. I turned so I could grab the white tablecloth in one of my bound hands. Oh, so carefully, I pulled it. Ice clinked in glasses and silverware scraped against empty plates. Most of the table had been cleared by the staff, but they had left a few items before being told to fuck off by their new boss. I winced at the noise and paused for a breath, waiting for my uncle to turn. When he didn't I pulled again until the steak knife was in reach. I clumsily grabbed it by the handle, and I tipped back until the chair's four legs hit the floor once more. I shuffled the chair back in place just in time for my uncle to turn around with a fresh glass of vodka.

I schooled my features to my disgruntled I'm-a-prisoner expression once more, hoping Yuri didn't notice the fine sheen of sweat breaking out on my forehead. If he did, he'd probably think it was due to the new bullet hole he'd given me. I turned the knife in my palm until the serrated edge touched the plastic around my wrist. This was going to take a hot minute, so I needed to keep him distracted. I wracked my brain trying to figure out something else to say, but as I opened my mouth, there was a knock at the door.

Yuri gave me a hard look like he knew what I was up to, before moving to open the door. There was some low discussion that I couldn't hear, but I didn't care. I was too busy trying to saw through the plastic attaching me to the chair. It was so tight that when the knife slipped it cut my wrist instead. Warm blood seeped from the wound making the knife slippery. The plastic, too.

I froze as Yuri glanced my way, but then he left and closed the door behind him. I couldn't imagine what was so important that it took him away from murdering his nephew in cold blood, but I was grateful. Then I heard the sound of scraping furniture and breaking class. Whatever my mother and sister were doing, it was bad enough that my uncle had to deal with them. Fuck. I had to get out of here. With the cuts I'd made and the blood slicking the zip tie, I squeezed my fingers to make my hand as small as possible and viciously twisted it against the biting plastic until it popped free.

Thank God! Twisting in the chair, I swiftly sawed through the zip tie on my other wrist. Switching hands, I moved to the door and stood to the side, waiting for someone to enter. It didn't take long. I heard them before the door opened, chatting about the weather like attempted murder and kidnapping weren't happening right under this roof.

My fingers tightened around the knife's hilt. The door opened, and I flattened my back against the wall behind it. I needed both men to enter completely, and when they did, I kicked the door shut. Then all hell broke loose. I leaped on the back of the man who'd come in second much to the anguish of my injured shoulder, and dispatched him with a swift jab to the throat with the point of the blade. He clutched his throat and went down, gurgling, blood spilling from his neck and mouth.

The other man whirled around and lifted his gun. I ducked and dodged as he fired one, two, three rounds, the sound deafening, but his hand was shaking so bad his aim was off and the bullets pounded the wall. Wood and paint chips sprayed my back. I grasped the knife's blade and threw it. It was like slow motion turning end-over-end, and I prayed it would stay true and hit its mark. Father made Valentina and me practice knife throwing until we could do it in our sleep, but I hadn't used the skill in over a year.

The knife lodged point-forward in the man's right eye and brain. He fell, dead. The gun shots would mean trouble, so I picked up the dead man's gun and checked the clip. Five rounds left. Better than nothing.

Pounding footsteps sounded in the hallway outside the door, and I rolled my eyes as I placed my foot on the dead man's face and yanked the knife free. My uncle wasn't kidding when he said he bought the loyalty of all my father's men. When was this going to stop? I wiped the blood and goo off on his shirt and slid the knife into my back pocket. The door opened, and I fired two rounds into the man who barreled in. He was dead before he knew what happened.

It was time for me to leave this room and find my mother and sister. And Uncle Yuri. It was time to end this. I carefully stepped over the dead man blocking the door and leaned against the door frame, listening for more footsteps. All was quiet. Slowly I tilted my head to peer into the hallway. No one was around, not even staff. It was eerie to have so much quiet in a house normally bustling with people.

A woman's angry scream echoed in the stillness, and I jerked my head to stare at the ceiling as if I could use x-ray vision and see through the layers of beams, plaster, and carpeting to find out what was happening. At least it answered my next question which was where the women were being kept!

Father had taught me how to be quiet walking heel-to-toe, and I used that now as I approached the wide staircase. I grew up in this house and snuck out of it enough that I knew every creaking floorboard and whining step. Soon I was crouched on the landing, surveying the hallway upstairs and down. From the sound of Valentina's shout, they were most likely being held in Katya's old room where there was very little they could use against the men holding them hostage in their own home.

I crept silently toward the door, a light blazing from the crack beneath. Voices argued from within. My uncle's voice was one of them. Great! I could kill him and whatever goon was in there with him terrorizing my family. It needed to be painful. It was one thing to try to kill me but no one messed with my family. When Father died—no! Was *gunned down*—, they became my responsibility. I couldn't fail them! Mother, Valentina, and now Katya, were my whole world. My entire existence and happiness depended on them.

With the fire of vengeance blazing in my belly, I sucked in a deep breath to steady my nerves, and then I kicked the fucking door down.

The door bounced off of the overturned chest of drawers and fell haphazardly askew. My uncle stood next to the window with his arms crossed over his chest. His goon was stationed by the closet while my mother and sister were seated on the bed, their hands bound once more behind their backs. The room was a wreck. Aside from the chest of drawers, the jewelry box was standing on its head and looked like someone had tried to break off one of the curving spindly legs to use as a weapon. Glass littered the floor from the vanity mirror and crunched under my shoes as I stepped inside the room.

"I don't know how you managed to escape the dining room, my boy, especially when I sent some men down there to take care of you, but you won't be leaving this room alive." my uncle rasped in his gruff tone. "Kill him."

The goon—this one I recognized as a long-time friend and employee of my father— hesitated. I could tell he didn't like this. Didn't want to be a part of it. "I already told you, Pakhan, I don't want to be a part of killing a Belov."

"I don't care, Lev. You agreed to be a part of my empire, and it starts with killing Constantine's son. Do it."

Lev's frown deepened and he looked between Yuri and me, trying to decide. "I'm not doing it."

"So be it." Yuri reached behind his back and pulled out a gun. Before I could react, he fired one shot, right through Lev's heart.

"No!" I shouted as Lev fell to the floor. My heart was beating so fast. That beating coupled with the ringing from all the gunshots made me deaf. I raised my own gun and fired at Yuri, but fire erupted in my chest and the world toppled around me.

"Misha!" Valentina's dark hair fell in a curtain around me as she knelt by my side. I gasped for breath. The scents of burning flesh mingling with smoke and Valentina's perfume choked in my throat."Misha, it's going to be okay," she sobbed. Her hands stroked my face, and I lifted one hand to cup the back of hers, holding her to me as tightly as I could muster. My muscles trembled, and my hand fell to my side.

"Your hands... how?" I whispered like it was important.

"Lev didn't tighten them much. Quiet, now. Rest." I felt her brush my fingers away from the gun, and she took it from me. Carefully she cocked the trigger, whipped sideways and fired three rapid fire shots at my unsuspecting uncle.

His body jerked with each bullet, and then he was falling backward. The window shattered behind him as he fell.There was a distinct smack when he hit the ground.

My mother ran to the window to look, and she breathed a sigh of relief. "Dead. I'll call the paramedics. Misha, my brave boy, stay with us until we can get you help. Don't you dare leave us." Her voice cracked on the last word.

I tried. I really did. But I was so cold and in so much pain. The lure of peaceful darkness was too much, and I reached for it, succumbing to oblivion.

Chapter 22

Kate

Present

A few days after I hung out with Lex, Derek texted asking to meet for breakfast. I knew he was dying to see me, but I was proud of his restraint. The text was short and to the point. No fluff. No extra questioning. It simply required a yes or no answer. An hour later, I found Derek sitting in a booth by a window in our favorite breakfast spot as kids. He stood and pulled me into a tight hug. "I'm so fucking happy you're home."

I rolled my eyes as I admonished, "Language, bro." I returned his hug with a squeeze that made him grunt. When he finally released me, I saw that he had already ordered for us.

A sheepish grin curved his handsome face. "I hope you still like chocolate chip pancakes."

Though my tastes had refined from when I was thirteen, the nostalgia of my childhood favorites was always hard to pass up. "Chocolate chip pancakes are perfect. Thanks."

We slid into our seats and dug into our breakfast. The minutes stretched to awkwardness as neither of us spoke.

We just kept glancing up at each other and then away until I finally cleared my throat. "Well, this is weird."

He grinned back and shrugged, "Yeah. I have so many questions, but I was ordered not to interrogate you."

Lex. I freaking loved that girl. She always had my back.

"It's okay to ask some questions. But only about me. The me I am today. I don't want to talk about what happened."

"Okay. Why don't you want to go to the police?"

"I already explained that to Lex, and I'm sure she told you."

"She did, but I want to hear it from you."

"Alright." I sighed. "I don't know my kidnappers. It was eight years ago, I was drugged, and I can't even remember what they looked like. Going to the police would only draw unwanted attention. I just want to move on with my life."

"I get it. But what about Mom and Dad? Don't you want to see them?"

"Yes... but I'm also scared because they, like you, will want to ask a bunch of questions I'm not ready to answer." I also wasn't ready for the tears, for the hugs and kisses from people I haven't seen since I was a kid. What if they didn't like the person I became? What if they started pressuring me to change? Even worse, what if they didn't like me and didn't want to see me again? I wasn't the same person I was at thirteen. And I wasn't the person I was destined to be when I was that girl. No, life and hard choices changed me.

Derek slid a hand over mine and curled his fingers into my palm. "What if I talk to them first so they don't make you uncomfortable?"

I turned my hand so it was palm-to-palm with his and linked our fingers. "I'll think about it. That's the best I can do for now."

He nodded and sipped his coffee with his free hand, not moving the other from its warm connection with mine. "What are your plans? For the future, I mean."

"I want to finish pastry school." The determination in my words surprised me because I'd felt listless for weeks.

Derek's brows shot up in surprise. "Pastry school," he repeated. "And why do you want to do that?"

"Bake, duh." I grinned at him. "I love everything about baking, and life's too short and unpredictable to spend time on things you don't love." My mind wandered to Misha, Valentina, and Larissa. My family away from home. I missed them so much. Talk about unpredictable. I often thought back to if there had been signs of what was to come at the wedding. It was impossible to say. "I started pastry school in Russia, and I want to finish. And then I want to open up my very own brick-and-mortar bakery."

"Don't take this the wrong way, Sis, but I don't think bakeries make a lot of money."

"Don't take this the wrong way, Bro, but money isn't my end game. Happiness is."

"Touche. Will you let me pay your tuition?"

"That I will do. As a loan."

"Deal."

The rest of our breakfast passed in companionable talk and laughter which my battered heart needed in order to heal from its ordeal of the past.

***

"So, as time went on, week after week, I was really enjoying myself. It had been such a long time since I had felt any semblance of freedom." I stared at the cottage cheese ceiling. Had any of those white pieces of plaster ever fallen on someone's face—or worse, in someone's mouth!—as they were lying here spilling their guts out on the therapy couch? Was I the only person weird enough to think about that? Probably. Lately my mind felt like a sieve—thoughts trickled in and out all day and night.

"And how did your relationship with Misha continue? Were you happy with him? Did you keep asking him to send you home despite enjoying your time in Moscow?" Dr. Reynolds was his usual stoic self, sitting in his overstuffed leather chair with a yellow notepad balanced on his knee and a pen poised between his relaxed fingertips. I bet he was getting enough from me to write a second dissertation.

I was really happy Lex had set me up with him. He was easy to talk to, and he didn't bat an eyelash when I broke down and cried about my thirteen year old self, my life, and my Misha. He simply passed me the tissue box. Now I was on my fourth counseling appointment, and though I wasn't feeling super great, I was feeling better. It felt good to talk about what happened with someone other than my brother and my best friend. The way I saw it, progress was progress. But I couldn't stop the little niggle of guilt in the back of my mind. Part of me kept saying it wasn't right for me to start feeling better when Misha was dead. That part wanted me to stay miserable for his sake. For his memory. But another part of me insisted Misha would hate for me to feel bad and would want me to get better. Dr. Reynolds told me that is the self I'm supposed to listen to. I was trying, but sometimes I felt like for every step forward, I took two steps back.

There was no other way to say it: grief sucked.

"I started to think he wasn't ever going to send me home. But I started not to mind either. I had a great boyfriend who cared about me, and I was learning a trade that I was passionate about. Not to mention, Valentina and Larissa had become my surrogate family. I was finally finding happiness when I had been uncomfortable at best, you know?"

Dr. Reynolds made a sound in his throat like what a hoarse vulture might sound like and scribbled something on his notepad. I noticed he did this every time I said something extra good that he could use in his next award-winning psychology article.

"Let's change gears a bit, shall we?" Dr. Reynolds said, looking at me over the rims of his circular glasses. "Last time we spoke, you were hesitant to see your parents. Has that changed?"

Ugh. Not this conversation again. "I don't know."

My clipped tone must have clued him into my mood on this topic because he set his notepad and pen down on a side table and leaned forward to rest his elbows on his knees. This was not the usual Dr. Reynolds stance, so it caught my attention. "I know you don't want to talk about this, Kate, but it's important."

"Are you going to try and guilt-trip me into seeing them like my brother does?"

"No. I don't think you should meet with them if you're not ready." He held a hand up when he saw the huge smile on my face. "But—" he enunciated clearly, "I do think you should write them a letter."

My smile dropped. "What would I say in it? Dear Mom and Dad, I'm sorry, but even though I was kidnapped and wanted to come home every day for a really long time, I freak out at the thought of seeing you." My chest burned with the guilt of it. "Yeah, that'll go over *really* well."

"Of course not. And I'm not expecting you to send it right away or at all. Sometimes writing down your feelings helps get them out more than talking about them to the ones who matter most. It might give you a direction you want to take when you do finally feel you can meet with them. Before our next session, I want you to write your letter and bring it with you when you come. We will look at it together."

My anxiety eased at his understanding and calm explanation. I should have known he wouldn't make me jump in the deep end when I wasn't even ready to swim. "Okay, Dr. Reynolds. I can do that."

***

"Are you sure this is what you want to do, Kate?"

A week later, Derek, Lex, and I were once again sitting in our favorite diner eating our childhood favorites. The doubt in my brother's eyes had me second-guessing my decision. Luckily, I was made of sterner stuff and gave him a decisive nod. "Yes. Dr. Reynolds said writing down your feelings is a great way to express yourself, and he was right. I do feel better. It makes the panic lessen a little bit. He and I went over the letter together with a fine-toothed comb until I felt comfortable with what I wanted to say to Mom and Dad. I want them to hear from me. Know I'm alive. I'm not ready to face them because I don't want to talk about it. This isn't forever, Derek. I just need time."

"You've been home for months now! How much more time do you need?"

"Derek," Lex's calming voice instantly smoothed the intense frown from Derek's brow, but the concern in his eyes lingered. She laid a gentle hand on his and squeezed reassuringly. "You were on the other side of this. And even when you were the one *doing* the kidnapping, it wasn't the same as being on the receiving end. With all due respect, you don't know how she's feeling. You have absolutely no idea. I do. At least a little. Give her the time she needs to recover. Stop pressuring and guilting her to do something she isn't ready for."

We sat in silence for a few minutes as I stared at a bead of condensation trickling down the side of my tall glass of iced tea. I was grateful Lex was here as a buffer for this conversation. When Derek and I were alone, we either spoke of mundane topics like baking and the weather or one of us would end up walking out. Usually me. Lex's demeanor calmed Derek's quick rebuttals and unwillingness to bend. He'd always been like that, even as a kid.

Finally, Derek broke the silence. "I'm sorry. To both of you." He brushed a kiss against Lex's lips, then nudged the tip of her nose with his. A small smile was shared between them, and I suddenly felt like a third wheel. Though seeing them together was still weird, I was now seeing it as sweet. I loved that they had each other. A stab of sadness overwhelmed my heart. They reminded me so much of my relationship with Misha. I turned away to catch my breath before speaking.

"It's okay. I know you want things to go back to normal, but they can't right now. Maybe not ever. I'm not the same girl I was at thirteen."

"I know that. But is it wrong for me to want you to be okay?"

"Not at all. I wish I could make it so, but I still need time."

"I want to hear the letter before I give it to them... if that's ok."

I nodded and pulled the letter from its envelope and smoothed the folds flat on the counter. I knew the letter by heart, but it was easier to read it than stare at my brother while he read it to himself. Kind of like an author who reads what they wrote out loud. It always sounds best from the author. Plus, at least if I'm reading, I'm not fidgeting or over analyzing every facial expression.

"Dear Mom and Dad,

So much has happened that I'm not sure where to start. The long and short of it is this: I was kidnapped, drugged, sold into prostitution, fell in love, and returned home broken. I want to see you. Speak to you. Hug you. But I am sad to my bones. It's hard to integrate back to a country and society I haven't known for eight years. It's taking time to recover. I need time and space to find myself again. When that happens, I will come see you. Until then, we may write to each other. I'd love to hear from you. I love you both so much!

Yours,
Kate"

I paused and looked up to meet the eyes of my BFF and big brother. And I waited. Lex swiped a tear off her cheek and smiled at me. "I like it. Don't you, Derek?"

"Yeah," he murmured quietly. His jaw ticked with emotion. "It's good. Perfect, even." He reached across the counter and took the letter and envelope from me. He refolded the paper and carefully slid it home into the envelope. "I'll deliver it to them today."

That was all I could ask for.

Chapter 23

Kate

Present

"Where did you say we were going?" I asked Lex for at least the fourth time. She'd knocked on my door at 5:00 this morning with not coffee but some sort of gross green shake. When I opened the door, she thrust the shake at me and said to put on a pair of leggings and sneakers.

I'd been seeing Dr. Reynolds regularly, and his newest idea was for me to spend less time at my hotel home and more time either communing with nature or being a productive citizen. I'd been doing a little of both, actually. Rain or shine, I took walks. Chicago wasn't really the epitome of 'nature', but it was what I had. I'd avoided the playground where I was kidnapped, and I carried pepper spray on my keychain, but the time outside cleared my head. But walking in Chicago wasn't what I would call 'exercise'. I did a lot of window shopping, and there were so many tourists that it was stop-and-go. The most exercise I got was for my eyeballs surveying my surroundings for kidnappers.

So, I was a little nervous of where we were going. Lex was a runner, after all. And I was not. My idea of exercise was whisking.

"You'll see when we get there. Stop asking." She glanced at me. "And drink your smoothie. It's good for you."

"It looks like something a cow would throw up."

She snorted a laugh. "Maybe so, but it doesn't taste bad. I already told you that the pineapple covers up the spinach flavor."

"But I can see little dark green flecks. What if there are chunks of spinach in it?"

"For a foodie, you sure are picky."

"I'm not a foodie."

"Whatever. Anyway, I blended it up really fine. I promise there are no chunks of spinach."

With a curl of disgust, I lifted the blender cup to my mouth and sucked in a mouthful of smoothie. And I didn't die from repulsion. In fact, I actually liked the taste. Pineapple was one of my favorite fruits, and I definitely tasted it. The rest of the smoothie went down easily enough, and I finished as we turned into a parking lot.

"Swallow Cliff Stairs. I completely forgot about this place!" I was out of the car as soon as it stopped and gazed at the map. The preserve was outside of Chicago and, from what I remembered, had walking trails, climbing stairs, and— "Wait, where are the toboggan slides?" The corners of my mouth tipped down in disappointment.

"They closed a while back. Why? Were you planning on getting a face full of mud like in the old days?"

"No, but I hate how much some things have changed since I was last here." It seemed like everything changed. I wasn't sure if it was the faulty memories of a traumatized kid or if things were actually very different now. Some things were the same like the old restaurant and the playground. The large buildings downtown. But some things were so different that I felt lost in my hometown.

She nodded and braced one foot on the curb by her car. "Okay, let's stretch. We're going to run up and down the stairs a couple of times."

"Um... maybe one time."

"We'll see." She winked at me as she bent over her leg in an elegant arch.

"Yes, we will," I pushed out my bottom lip stubbornly and then mirrored her action only losing my balance once before we switched to the other foot.

When we finished stretching, Lex led the way to the long stone stairway. I frowned at the swathe of green grass blanketing the hill between the two staircases. A distant memory of sliding down the metal toboggan slides with my big brother tickled my brain. It would have been fun to go down one of those slides for old times' sake, mud in the face or not.

"Kate."

I blinked back to the present and smiled at my BFF. "Yeah?"

"Ready?"

"Uh, no."

"Too bad. On the count of 3, we are going to run together up these stairs."

Lord help me. I hated exercise.

"One. Two. Three. Go!"

With a groan, I jogged up the stairs. Halfway up, my legs and lungs began to burn. "I can't!" I wheezed, slowing down.

"Don't you dare stop! Breathe and push through the pain!"

If I was a cussing person, Lex's ears would be blistered from my words right now. She could be such a bully when it came to coaching. But I followed her directions and pushed myself to the top. And promptly collapsed on my butt, panting. "Oh, my God." Pant. "I'm dying." Pant.

Lex hadn't even broken a sweat despite the warmth of the morning and the exercise. In fact, she was jogging in place next to me! "C'mon! Get up. Let's run down and jog up again!"

"Yeah, that's not happening. If we are going to make this a thing, I'm going to need to work up to that."

She laughed and reached down to help me up. "I know. It was wishful thinking." I put my hands in hers and allowed her to pull me to my feet. "Now, we are going to do something to get rid of some of that pent up anger." She led me to a look out spot where we could see a large area of the park from above. "One thing that's special about coming back home after a life changing ordeal like you and I had is that no one expects you to be the same exact person you were."

"What do you mean?" I crossed my arms on the guardrail. I had the feeling everyone expected me to be exactly who I was at thirteen when I was kidnapped. Even Derek. Even Lex. But maybe I was putting my own expectations on them and not truly listening to what they have been saying.

"I mean exactly that. You can choose who you are now. If you could change something from the person you were, what would you choose?"

I shrugged. How the heck was I supposed to know?

"Well, let's try something. Do you get tired of watching your language all the time and policing other people's?"

I'd never considered that I was policing other people's words, but now that she mentioned it, I had been. And it was exhausting. And probably really annoying to everyone else. I didn't want to be that kind of annoying. "Yes."

"Good. One thing I did when I came home after being kidnapped is stand up here and scream. I want you to scream 'shit' at the top of your lungs."

"Won't people hear me?" A glance around showed there were several people jogging up and down the stairs or walking the trails, but it wasn't very busy yet.

"So what? There aren't any children."

Good point. "Okay." I sucked in a deep breath, and then I said, "Shiiiiiiit!" loudly. Screaming wasn't my jam.

Lex was not impressed if the cocked brow was any indication. "That was pitiful. I guess we need to practice screaming first. No words, just screams. Kate, you need to let go. Let go of the anger, the resentment, the frustration, and any other emotion you feel about what happened to you. Don't worry about anyone else. They are minding their own business. This is a public place, and we aren't taking our clothes off or anything *that* inappropriate. Just let it go."

Let. It. Go. Like Elsa.

I loosened my arms and gripped the railing instead. Then I closed my eyes and let the anger and unfairness of losing eight years of my life to the sex trade fill me to the brim.

And I screamed.

And screamed.

And then the words came. "I FUCKING HATE YOU! FUCK YOU! FUCK YOU! FUCK YOU FOREVER 'TIL THE DAY YOU FUCKING DIE!! MISHA! I WANT MY MISHA BACK!"

They kept coming until my throat was raw and hoarse. And then warm hands grasped mine, pulling them from the railing and turning me until I was embraced in warmth and soothing words filled my ears. Only then did I realize I was crying. I wrapped my arms around Lex's waist and sobbed into her neck until I had no tears left.

Chapter 24

Kate

Present

"Well?" I crossed my arms and leaned against the back counter as I watched my brother stare down at the slice of mousse cake I'd set down in front of him.

He lifted the plate and jiggled it, watching the firm mousse wiggle a bit before he raised a brow at me. "What is it?"

"It's called Bird's Milk Cake. I learned to make it in Russia."

"But what *is* it? Why does it move like that? *Should* it move at all?"

"Derek." Lex grumbled a warning and lifted the fork. She dug through the creamy layers and popped it into her mouth. "Mmm..." her eyes closed. My brother turned to look at her, and his stared intensified. And heated.

"Gross. Don't look at my best friend that way in front of me."

Before he could retort, Lex had scooped up another bite and thrust the fork into Derek's mouth. "Don't pick fights. We've talked about this," she murmured before taking another bite. "So yeah, what's in this? It's divine!"

"The bottom layer is yellow cake. It has a layer of vanilla custard buttercream. On top of that is an airy lemon mousse. The whole thing is covered in chocolate ganache. It's my current favorite thing to make. Lex likes it. What about you, Derek?"

"S'good," he said around a second mouthful of cake.

"We will take another slice to go," Lex said with a smile.

"Two slices," Derek corrected, brandishing his credit card. "And one of those sticky buns. You want anything else, baby?" He gave Lex a sticky kiss on the cheek.

"Two petit fours and some of those pink rose macarons. I can already tell you working here is going to be very, *very* bad for my waistline."

I snickered as I carefully transferred two slices of Bird's Milk Cake into a box and placed it on the counter next to the register. A Slice of Heaven Bakery.

"Thank you both for coming in to see me."

"Of course! We've been meaning to. I had to promise Derek sex to keep him home on your first day."

"Gross," I laughed and swiped Derek's card. Then I made a show of pumping the hand sanitizer twice on my hands. He snorted and rolled his eyes. "A week was the perfect amount of time to wait."

Derek leaned over the counter to kiss my cheek and then ruffled my hair. "See ya soon, Kate. Come for dinner tomorrow."

"Okay, budder." I watched them leave with their boxes, and I quickly took inventory of the food in the glass case. We baked most of these items fresh daily, but some were still good for several days like the cakes, cookies, and sticky buns as long as the case was air tight. We donated the rest of the items like the macarons, muffins, and anything on the verge of getting stale to the homeless shelter. There was only fifteen minutes left before we closed for the night, so it was time to gather those items into their boxes.

The bell dinged as the door opened. "Be right with you!" I called out, but as I turned to get one of the boxes I'd built earlier, my foot slid on spilled coffee I'd forgotten to clean up, and I went down. Hard. "Damn it!" I growled with a sigh, more angry than hurt, though I knew my knee would be sporting a bruise tomorrow.

"Tsk. Language."

I froze. That voice. My heart stuttered in my chest and I forgot to breathe. It couldn't be him. He was dead. This had to be my imagination—my desperate yearning for Misha— making me hear his voice when it could only be a random customer. Deep breath in. Deep breath out. I got to my feet and turned to face the customer.

And there he was. My Misha. Grinning at me from ear-to-ear. He looked exactly as I remembered. His dark hair artfully disheveled. His face clean-shaven. His eyes shining with mirth. He looked paler than usual. And tired. Really tired, if the dark circles under his eyes were any indication.

"Misha!" I clutched my hands to my chest as I lost my breath for another reason entirely. And then I began to cry. "You're alive! My Misha!" I ran around the counter and threw myself into his arms.

He winced as I barreled into him. "Careful, Katya. I'm still a little tender." Despite his words, he hugged me tight and rested his head on top of mine.

"Misha, I didn't think I'd ever see you again!"

"I missed you so much. I've been worried about you, but it looks as if you are doing okay for yourself."

"As okay as I could be thinking the love of my life was dead! How are you here? Are Larissa and Valentina okay?" I sniffled against his neck, breathing in his spicy scent.

Misha carefully grasped my upper arms and set me back just enough to dip his head down to look in my eyes. He drew his hands up my shoulders, my neck, until he cupped my cheeks and used his thumbs to wipe away my tears. "Mother and Vally are fine, sweetheart. They are settling into our hotel room. We just landed, and I wanted to come straight here."

"How did you know where I was?"

Misha gave me one of his rich boy condescending looks. "Katya, I was in the Russian Bratva. I could find a lost penny if I needed to."

An hour later we were snuggled up together in my hotel room. We'd picked up Chinese on the way over, something Misha had never tried before despite living in a country so close to China. We dropped the food on the small, round table in the corner of the room and dropped ourselves onto the bed just to be connected and close to each other.

"You said earlier that you *were* a part of the Russian Bratva. Are you not anymore?"

"Caught that, did you?" He lifted my hand to his lips and kissed each fingertip. "Well, yes. I left that life in order to move here to be with you. And I wanted to get my family out of there. I had to promise never to return to Russia."

"Are you going to miss it?" I asked, worried that he wouldn't be happy doing something else. What if he decided later that he'd made a huge mistake? The idea rankled. I was glad we were having this discussion now instead of months or years later.

"Hell no. I never wanted that life. Was the money good? Sure. Who wouldn't want to live in luxury? But I didn't like the price that came with it. Now I feel free in ways I've never felt before. And my sister can now pursue her dreams, too. And my mother can live worry-free now that no one will make her remarry or live in the guest house like before. She can do what she wants."

Relieved, I leaned in and pressed my lips to his in a gentle kiss, but he stopped me when I tried to roll on top of him.

"I want to do this more than anything in the world, but I can't. Not yet."

"Why not?" My tone was more defensive than I would have wanted, but he had never denied me sex before.

"It's just that... I'm still healing." He sat up and lifted his shirt to show off the large bandages on his chest and shoulder.

"Damn, how are you still alive?" I whispered, carefully running a finger over the bandage on his chest. It was way too close to his heart.

"Baby, I don't think I'm ever going to get used to you using bad language." He laughed. "It's weird. But anyway, I'm alive thanks to Valentina and Mother. Valentina shot my uncle, and Mother called for an ambulance while Valentina put pressure on my chest wound. At least that's what they said when I awoke in the hospital."

Before I could respond, my stomach decided that was the perfect moment to rumble, breaking the tension and causing both of us to smile. "Let me introduce you to the finest Chinese food in Chicago."

Epilogue

Kate

A few weeks later

The house looked just like I remembered. A large brownstone with simple white pillars, brick stairs, and a white porch swing swaying in the breeze. A tug at the box had me looking up at Misha. My face felt frozen in a perplexed expression that I couldn't seem to melt away into something normal.

"Why don't I carry the box?" Misha asked for the third time. He'd offered in the car, then on the way to the door. I know why he wanted it. It was going to be really weird and awkward when my parents tried to hug me with a humongous, white pastry box clutched to my chest.

With a sigh, I carefully handed it over as if it contained my first born, not a coconut cake and an assortment of French macarons. "Thanks." The summer wreath on the door caught my attention. I remember my grandmother telling me one Christmas as she shoved evergreen fronds into a homemade wreath that the circle symbolized the everlasting life after death. She also told me that flowers in a spring and summer wreath meant life and resurrection.

It was not lost on me that I had come so far since I was kidnapped at thirteen. I went through unimaginable ordeals. Sacrificed parts of myself to survive. And now I had been resurrected into a new life as an adult with family—old and new—and dreams I could actually see ahead of me.

The anxiety melted away, and I raised my hand. The knock was firm and sure. The door swung open, and the faces inside showed the purest joy and welcome. All for me.

Life. Was. Sweet.

Kartoshka Recipe

This recipe is provided by Valentina Sushchik of food blog, "Valya's Taste of Home".

https://www.valyastasteofhome.com/kartoshka-chocolate-cake-truffles-potato-pirozhnoye/

Ingredients:
8 eggs
1 cup sugar
2 cups flour
8 oz. unsalted butter (softened)
14 oz. lightly cooked condensed milk
4 tbsp cacao powder +2 tbsp for dusting
1 cup pecans
⅛ tsp sea salt
2 tsp pure vanilla extract

Instructions:

1. Preheat the oven to 350F. Make the sponge cakes: Beat 8 eggs and 1 cup of sugar for 5 minutes or until fluffy and pale yellow in color. Sift in 2 cups of flour two additions. Mix in the flour carefully not to deflate too many air bubbles.

2. Divide batter equally between 2 – 9" pans greased with butter. Bake in the oven at 350 F oven for 18 minutes or until light golden brown. Remove from the oven and let the cake sponges cool completely (I make the sponge cakes and cook condensed milk the night before making kartoshka).
3. Crush sponge cakes in the food processor ½ sponge at a time.
4. Transfer the crumbs onto a large baking sheet lined with parchment paper.
5. Bake/toast crumbs for 15 minutes in a preheated oven to 350 F (180 C). Remove from the oven and let it cool completely.
6. Crush pecans in the food processor.
7. Transfer to a small baking sheet lined with parchment paper and bake/toast for 7 minutes. Remove from the oven and let it cool completely.

Assembling Kartoshka Truffles

1. Cream softened butter on high for 5 minutes using pedal mixer attachment. Add lightly cooked condensed milk and beat it together for 2 minutes, scrape the sides of the mixer bowl and beat it again for a minute or so.
2. Add cake crumbs, pecan crumbs, cocoa powder, salt into a mixer bowl with cream. Using pedal attachment mix all of the ingredients on low for 30 seconds. Add vanilla extract and mix for another minute or until all combined. Using an ice cream scoop (the amount of

mixture is roughly ¼ of a cup), scoop the cake mixture, roll it into a ball, then into an oval shape.
3. Place shaped kartoshka onto a platter.
4. Dust with cocoa powder, then transfer into mini cupcake liners. Store it in the container covered with a lid.

Bird's Milk Cake Recipe

The following recipe is provided by Marina Rizhkov, founder of the blog, "All We Eat".

https://allweeat.com/birds-milk-cake/

Cake Ingredients:
3 large eggs
½ cup sugar
½ tsp baking powder
½ cup all-purpose flour (unbleached)
Bird's Milk Ingredients:
1 cup + 2 tbsp water
2 tsp agar-agar
4 cups powdered sugar
¼ tsp dry vanilla
3 egg whites (room temperature)
3 oz. lemon flavored jello mix
Yellow Cream Custard Ingredients:
½ cup sugar
3 tbsp milk
3 large egg yolks
½ cup unsalted, softened butter (1 stick)
Chocolate Glaze Ingredients:

1 cup chocolate chips
½ cup heavy whipping cream

Instructions

Sponge Cake

1. Preheat your oven to 350F.
2. Butter up a 9" round cake form.
3. In a stand mixer, beat together eggs and sugar until pale and well blended on high speed. On low speed, add baking powder and flour.
4. With the help of a spatula, transfer the batter to the prepared cake pan.
5. Bake for 25 minutes. Set on a cooling rack.

Bird's Milk

1. Combine a package of lemon-flavored jello with water. Microwave for 30 seconds (another healthier option is to warm it up on the stove). Set aside until ready to use.
2. In a stand mixer on high, beat egg whites from large eggs. Add in the dry vanilla. Keep beating until you combine the other ingredients.
3. On the stove, in a medium-sized saucepan, combine water and agar-agar on medium heat, and bring to a boil.
4. Add in powdered sugar, whisk together and boil for exactly 6 minutes (no less – no more). Take off the heat and quickly do the following two steps.
5. Add the jello mix to the egg whites. Keep mixing.

6. With the mixer still beating, pour in the sugar powder syrup. Mix for 3 minutes.
7. Transfer the bird's milk mousse into the same size cake pan that you used for the sponge cake.
8. Refrigerate for 45 minutes. Meanwhile you can make the cream.

Custard Cream

1. On the stove or the microwave, bring to a boil sugar, milk, and egg yolks from large eggs.
2. Place in the refrigerator to cool down.
3. After it cools down completely (30 minutes or so) in a mixing bowl, combine with unsalted butter using a hand mixer.

Put the Bird's milk Cake Together

1. Spread the buttercream on the sponge cake.
2. Gently take out the bird's milk mousse from the form and place it on the buttercream.
3. Place it back into the refrigerator until the ganache is ready.
4. Important! The bird's milk layer must be completely cooled down to pour the ganache over; otherwise, your cake will melt.

Ganache

1. Melt chocolate chips and combine with heavy whipping cream to make the ganache. Spread the ganache all over the cake.

2. Keep in the refrigerator until ready to serve.

NOTES
- Prepare the ingredients ahead of time. The process of baking goes smoother when you don't have to worry about where your ingredients are and the time it takes to get them out! Pulling them out and measuring them beforehand makes baking go a lot smoother.
- Make sure you have the time. Although this cake is not complicated, you need some patience for it. It comes together with a few different layers of cake and needs time to set. You can make the cake 2 days in advance and then serve it. The end result is worth it though.
- Use lemon-flavored jello, and don't substitute for another flavor. The taste of the bird's milk will not be right if you do so.
- Use visuals! Learn how to make an easy sponge cake from our YouTube channel. You will love this delicious dessert; the sponge cake is so simple to make, and you can with just 4 ingredients. The delicate mousse-like marshmallow layer is made in the same 9-inch cake pans as the sponge cake.
- The white bird's milk mousse needs to be completely cooled down to pour the ganache over; otherwise, your cake will melt.

Sneak Peek of Twisted Vows

Chapter 1
Marcus

I usually love being an attorney. Solving legal problems is my forte. I like to think of myself as the LeBron James of corporate law. With less whining. I love speaking in the courtroom. I love rules, laws, and finding ways around them. And I love helping a business 'stick it' to a competitor or a Karen with too much time on her hands. But what do I love most of all about being an attorney? Making money.

What I don't like about this business is schmoozing. I'm not that kind of guy. Nattering on with compliments to persuade a CEO to sign with Dexter, Dexter, and Rooney (and soon-to-be Ashby) was not something I liked doing. Put me in a courtroom against a rival law firm, and I will outperform all their antics, but stick me in a steakhouse, high end club, or—in this case—strip club, and I feel out of place and off my game.

But this was the condition set to me by Joseph Dexter last night in his office: meet the CEO of Ranger Records in Nashville and get him to sign with us. Not only will I receive a bonus for the account, but I will also make partner in the firm. This has been my dream for the seven years I've worked for D, D, &R.

So here I am in a smoky strip club not even in the nice part of Nashville. If I hadn't just met Chet Ranger, I would wonder why the CEO of a prestigious recording company would ask me to meet him in such a grimy place when there is literally a whole strip of elite clubs downtown. But, like I said, I *have* met Chet Ranger, or as I like to call him: wannabe Colonel Sanders. I cannot not tear my eyes away from how he was shoving chicken parts between his greasy lips like they were going out of style and then stuffing dollar bills in the g-string of a dancer with those same fingers.

I want to hand her a wet wipe. Yes, I carry those in my briefcase because you never know when you might need one. I like to be prepared for any eventuality. Being unprepared is what gets you in the kind of trouble when you might need—you guessed it—an attorney. Like me.

"Eat up, Ashby! The all you can eat buffet isn't really all you can eat, right boys?" He nudges the men on either side of him and they all laugh at what I can only assume is an inside joke because it really wasn't funny.

The plate in front of me is a disgusting mix of fried everything sitting in little puddles of oil. This does not meet my dietary restrictions. I assume some of the oblong fried things are vegetables—it can't all be meat, right?— but I can't tell the difference. Every fried nugget looks like every other fried nugget. I lift a piece and bring it to my nose for a sniff. The way the men are chowing down, I know this stuff is edible, but...ew. Chet Ranger and his goons are staring at me, eyes laughing with their smiles. Time to man up. I shove the nugget into my mouth and chew. The inside has the consistency of creamed corn. Wow, you really can fry anything. And it isn't as disgusting as I thought it would be, but this one nug will have me running an extra mile on the hotel's treadmill tonight.

"Atta boy!" Ranger crows, pounding the table with a meaty fist. "I can't do business with a man too pussy to have a good time at a fine establishment like Lefty Loosie."

Fine establishment, my ass. This place is only a step up from Hulk Hogan's PastaMania—yes, that was actually a restaurant. My bouncing leg under the table indicates I'm antsy to leave. Just have to stay long enough to get Ranger to sign the damn document.

"So, as I was saying, you won't be sorry for signing with Dexter, Dexter, and Rooney. Despite being housed in Chicago, we represent many recording companies from all over the U.S. And we do an exceptional job representing them in co—"

"Let me stop you right there, Ashby. I've heard every sales pitch you can throw at me. All you lawyers are the same. 'We represent the best. Blah blah blah.' I get it. But what do you have that's different from everyone else? Ranger Records represents blazing a path through uncharted territory. That's what makes us different, and we need a corporate law firm that understands that."

Blazing a new path? What part of the music industry is considered 'uncharted territory'? Most music these days is pieced from older songs and meshed together with a bunch of electronic AI bullshit. I school the annoyance from my face and think. There has to be a way to convince Ranger that D, D, &R is the right move. What makes us different? Ding-ding! I am going to crush this deal. I hope Joseph Dexter has the sign ready with my name on it!

Leaning forward, I indicate for Ranger and the other men to come closer. They glance at each other and then lean in. "Listen. Do you know Evangeline?"

"You mean *the* Evangeline? The up-and-coming operatic country singer?"

"The one and only. My firm represents her agent, and I happened to have a discussion with said agent who mentioned Evangeline was looking for a new recording company."

"And why would she be doing that?" Chet asked, doubtfully. "She's doing very well for herself right now."

"Oh, sure, she is. But I can't divulge specifics because of, you know, attorney-client privacy." Damn, I am good. I sit back and pop another corn nugget into my mouth, not even caring about the calories. I chummed the waters, and now all I have to do is wait for the shark to take the bait. It won't take long.

"If you can set up a meeting between Evangeline's agent and Ranger Records, you have yourself a deal."

I extend my hand across the table. "You've got yourself a deal."

Chet Ranger gives my hand a strong, but greasy, pump. Beneath the table, I wipe my hand on my napkin. Ranger looks around and snaps his fingers at a passing waitress. "A bottle of champagne, sugar." His fingers, those same greasy, nasty fingers, slide down her back to cup her ass. And pinch.

The girl pinches his thumb between two fingers and removes his hand from her backside. Ranger laughs, and I glance up to see how she takes this.

And freeze.

Bouncy black curls.

Gorgeous brown eyes staring right back at me.

Rosita.

And she is not happy to see me.

Acknowledgements

My Editor

This novel has been a work of a lot of labor, a lot of frustration, and a lot of love. I want to personally thank my wonderful editor, Kelly Helmick, from Dog Star Creative Co. for making me put my big girl panties on and re-write the entire plot. I was so mad and creatively lost even though she helped me restructure the plot. But then I just dug in, and ya know what? She was right! Kelly, the story was so much better after I re-wrote it! You never steer me wrong, and you always, always, always have my back. I've learned to trust you and your judgement. Thank you so much!

My Proofreader

I asked my childhood friend, Rachele, elementary teacher extra-ordinaire, to proofread my novel. She was an ARC reader for Twisted Redemption and found some errors in that manuscript, so I figured, "what the heck?" And she rocked it! Thank you, Rachele, for being a great proofreader and a great friend!

My Fans

To my sweetest fans, Saasha, Melinda, Nancy, and Rachel, thank you for encouraging me to continue. Saasha and Nancy, especially, thank you for pestering me about when my next book was going to come out. Seriously, knowing someone--anyone--wanted to actually read my stories made all the difference in the world for me to continue. Love you!

The Food Bloggers

To Valya and Marina, thank you tremendously for allowing me to use your recipes in the back of this novel. My character, Kate, was so influenced by these specific Russian delicacies, and I found a love for them, too. Thank you for making it come alive to my readers.

Georgia Blake lives--surprisingly not in Georgia--in East Tennessee with her husband, son, two dogs, and two cats. While writing is not her full time job, she loves the creative release it provides. Besides writing, she enjoys reading all the romance novels she can (usually a book on Kindle and an audiobook), snuggling her son, forcing snuggles on the cats, and annoying her husband by putting her earbuds in when she doesn't feel like talking. She is super happy to have readers reach out on social media if they enjoyed her books. Those messages are what keep her writing.

Join Georgia's Facebook Group: Georgia's Gorgeous Captives
Follow her on TikTok: @georgiablake097
Instagram: authorgeorgiablake
Visit her website and join her newsletter: https://authorgeorgiablake.com/

Milton Keynes UK
Ingram Content Group UK Ltd.
UKHW022335230424
441619UK00015B/785

9 798218 400101